A Devon Night's Death

By Stephanie Austin

Dead in Devon

Dead on Dartmoor

From Devon With Death

The Dartmoor Murders

A Devon Night's Death

a&b

A Devon Night's Death

STEPHANIE AUSTIN

Allison & Busby Limited
11 Wardour Mews
London W1F 8AN
allisonandbusby.com

First published in Great Britain by Allison & Busby in 2022.

A CIP catalogue record for this book is available from the British Library.

First Edition

ISBN 978-0-7490-2892-3

Typeset in 11.5/16.5 pt Sabon LT Pro by
Allison & Busby Ltd.

Printed and bound by
CPI Group (UK) Ltd, Croydon, CR0 4YY

For Di

PROLOGUE

When you consider my nasty habit of discovering corpses, it's curious that I've never found one when I'm walking the dogs. Dog walkers are the perfect candidates for finding dead bodies. Up early in the morning, they are the first to come across those things dumped secretly in the hours of darkness: a roll of old carpet, a dead microwave, a corpse. They stroll across empty waste grounds, past derelict buildings, their concrete walls garish with graffiti, or by stagnant canals, under bridges where skeletal shopping trolleys rise from shallow water. They amble along shady lanes edged with deep ditches, over rough pasture where nettles and yellow ragwort run riot, through thorny scrub, or in woods where leaf litter lies deep, the perfect place to abandon the odd corpse. To be honest, it's usually the dogs, rather than their owners, who make the discovery. They possess the superior sniffing equipment.

A dog walker once found a body in Ausewell Wood, near Ashburton where I live. It was actually a skeleton in a sleeping bag, and presumed to be a camper or rough sleeper who'd succumbed to exposure. Poor bugger, he must have been lying there a long time. No foul play was ever suspected. It was reported in the local paper, but I don't believe the identity of the unfortunate person was ever discovered.

I get up early each weekday morning and walk five dogs for their owners. The Tribe, I call them – Dylan, Nookie, Boog, E.B. and Schnitzel, in descending order of size. You might think that with an enthusiasm for digging and five times my sniffing power, the Tribe might have unearthed the odd cadaver on our woodland walks, snuffling about under all that undergrowth, but they haven't.

I may have an unfortunate reputation for finding corpses – a member of the local police force laughingly refers to it as my *hobby* – but despite this, I have never discovered a dead body whilst out walking the dogs. Until now.

CHAPTER ONE

People who seem too good to be true usually are. I should have remembered that when I met Frank Tinkler. But when he walked into *Old Nick's* at the end of a long, quiet afternoon, he seemed like the answer to a prayer.

'This is a very interesting shop,' he observed politely. He was somewhere in his sixties and sported a neatly trimmed grey moustache. He wore a blazer, and Panama hat, which he doffed on entry and which gave him the air of an old school cricket umpire. 'What would you call it exactly, art and crafts?'

'It's really antiques,' I jerked my thumb in the direction of my own selling space at the rear of the building, although *antiques* is a rather grand title for the odd assortment of stuff I currently have to sell, 'and vintage clothes. And over there,' I gestured towards the bookshelves, 'we have second-hand books. We run a book exchange.'

'Ah!'

I got the annoying feeling that he hadn't come in to buy anything. That's the trouble with owning an antique shop: as many people come in to sell you things as come in to buy. I'd just refused a woman who took it personally when I didn't want to purchase her Royal Doulton figurines. As I tried to explain, however dainty and finely crafted they were, there is no market for porcelain ladies in crinolines at the moment.

I frequently wonder why I don't sell *Old Nick's*. I'd never wanted to own an antique shop but Nick left it to me in his will. Quite why is something of a mystery. I had only been working for him for a matter of months when he was killed. His family think he left it to me out of spite, although whether it was to spite them or me, I've never been sure. It was getting on for five-thirty, closing time and I didn't want to hang around for a chat with this man if there wasn't going to be a satisfying ping on the till at the end of it. 'Were you looking for anything in particular?' I asked, hoping to speed things up.

'I heard a rumour you have spaces to rent.'

I must have beamed. I've had trouble renting out selling space. My last paying tenant, Fizz, only stayed a few months and by then I was glad to see the back of her. She now runs a swanky gallery of her own in North Street. 'You heard correctly.' I gestured towards an empty area by the bookshelves that I'd long been wanting to fill. 'That space there is available—'

'No, no.' He cut me off with a firm sweep of the hand. 'I need my own room. You see, I've always had a workshop at home, in the spare bedroom. But my daughter and her children have come back to live with us – lovely to have them with us, of course,' he added hastily, 'but I've lost my working space.'

'I've got two rooms upstairs.' These had once formed part of Nick's flat and I led him up to what had been his former living room. It was also the room where he'd been murdered but I didn't mention that.

He pointed to the sink in the corner. 'That's excellent. I need running water for my work.'

'What do you do exactly, Mr . . . er . . .'

'Tinkler,' he answered with a charming smile. 'Call me Frank.'

I pointed to myself. 'Juno.'

'I know who you are, Miss Browne. All of Ashburton must be aware of your exploits.'

'What exactly do you sell?' I asked, anxious to move on before the conversation turned to my unfortunate sleuthing activities in any more detail.

'Marbled paper.'

I wasn't sure I'd heard right.

'I marble it myself,' he went on. 'I used to be a bookbinder by trade and I still do the odd bit of restoration work, but I'm retired really. The paper-marbling is just a hobby.' He opened a book that he'd been carrying tucked under his arm since his arrival. 'Here are some samples.'

I took the book from him. Each page was different, patterned with coloured inks to look like marble or rippled sand, feathers or leaves, or peacock tails in shades of red and gold. Some were just abstract works of art in wild swirling colours. I ran my fingers over the paper. 'You do this by hand?'

'Oh yes,' he answered modestly.

'It's beautiful,' I breathed. 'Is there a market for it?'

'Indeed, there is. I sell my work to bookbinders for the endpapers of bibles, atlases, legal and medical journals – that sort of thing – as well as for the antiquarian market.' He looked around him. 'This room would make a splendid workshop.'

'It's actually a retail unit,' I pointed out. When I'd converted Nick's old flat into rental space, I'd had to apply to the council for a change of use. I didn't want to fall foul of the regulations.

'I could sell these.' He opened his blazer and pulled some greetings cards from his pocket, abstract patterns in bright, fresh colours. 'I do these greetings cards and notebooks just for fun.'

'They're lovely.' I took one from him. 'We could display them downstairs.' On some of those empty shelves, I added to myself.

'I'd like to move in as soon as possible, if that's all right with you. We need to discuss rent of course, but one or two questions first if I may.'

I was eager to discuss rent too. 'Please, fire away.'

'I often find myself burning the midnight oil, particularly if I've got a large demand to fill. Would it be in order if I were here working after hours, when the shop was closed?'

I nodded, anxious to please. 'I can give you a key to

the old flat door at the bottom of the stairs. It opens on to the alley at the side. Then you can let yourself in and out when you like without having to go through the shop.'

'That would be perfect,' he smiled. Then he added, after a slight hesitation, 'Also, would you object if I put some kind of lock on this door, for when I'm not here?'

I wasn't so sure about that. I didn't like the idea of not being able to get into the room. What if he left a tap running and caused a flood in the shop downstairs? That's exactly the sort of thing Fizz had been likely to do.

'Some of the books I am asked to restore are quite rare volumes,' he pointed out, 'and naturally I am responsible for them while they're in my care. And I notice you don't seem to have a burglar alarm or any CCTV on the premises.'

He was right there. I hadn't got around to affording any. 'No,' I admitted. 'I suppose . . .'

Frank smiled. 'I don't smoke. I promise you I won't start a fire.'

'Well, in that case.' A voice in my head still niggled, but somehow his polite, persuasive manner made my fears seem unreasonable. Besides, I was anxious to let the room and once we'd agreed a figure, he was ready with the rent. Paid up front, in fact. When I first opened the shop, I had intended to insist on a six-month tenancy agreement for anyone renting space but my experience with Fizz made me wary of lumbering myself with someone I couldn't easily get rid of. Frank and I agreed on one month's notice, either way.

I phoned Sophie after he'd gone, and Pat, as they'd both be on duty in the shop next day, to warn them of Frank's arrival and make sure one of them gave him a key to the side door. They're both too penniless to pay me any rent, so they man the shop in return for free working and selling space, an arrangement that allows me time for my proper job working as a domestic goddess, which basically means clearing up after other people.

'He's not going to play loud pop music all the time, is he?' Pat demanded, 'Like that last one.'

'I wouldn't think so. Frank strikes me as more of a Radio Three man.'

Pat grunted. 'Is he going to be minding the shop?'

'I haven't asked him to,' I admitted. 'I thought we'd see how he settled in before I suggested leaving him on his own.' At one time I'd thought everyone could take it in turns to man the shop, but Fizz had been a disaster.

'Good thinking,' Pat agreed. 'Besides, Sophie and me manage things OK between us. And Her Ladyship comes in to cover now and again. I don't think we want too many people left in charge.'

I stifled a laugh. By 'Her Ladyship', she meant Elizabeth, a friend who helped out in the shop when she wasn't busy as a part-time receptionist at the doctors' surgery. She's a retired teacher with a gracious but crisp, no-nonsense manner, which seems to inspire Pat with a grudging sense of awe. 'You're probably right. Anyway, as long as you and Soph know he's coming.' I wouldn't get to *Old Nick's* until the end of the day myself, I'd be busy working.

It was a relief to close up, to escape the gloom of Shadow Lane and be released into the early evening sunshine. June had been hot and dry with very little rain and July was promising to be even hotter. I strolled down the narrow lane to my little white van. Every time I see it, it reminds me that it's time it had a new paint job. Its white anonymity is a waste of advertising space. I used to call it White Van, till a friend christened it Van Blanc, which I prefer. I'd parked it in the shade, but I still felt as if I was climbing into an oven, the hot plastic smell of vehicle interior overwhelmed by the even stronger aroma left by the Tribe who got picked up in it every morning, the unmistakeable, comfy smell of dog.

I drove out of Ashburton, up the hill, a shady road through green woods, which eventually wound its way on to the open moor. I turned off at Druid Cross, towards my old friends Ricky and Morris's place. They live in an impressive Georgian pile high above the town, looking down over the valley. From here they run their theatrical costume hire company. I'd phoned them earlier to see if I could borrow their shower. The boiler in my flat had gasped its last, leaving the entire house without hot water for days.

When I got there, the hallway was blocked by several large laundry hampers, costumes returned from a recent theatrical production and waiting to be unpacked. It's the kind of job I often help Ricky and Morris out with.

After my shower, we all sat in the breakfast room, drinking wine, the garden doors flung open to let in the shimmering summer evening, my damp curls fluffing up horribly because I'd forgotten to bring my conditioner. I told them about my new tenant.

'Tinkler?' Ricky looked thoughtful. 'That name rings a bell.'

'Spare me the dreadful jokes. He seems very nice. Anyway, I need his rent so unless he's a secret axe-murderer I'm prepared to take his money.' I took a sip from my glass. 'How's the theatrical project going?' They were planning to stage *A Midsummer Night's Dream* in their garden at Druid Lodge. The rolling lawns and thick shrubbery make it the perfect setting for outdoor theatre. It was to be a community production with all the profits going to local charities.

Ricky moaned, performing a dramatic roll with his eyeballs. 'I wish we'd never got involved now. We should never have applied for that funding.'

'You mean the Arts Council Funding?' I asked. 'Why not? What's the matter?'

'It's Gabriel Dark,' Morris murmured.

'Who's he?'

'He's the professional director the Arts Council are sending us.' He blinked, his round eyes solemn. 'Of course, we don't get a choice but . . .'

Ricky blew cigarette smoke down his nostrils. 'I wish we were still directing the show ourselves.'

'I don't understand why you're not.' The original plan was that they would direct the play between them. They've done it before. They're old hands at all this theatrical stuff, they've been doing it all their lives. But they'd learnt about an Arts Council Outreach Project that would pay for the services of a professional director from London.

'We thought it would be good for the cast, being directed by a young, professional director,' Morris explained, 'someone who's actually working in live theatre today—'

'—instead of a pair of knackered old has-beens like us,' Ricky finished for him.

'You're not has-beens.' I kept quiet about the knackered old bit. But they were making a mistake. I was sure no one could do a better job than they could. 'So, what's wrong with this Gabriel Dark?' I asked, apart from sounding as if he'd come from some kids' book about wizards.

'Well, I haven't worked with him personally,' Morris admitted, laying a plate of bread and olives on the table, overcome as always by the compulsion to feed me, 'but he has a certain reputation.'

'No one wants to work with him twice.' Ricky laughed slyly, 'That's probably how he's ended up doing outreach projects with amateur provincials.'

Morris returned from the kitchen with crackers and cheese. He cast Ricky an anxious glance over his little gold specs. 'Perhaps it was just a case of you and him not getting on,' he suggested, 'after all, it was a long time ago.'

'It was,' Ricky agreed. 'I was in his production of *Hamlet,* it must be twenty years ago. He was a real brat, fresh out of drama school, trying to make a name for himself.'

He lobbed his fag end into the garden and strolled to the table, walking his long fingers across the surface to pinch an olive.

'Perhaps he's changed over the years,' Morris said optimistically.

Ricky shook his head. 'There'll be trouble, you'll see.'

I was grateful I'd only volunteered to help with costumes. Acting is not my thing.

After a glass of Malbec, some excellent local cheese and an hour of listening to Ricky prophesying that their theatrical production was doomed, I made my excuses and came away.

The van rattled down the hill into Ashburton. I turned over the little stone bridge that crosses the shallow Ashburn and past a row of old weavers' cottages. Drinkers enjoying the last of the evening sunshine lingered on the grass outside of the Victoria Inn, the pink sky behind the surrounding hills promising another fine day tomorrow. The air was still warm. I passed the town hall with its little clock tower, the ramshackle row of old shops. Then on an impulse, I turned and made a detour down Shadow Lane.

In the dimness of the narrow alleyway, *Old Nick's* shone like a jewel, its pale green paintwork, its name on the swinging sign above the door picked out in gold, the displays in the windows highlighted by spotlights. I felt a little stab of pride, remembering what a shabby, run-down hole it was when Nick was alive. If I sold it, I could afford to buy my own home and stop renting the upstairs of Kate and Adam's decrepit house. Except that they need my rent, and probably wouldn't find another tenant without having to spend squillions doing the place up. And if I sold the shop, where would Sophie find a place to paint, or Pat sell the things she makes to raise money for the animal sanctuary she runs with her sister and brother-in-law? There's the problem: it's not just about me any more. And even if the shop is stuck down a dark alley where the sun never shines and tourists fear to tread, I want to make a success of it. And I had a new rent-paying tenant now, Frank Tinkler. Perhaps things were about to look up.

Kate appeared in the hallway as soon as I got home, glowing and beautiful and all mumsy-to-be, her thick dark plait hanging down over her shoulder. 'Juno, can I have a word?' There was a worried look in her eyes.

My own must have narrowed in suspicion. 'What's up?' I demanded. 'Are you OK?'

Instinctively, she stroked her rounded tummy. 'Yes. I'm fine. It's nothing like that.'

She smiled brightly. 'The good news is, the boiler's in.'

'We've got hot water again. Excellent. And the bad news?'

Her words tumbled out in a rush. 'Well, there's been a slight accident in your bathroom.

'Adam and I thought it was time you had a proper shower, so we'd asked the plumber to put one in over your bath—'

Yay, I thought. I'd be able to wash my hair without having to submerge myself in the bath every time.

'But when he drilled the wall to fix the shower unit in,' she plunged on, 'most of the tiles fell off, bringing the plaster down with them and well . . . the whole bathroom needs plastering and retiling. We've got to get a plasterer in.'

'Ah.'

'The plumber had to rush off and he's left it in a bit of a mess. Adam's up there now. He was trying to clear it up before you got back.'

'I'd better go and see how he's getting on.'

'It is a bit of a mess,' she repeated with an apologetic shrug. 'I'm just warning you.'

As I approached the door of my flat, I could hear a noise like someone shovelling shale. I called out 'Hi!' and detected muttered cursing. I poked my head gingerly around the bathroom door.

A bit of a mess was an understatement. The bath was full of broken shards of white tile and chunks of wet red plaster. Adam was on his knees with a dustpan, shovelling the mess into a garden bucket. Red dust coated his hair, beard and eyebrows and clung to his sweaty face. It hung in the air and covered the walls, as well as my soap and toothbrush. He squinted up at me and coughed. 'Sorry about this.'

'Hmmm. Shall I fetch some bin bags?'

'They're not strong enough.'

'Well, there's obviously not room for two of us in here,' I said benevolently, 'so I'll leave you to it, shall I?'

He slid another dustpan full of broken tiles and dust into the rapidly filling bucket, groaning as he got off his knees. 'I'll just lug this down to the back garden,' he croaked, wiping his face with his sleeve. 'It's only my eighth trip.'

'I can tell it's not your first by the state of the living room carpet.'

'Sorry.'

'It's a bit late to put newspaper down now,' I observed as he crunched across the living room, grinding gritty dust into the pile. 'Perhaps we could consider a new carpet?' I called out after him and heard more swearing as he lugged the skip downstairs.

I didn't really care about the carpet. It's threadbare in places with a beige swirly pattern that was probably the height of internal decor fifty years ago. And as a domestic goddess I spend too much time hoovering other people's carpets to fuss with housework when I get home. But Daniel was coming at the weekend and, whilst I suspect my lover is not fussy either, we haven't been together long and I don't want to give him the impression that I wallow in filth. The idea that the bathroom might not even be operational was depressing. A cosy romantic soak surrounded by scented candles was obviously off the agenda.

'Do you think this will be sorted out by the weekend?' I asked as Adam reappeared with his empty bucket.

We stared together at the ruined bathroom walls, the chunks of missing plaster, the old lath strips showing underneath, and he puffed out his cheeks in a sigh. 'We'll do our best. The plumber's promised he'll come back and finish the shower tomorrow. It's the plastering and retiling that might hold things up.'

I nodded sadly. There was obviously nothing more he could do. I grabbed a dustpan and brush from under the sink and whilst he lugged the next load of tiles and plaster downstairs, began to brush down the surfaces. Four buckets later the bath was empty.

'I'll wash it all down,' I told Adam. 'You've done enough.' In the morning he had to be up even earlier than me, to cook breakfasts at *Sunflowers*. Kate's morning sickness was preventing her from going in to help him in the cafe first thing and they couldn't afford to pay for extra staff. If the dog walking hadn't prevented me, I'd have gone in to help him myself. We wished each other goodnight and I set to washing down the bathroom. Finally, I lathered the dust off my soap. I decided to junk the toothbrush. Then I ran the vacuum cleaner over the living room carpet, the gritty dust rattling inside as if it was crunching on muesli.

It was only when I flopped into a chair at the end of all this labour, my thoughts turning towards a cosy read in bed, that I noticed the light on my ancient telephone answering machine winking at me like an evil red eye. Full of foreboding, I pressed *play*. It was Daniel's voice, asking me to ring him back.

'Is that Miss Browne with an "e"?' he asked as soon as he picked up. The warmth in his voice made me smile.

'It is, Mr Thorncroft. What's up?'

'I'm sorry, Juno, change of plan. I'm not going to be able to make it at the weekend.'

I ignored the sinking feeling. He was currently working

in Ireland on a peat conservation project. 'Stuck in the peat bog?' I stifled a sigh. I could hardly complain when he's trying to save the planet.

'Up to my neck,' he responded. 'There's a problem and it'll be better if I stay here and get it sorted now.'

'You'll miss the concert,' I reminded him. 'I've bought tickets.'

'Blast! Sorry, Miss B. Can you find someone else to go with?'

'Expect so,' I muttered glumly.

'Then I'll definitely be free to come over the following weekend when the caravan arrives.'

'Caravan?'

'I've bought one online. It's being delivered to Moorview Farm a week on Saturday. I'll need to be there for that.'

I cheered up a little. The farmhouse Daniel had inherited was a ruin and he'd been planning to buy a caravan so he could stay onsite whilst the building work was done. It was also intended to be a private place where he and I could satisfy our passion for each other without worrying about disturbing the slumbers of Kate and Adam downstairs. Now he'd finally got around to buying it. Despite the fact that I wouldn't see him for another ten days I came off the phone feeling cheerful and celebrated by making hot chocolate and snuggling down in bed.

I'd barely opened my book before there was a light thump next to me and Bill meowed a welcome. He'd been keeping out of the way during the bustle in the bathroom, although the trail of pink paw-prints he left across the duvet meant he must have been sniffing around in there since. 'You're not my cat,' I told him. 'Why aren't you downstairs with Kate and Adam where you belong?' He didn't have an answer, just curled up next to me, purring.

I tried a second question. 'What can go wrong in a peat bog?' But he didn't have an answer for that either, just closed his one green eye, tucked his paws under and left me to my reading. I must have been tired. I woke up next morning with the bedside lamp still on and hot chocolate coagulating in its mug.

CHAPTER TWO

Even in the cool of the early morning, the sky pale and soft, a delicate mist hanging over grass silvery with dew, I could tell it was going to be a hot day. Later the sun would be fierce.

I walked the Tribe along lanes shaded by hedgerows thick with summer growth, with fresh hawthorn and hazel and flossy with the creamy heads of elderflowers. We walked in cool, green woods, where amongst the tumbled, mossy stones we could find streams to splash about in and the dogs could chase the sunbeams flickering on the water.

After I'd delivered the canines back to their various homes, then scrubbed my way around a client's kitchen and bathroom, I'd begun to wish it wasn't quite so warm. I emerged from their house squinting into the sunlight, sweaty and smelling slightly of bleach, longing for a cold drink before I headed off to my next appointment. I dropped in at the shop where I knew there were some cans in the fridge upstairs.

Unfortunately, my way to the kitchen was blocked. Frank had already started moving in and was in the process of dragging some metal shelving up the stairs towards his room. He had a helper, a good-looking fella of about twenty, with short-cropped fair hair, who was pushing from the other end. He introduced him as Scott, a nephew of his. I decided I'd better forget about the cans in the fridge. Sophie was at her easel, rapt in contemplation, not of her current painting, but the muscles rippling beneath Scott's fitted t-shirt. I snapped my fingers beneath her nose and she jumped, grinning at me as I waved goodbye.

On any weekday morning the corner of North Street is alive with shoppers and busy with delivery vans half-parked on the pavement trying to unload outside of the shops. I nipped into the Co-op to buy myself a drink and a sandwich for lunch, almost bumping into a woman in the doorway as I came out. 'Aren't you Juno Browne?' she smiled.

She was a slim, middle-aged lady with mild blue eyes and wispy fairish-brown hair. I didn't recognise her. 'Um . . . yes.'

'You don't know me,' she added, seeing my blank look, 'but my husband has just rented a room in that lovely shop of yours. Frank Tinkler?'

'Oh, you're Frank's wife? Hello!' We exchanged smiles and handshakes. 'Yes, I've just seen him, he's just moving in.'

'I'm Jean.' She must have been a bit younger than Frank, with the same well-mannered charm, a slightly faded English rose-type dressed in a summery white blouse and floral skirt.

'I hear you're claiming back your spare bedroom,' I said.

'Not just the spare bedroom,' she laughed, 'the conservatory, the utility room. The boxes full of old books are bad enough, but I'm fed up of finding sheets of marbled paper spread out to dry everywhere. I don't know why he can't do it all in the garage, but he says it's too damp. It'll be such a relief to get rid of all his stuff.'

We were interrupted by a breathy Welsh voice as an ample, fair-haired woman wearing a dark business suit one size too small bore down on us from across the street. 'Hello, Mrs Tinkler!' she cooed as I groaned inwardly. Sandy Thomas, who worked in the office of the *Dartmoor Gazette*, fancied herself as an ace reporter and was a right pain in the arse where I was concerned. 'Hello, Juno!' she added, as if we were old friends. 'How is Frank, Mrs Tinkler?' she asked solicitously, 'has he got over that nasty business from last year?'

I could see Jean Tinkler stiffen. Her laugh evaporated. 'Yes. Yes, he's fine, thank you.'

'No lasting consequences, I hope?'

'No. No, Frank was very lucky. He got away with a few bruises, he really wasn't hurt, you know.'

I must have been looking as baffled as I felt because Sandy explained, 'Mr Tinkler was the victim of a hit-and-run driver last year, right here in Ashburton.'

She turned to Jean for confirmation. 'On Eastern Road, wasn't it? He was just crossing the road—'

It was obvious Jean Tinkler didn't wish to discuss it. 'Would you excuse me?' she asked, cutting Sandy off short. 'I really must get on. Nice to have met you, Juno,' she added and hurried away.

For a moment we watched her departing back. 'What happened?' I asked.

Sandy could always be relied upon for information. 'Well, like I said, Frank Tinkler was crossing Eastern Road and this driver nearly knocked him down. He managed to jump out of the way just in time. He was a bit bruised and shaken, that's all.'

'But the driver didn't stop?'

'No, went speeding off, apparently.' She dropped her voice and laid a conspiratorial hand on my arm. 'I'll tell you one thing, though . . .'

'What?'

'There was a witness, been chatting on the pavement with a friend, saw the whole thing, swore that the driver aimed the car at him deliberately.'

'Tried to run him over?'

'Yes. But swerved at the last moment, the witness said.'

'Perhaps the driver simply didn't see him until it was almost too late.'

'No, no,' Sandy assured me with a solemn shake of her head, 'the witness was sure it was deliberate.'

I could see it made a better news story that way. 'But this witness didn't manage to get the car's number?'

'Unfortunately, not,' she added sadly. 'I think he was more concerned with making sure Mr Tinkler wasn't injured. So, I don't suppose we'll ever know what really happened.' She sighed and then slanted a glance at me. 'What about you?' she asked, her little newshound's nose twitching. 'Aren't you investigating anything at the moment?'

When I'd escaped from Sandy, unable to convince her that I don't investigate things, they just happen to me, I made my way up to Stapledon Lane. My long-standing client, Mrs Berkeley-Smythe, has a cottage there. She spends most of her life away on cruise ships and her garden needs regular watering during her absence. She's had the lawn paved over, in favour of fashionably expensive stone, so there's no mowing to worry about, but terracotta pots dry out quickly and I didn't want Chloe to arrive home to find her cosmos fried to a frazzle. Why she wants to bother with so many plants when she's so rarely on dry land to admire them, I can't imagine, but in this dry heat a thorough soaking would only last them for a day or two. Recently, she's taken to statuary. A serene stone buddha sits in the shade of a Japanese maple and an impossibly large and happy frog smiles amongst the ferns in a shady corner. I'd reeled out the hosepipe and was just filling up the ornamental birdbath, a bronze-coloured shell mounted on an ornate pedestal, when my mobile phone rang. I reduced the gushing hosepipe to a dribble. It was Ricky. 'What's up?' I asked.

‘Sorry to bother you, Princess, but I don’t suppose you could do us a favour?’

‘Anything for you,’ I responded recklessly.

‘It’s that bloody Gabriel Dark,’ he explained. ‘He’s coming down from London this afternoon to talk about the Shakespeare project. He wants to take a look at the performance space before he arrives to start rehearsals. ’Course, we’ve had to offer to let him stay the night. But the point is, the old Saab is in for a service and won’t be ready till five-thirty, and he needs picking up at the station at four so . . .’

I glanced at my watch. ‘I can do it after I’ve finished this. Where will he be? Exeter?’

‘No, Newton Abbot. Thanks, darling, you are a star.’

‘As long as he doesn’t mind riding in the doggy van.’

Ricky snorted. ‘He’s lucky to get a ride at all. I’ll ring him and let him know, tell him to look out for a flame-haired goddess.’

I ignored this. ‘And how will I recognise him?’

‘That’s easy,’ Ricky chuckled. ‘Just look for the horns and tail.’

Despite the satanic appearance Ricky tried to give him, Gabriel Dark was a normal-looking human being of about forty, shortish, with floppy black hair, blue eyes and a charming smile. He was quite attractive, actually. *Don’t let the boyish grin fool you*, Ricky had warned me, *he’s got an ego the size of Jupiter.* That’s rich, coming from Ricky. His description of me must have been more accurate because Gabriel Dark approached me as soon as I reached the station entrance. There weren't any other six-foot redheads about.

'Juno?' he asked, and when I nodded, proffered his hand. He looked me up and down as we shook. I must have looked a treat in my old gardening trousers. 'Please tell me you're auditioning.'

'No, sorry.'

'But you'd make a perfect Helena.'

I admitted to having studied the play at college and pointed him in the direction of my old Van Blanc. 'I hope you're not allergic to dogs, I take five of them out in this every morning. Ricky and Morris send their apologies for not picking you up, by the way. Their car's being serviced.'

'So they explained. Listen, Juno,' Gabriel slid into the passenger seat and buckled up his seat belt, 'help me out here, will you? Can you tell me a bit about my hosts, the initiators of this project? This . . . um . . .' he unfolded a piece of paper from the leather manbag he carried, 'Morris Greenbaum and Ricky . . . erm . . . Steiner, is it?' he frowned as he donned a pair of designer reading specs.

'You've met Ricky before,' I reminded him. 'He was in your production of *Hamlet* years ago.'

Gabriel frowned. 'The name doesn't mean anything.' He glanced at me sideways. 'You don't know which part he played?'

'The ghost, I think.'

He shook his head as if he was still at a loss. I was amazed. How could anyone forget Ricky, even if the production was twenty years ago? Apart from the fact he's always memorably rude, Ricky had the charismatic good looks you don't forget. He still has, in a grizzled kind of way.

'Nope, perhaps I'll recognise him when I see him.'

There was something about his careless shrug as he spoke that got my antennae twitching.

I suspected that he remembered Ricky perfectly well, but for some reason chose to pretend he didn't.

'I understand they've got some kind of theatrical background,' he went on dismissively. 'I really should have studied their info,' he admitted, waving his piece of paper about, 'but I haven't had a minute.'

He'd just had three hours sitting on a train but perhaps he'd been occupied with other things. I explained that Morris sang and Ricky played the piano and that though they claimed to be retired they still entertained as a double act, Sauce and Slander.

Gabriel groaned. 'They sound dire!'

'No, actually, they're very funny,' I responded, stung on their behalf. 'They write satirical songs. They only perform to raise money for charity these days. And of course, they make costumes.'

Gabriel Dark raised an eyebrow. 'Do they now?'

He really hadn't read any of that piece of paper. 'They run a theatrical hire company. They send costumes to theatre companies all over the place.'

'Do you think they'll make costumes for this show?'

I had to smile then. 'Let's put it this way, they'll be very offended if they're not asked.'

Gabriel laughed. 'That's a relief. I thought I might have to find some old dear with a sewing machine and get down on bended knee.'

His phone trilled *The Ride of the Valkyries* and he slipped it from his pocket. He frowned briefly at the screen but didn't take the call and returned the phone from whence it came.

'Is this your first community production?' I asked.

He grimaced. 'I'm afraid I drew the short straw.' He made it sound as if he'd had no choice in the matter. His phone went, it was the Valkyries again. This time he didn't bother to look at it. I asked him about his own career and he launched into a long story about how he'd been blighted by a succession of short-sighted theatre administrations and ignorant audiences. Eventually he asked about me. What did I do, apart from driving dogs around?

'I actually *walk* the dogs,' I explained. 'I've had my own business as a domestic goddess for several years now, basically cleaning and caring, with a bit of dog walking and gardening thrown in. Then I inherited an antique shop.'

'Wow!' he grinned. 'That's cool.'

'Well, it is and it isn't. At the moment I'm trying to keep both businesses going at once.'

'Can't you give one of them up?'

'Neither of them makes enough money on its own.'

'Ah!'

His phone went a third time. The Valkyries were getting impatient. He grinned apologetically. 'I'd better take this . . . Yes?' He listened for a moment, then hissed into the phone. 'How did you get this number?'

I concentrated on the road ahead, trying not to look as if I was eavesdropping. After a few more moments Gabriel ended the call. 'I can't talk now.' He flicked me an embarrassed glance as he returned the phone to his pocket, 'These damned call-centre people, they never stop pestering, do they?' He laughed weakly and I murmured sympathetic noises. He lapsed into silence as I turned off the main road into Ashburton. From the way he was frowning and chewing his lip. I'd have said the damned call-centre people had rattled him for some reason. But as I drove through the narrow streets of the town, he began to take notice. 'This place really is old. I had no idea.' I restrained myself from launching into its history, fascinating though that is. I just let him soak it all up, its steep roofs, crooked beams and stone archways spoke of its age more eloquently than I could. I turned up the hill, the steep road taking us towards Druid Cross through a long green tunnel of trees. Sunlight glimmered through the leaves in specks and freckles of gold. 'Wow!' Gabriel cried, delighted, 'This is real fairy glade stuff.'

I turned along the lane, the hedgerows parting suddenly, a five-bar gate allowing us a glimpse of gold fields ripe with corn dipping down to the town below, the towers of St Lawrence Chapel and St Andrew's church rising above huddled rooftops. Shortly afterwards, we swung in through the gates of Druid Lodge and followed the curving drive through the gardens. Then the house came into view and hit Gabriel full wallop with its grand

Georgian architecture. He was momentarily silenced. 'My God, this isn't where they live?' The van crunched to a halt on the gravel outside. He gazed at the row of long windows, the columns and the stone portico above the front door. 'Lucky bastards!'

'They share it with several thousand costumes,' I reminded him, but he wasn't listening. He got out of the van and stood gazing at the white frontage of the house, one hand shading his eyes. 'It's fantastic,' he muttered enviously.

'Let's go inside. Ricky and Morris are dying to meet you. And I'm sure they'll give you the grand tour if you want it.'

'I certainly do,' he told me, and the *Ride of the Valkyries* started up again in his pocket.

Morris begged me to stay for dinner. It wasn't the prospect of his wonderful cooking that made me agree to his invitation as much as the note of desperation in his voice and the pleading look in his eyes.

Ricky already had a dangerous look about him. Gabriel was insisting that he couldn't remember his Hamlet's Ghost at all. 'Are you *sure* it was my production you were in?'

'It was set in a concrete bunker,' Ricky retorted. I couldn't help noticing his voice had lost its slight London twang and assumed the richer, fruitier tones he used on stage.

'Oh yes, yes!' Gabriel clicked his fingers annoyingly. 'I do remember vaguely.'

Ricky had photographs at the ready and thrust them under his nose. There were colour pictures of him dressed as the ghost, magnificent in ghostly silver make-up and full body armour, and several black and whites taken at a rehearsal, with one of him and Gabriel looking as if they were in the midst of a heated argument.

Gabriel took them from him, leafing through. 'Of course!' He nodded as if it was all a wonderful memory that had suddenly come flooding back to him. 'How could I forget? A towering performance, Ricky! Bloody wonderful!'

Ricky is nobody's fool. He'd predicted that Gabriel would wind him up and I could tell by the narrowing of his eyes and the grim set of his jaw that he wasn't wrong. Morris began nervously polishing his spectacles. I laid a comforting hand on his arm and promised I'd come back in time for dinner. I wanted to change, and I always try to pop into *Old Nick's* before closing time.

'I'll be back at seven,' I whispered to him. 'Try to keep the lid on.'

CHAPTER THREE

I'd been so distracted by picking up Gabriel Dark that I'd almost forgotten about Frank Tinkler moving in. Sophie was cashing up when I arrived, her dark head bent low as she counted piles of change for the float, her lips moving silently. She might be a brilliant artist but cashing up takes her ages. Frank had moved in all his shelving and bits of equipment, she told me. 'He's bringing his inks and papers tomorrow, and he's promised he'll show me how to do marbling when he's all set up.' She smiled. 'He's nice, Frank, isn't he? Sort of old-fashioned and very polite.'

'Gentlemanly,' I agreed. The idea that someone might seriously aim a car at him with the intention of killing him seemed ridiculous the more I thought about it. Perhaps whoever had witnessed the incident enjoyed dramatising in the same way Sandy Thomas did.

Sophie's brows drew together in a frown. 'Did you tell him he could put a padlock on his door?'

I nodded. 'Some of the books he repairs are valuable, apparently.'

Her dark eyes widened. 'They must be encrusted with gold, judging by the size of that padlock.'

We went upstairs so she could show me. The door to Frank's room stood open, there was no need to lock it yet as all it contained were racks of empty shelving, a table and chairs and a pile of wide, shallow trays that I assumed were used in marbling. But a steel plate had been screwed to the door with a thick metal hasp from which hung a very chunky padlock. I weighed it in my palm. 'I didn't realise it was going to be this big.' It wasn't the sort of padlock you opened with a key either. It had a combination on it, a row of numbers set on tiny rollers; you needed to line them up in the correct sequence for it to open. 'He's obviously very security conscious.'

Sophie puffed out her cheeks, 'Seems a bit over the top to me.'

I glanced into the room and noticed a heavy iron safe on the floor in the corner, its door wide open. It was empty inside. 'That must have taken some heaving up the stairs.'

'It did,' Sophie nodded. 'It was a good job he had help from Scott. He couldn't have managed it on his own.'

'He must be expecting to take more money than the rest of us do. Still, if it keeps him happy. After all, we don't have a burglar alarm and we need his rent.' I turned to frown back at her as we trod downstairs. 'You haven't mentioned that you and Pat don't pay any, have you?'

'Of course not.'

'Good. He doesn't need to know what our arrangement is. Just keep it under your hat.'

I dropped Sophie off at her mum's and went home to change. When I arrived back at the flat, I found a transformation had taken place in my bathroom – or at least, in half of it. The shower had been put in over the bath, a glass screen fitted, and one wall was clad in what looked like marble panels, white with a sparkly gold fleck. They were actually made of plastic, but I wasn't about to complain. They looked clean and modern and were a great improvement on broken tiles and missing plaster in the rest of the room. I bounced downstairs to knock on the kitchen door.

'It's good stuff, isn't it?' Kate said brightly. 'The plumber suggested it. It's cheaper and quicker than getting new tiles. He just sticks the panels straight on the wall. Is the colour OK? I didn't think you'd want pink. He says he'll finish it tomorrow.' She grinned, 'In time for the weekend.'

I sighed. 'Daniel's not coming now. There's trouble at t'bog.'

'Oh, what a shame!' She disappeared for a moment and reappeared with a small consolation prize wrapped in foil, a leftover offering from *Sunflowers*. 'Bombay pie,' she explained, 'curried veggies with chickpeas and paneer.'

'Thank you.' It was only a small package but a goodly weight. A little while ago Kate and Adam were thinking of selling *Sunflowers* and, thank God, they'd changed their minds. Without their cafe leftovers I might starve.

Half the walls in the bathroom might still be bare and crumbling plaster, but the new shower worked. I lingered under it for ages, holding my hair up, enjoying the rising steam, the tingling needles of hot water pouring over my neck and down my spine. Then I washed my hair, towelled it dry, changed and made it back to Druid Lodge, only ten minutes late.

I needn't have hurried; dinner was not yet on the table. Gabriel, Ricky and Morris were in the garden, surveying the potential performance space.

'The main acting area is down there where the lawn levels out, with the lake and woods as a backdrop.'

'We thought it would look so pretty,' Morris added, 'with lights in the trees reflecting on the water.'

'Pretty,' Gabriel repeated, as if this was an entirely alien concept, his palms closed together in front of his mouth, eyes narrowed, as if he was deep in thought.

'And it would be so lovely,' Morris continued with a catch of sadness in his voice, 'if we could make it a place of happy memories again.' He began polishing his glasses, always a sign of stirred emotion with Morris. Not long ago the lake and the wood had been the scene of tragedy. A body had been found floating in the water and the young gardener, Luke, who had transformed the lake and little woodland from a dark, weed-choked, overgrown wilderness, to an airy glade filled with dappled light, had committed suicide.

'Actually, I like the lake,' Gabriel declared after a

brief silence. 'Wouldn't it be great if the fairies could rise up out of it like water spirits?'

Ricky wasn't impressed. 'They'd get their costumes wet.'

But Gabriel seemed inspired. 'They could be naked.'

'Oh, I don't think so.' Morris settled his specs back on his nose. 'This is a community production, you know, there may be children involved. And in any case, the water is quite deep in places. We wouldn't want any accidents.' He was getting emotional again and I squeezed his arm gently.

'Health and Safety,' Gabriel moaned. 'Why does it always stand in the way of creativity?'

Ricky and I exchanged disbelieving glances over the top of his head.

'I'm hungry,' I said loudly to Morris. 'Isn't dinner ready yet?'

He seemed relieved to turn his attention to food. 'Yes. It's all ready,' he said and we trooped inside.

The Valkyries didn't turn up during dinner. I think Gabriel must have switched off his phone. 'Don't you think we should persuade Juno to audition?' he asked, as we lingered over the salmon and dill tart, minted potatoes and salad that Morris had placed on the table. 'She'd make a lovely Helena.'

Ricky kicked me none too gently on the ankle. 'You won't get her onstage. We've been begging her for years.'

'I stood in for Jenny when she hurt her back in *Jack and the Beanstalk*.'

'The arse end of a pantomime cow doesn't count,'

Ricky argued. 'You could've been anybody.'

'Well, there's gratitude for you! There I was, bent double, tripping over those bloody udders because I couldn't see where I was going . . .'

Gabriel was laughing.

'Strangely enough,' I added, 'I do not feel any desire to perform.'

'That's a pity,' Gabriel said. 'But will you be involved in some other way?'

'Well, if they ask me *nicely*,' I replied, giving Ricky a baleful stare, 'I might help with the costumes. And I'm usually the one at auditions running around with a clipboard making sure that we've taken everyone's contact details.'

'You wouldn't like to do the same for me next Sunday, would you?' he asked. 'That would be a real help.'

During dessert he asked if he could see around the house and look at the costume collection. 'Do you have any ideas about costumes?' Morris asked.

Gabriel shrugged, a spoonful of raspberry mousse poised in mid-air. 'I was thinking about modern dress.'

'Modern dress?' Ricky repeated, scandalised.

Gabriel flicked him a tiny glance. I suspected he was trying to wind him up.

'That does seem like a wasted opportunity,' I put in hastily, 'when you've got professional costumiers here ready and waiting.'

'You're probably right.' Gabriel shrugged. 'Show me around this wardrobe of yours,' he added loftily. 'Maybe I'll find something in it to inspire me.'

I helped Morris clear the plates as he went to make coffee, really just an excuse for the two of us to whisper in the kitchen.

'Thank God he's only staying one night,' he muttered, shaking his head. 'There'll be bloodshed if he stays any longer. We can't possibly put him up for six weeks.'

'Is he expecting you to?'

'He's been dropping heavy hints. But we'll have to find him a guesthouse.'

'Do you want me to drive him back to the station tomorrow?'

'No, no, my love, we've got the car back now, there's no reason why you should have to bother with him again.' He stopped loading up the tray with coffee things and looked at me. 'Are you all right about helping out next Sunday?'

'Of course. I'd have come anyway.'

He sighed heavily as he picked up the coffee tray. 'Good. I've got the feeling we'll need all the help we can get.'

CHAPTER FOUR

Frank Tinkler seemed to have made himself at home in *Old Nick's* by the time I arrived the following afternoon. The empty shelves in the shop had been brightened by a display of his cards and notebooks and there was a discreet sign – *Marbled Papers by Frank Tinkler* – on the counter. Pat was on duty, squinting with concentration as she threaded coloured beads on long silver pins to make earrings. On the table in front of her was an assortment of chipped saucers that she had filled with all her different beads and jewellery findings. There was no sign of Sophie. The watercolour she was working on, a dramatic view of Brentor church, lay abandoned on her easel.

'She's upstairs,' Pat told me before I could ask, 'with Frank.'

I leant over to remove a silver earring hook that had become entangled in the crocheted sleeve of her cardigan.

'Everything OK?' I asked.

'If you mean, have we sold anything? No, we haven't,' she responded without taking her eyes off what she was doing, 'but if you mean, is Frank OK? Yes, he is. Except he was a bit put out when he found out he couldn't get a signal for his mobile phone in here.'

'Oh, hell's teeth! I should have mentioned it when he was here the other day. I forgot. Did you tell him he could use the landline?'

Pat pushed a strand of lank brown hair behind her ear. 'I did.'

I went up to say hello. I could hear Sophie giggling as I climbed the stairs. Frank had rolled up his sleeves and wore a green apron over his immaculate clothes. He and Sophie were bending over the table, their attention fixed on a shallow metal tray filled with some kind of viscous liquid. Floating on its clear surface were blobs of coloured inks like virulent moulds growing in a Petrie dish. Sophie dropped red ink from a paintbrush and I watched the blob spread out into a pink haze.

'Now, Sophie, are you happy with your colours?' Frank asked.

She thought about it for a moment, her dark head tilted. 'Can I add some orange?'

She made to pick up one of the bottles of ink ranged on the table, but Frank almost snatched it from her hand. 'Not that one, if you don't mind. Not Sunset Orange. It's rather expensive,' he smiled apologetically. 'I only use it for touching up.' He handed her a different bottle. 'Use this orange instead.'

He took a sheet of thick, white paper and laid it lightly on the liquid surface, peeling it back almost immediately. The coloured spots and splashes had transferred themselves to the paper and he laid it down flat on the table. 'Hey presto!' The resulting sheet looked like the cards he had on display down in the shop, streaks and blotches of random colour in an abstract work of art. 'Good afternoon, Juno,' he greeted me politely.

'Frank, I'm sorry—' I began

He held up one finger in a schoolmasterly fashion. 'Bear with us one moment. So, Sophie, this is what results if we just drop the colour on to the liquid without taking any further action. But,' he went on, picking up a metal skewer, 'this is where it gets more interesting.'

He dipped the skewer into the liquid and began to drag it from one side of the tray to the other, creating a pattern of colours as he went. 'This is what we call feathering,' he explained.

The liquid seemed to be offering a slight resistance. 'Is that just water?' I asked.

'It's thickened with carrageen moss,' he explained.

'The stuff you use for setting jellies?'

He smiled. 'Quite so.' The random streaks and splodges of colour had now coalesced into a repeating pattern. Frank laid another sheet of paper on the surface and then pulled it off. 'You see, the same colours, but a completely different effect.'

'And is that permanent?' I asked, staring at the paper. 'You don't have to fix the colours in any way?'

'No, that's all there is to it, although once it's dry you

can touch it up by hand, if you want to add other effects.'

Sophie picked up a vicious looking metal comb. 'Can I use this?'

'Try it,' Frank offered. 'The more you comb and rake the inks, the more intricate the pattern becomes.' Sophie began to scrape the comb across the watery surface, the tip of her tongue poking out in concentration

'I'm sorry, Juno,' Frank turned to me. 'I interrupted you.'

'I only came in to apologise about the phone signal – or rather the lack of it. I should have mentioned it the other day.'

He laughed. 'My goodness, I've lived in Ashburton long enough to know how unreliable the phone signals are.'

'Please use the landline downstairs if you need to.'

'My calls are hardly vital,' he assured me.

'This is fascinating,' Sophie declared. Her comb had sliced the feathered pattern up into loops of interconnecting colours. 'Can we see?'

Frank obligingly laid on another piece of paper and peeled it away. Sophie put down the comb and brandished a metal rake.

'You could be stuck with her for hours,' I warned Frank. 'When you get fed up of her, remind her she's got a customer waiting for her to finish that painting downstairs.'

'I'll be down as soon as I've done this,' she promised, without looking up.

I knew better. She'd be another hour at least.

* * *

I called in on Maisie next morning, another of my regular clients. She's ninety-six. I could see her as I walked up the garden path to her cottage, standing in her glass porch. She was dressed, which meant a carer from the agency had already called to get her up that morning, although the tumbled state of her apricot curls meant it hadn't been her favourite. Only Maria was allowed to comb Maisie's hair. She was leaning on her zimmer frame, swiping the air about her with a feather duster as she tried to shoo out a bumble bee as big as a marble. It kept banging itself against the window, buzzing with indignation. I fetched a tumbler and a sheet of paper to trap it against the glass pane and then released it into the garden. We watched it fly off into the blue on wings that seemed too tiny to support its furry body.

'They find their way in easily enough,' I said. 'How come they can never find their way out?'

Maisie shook her head. 'Bees is precious. Can't afford to waste 'em.'

At this moment Jacko, her beastly little terrier, trotted around the side of the house with the smug look of a dog who's been up to something. Whilst I cleaned her living room, Maisie sat in her chair, Jacko dozing on her lap, and I told her about my new tenant, Frank.

'There used to be family called Tinkler lived up by the cricket ground.' She sniffed dismissively. 'Bad lot, if you ask me. One of 'em got done for smuggling cigarettes from trips abroad. Don't remember the name Frank. I wonder if he's related?'

'I hope not. And actually, I've no idea where he lives.

In Ashburton somewhere. His wife is called Jean.'

'Jean?' Maisie scowled and then shook her head as if the name meant nothing. 'You wanna ask him,' she went on, 'ask him if he has family live up along Cuddyford way. There was another lot of Tinklers lived up there. They were another bad lot an' all.'

I laughed. 'Why, what did they do?'

Maisie shook her head. 'Don't remember now. But you ask him if he's related.'

Perhaps I won't. I thought of Frank up in his workroom, mixing up his colours, dropping spots of marbling ink on to moss-thickened water, raking through the colours with a comb. Odd, what some people spend their time doing. But Frank was pleasant, polite and had paid his rent upfront. If he had dubious relatives, it was no affair of mine.

Later that evening Sophie and I loaded up, carrying blankets to sit on and coats for when it got cold as darkness fell, together with leftovers from *Sunflowers* I'd scrounged from Kate. The weight of my backpack was further increased by glasses and a bottle of wine. Sophie had brought a giant bag of crisps and large bottle of cider, probably not a good idea because, tiny as she is, it only takes about a thimbleful of any alcohol to get her drunk. We'd also bought torches to prevent us from tumbling into any ditches on our way home.

'Thanks for coming to the concert, Soph.'

'A free ticket is a free ticket,' she responded practically. 'Anyway, I'm only really coming for the picnic. I don't know what sort of music you're subjecting me to.'

'It's a string quartet. It'll be very easy listening,' I lied as she wrinkled her nose. I wasn't sure if the programme would be to her taste, but I'll listen to just about anything, especially if it's live. This concert was part of the summer music festival, with events going on all week at various places in and around Ashburton. I'd already been to a folk concert at the arts centre and chamber music in the town hall.

We trudged up Bowden Hill, past the last of the houses. The tarmac ended a few yards further on and we carried on up the rough track between high hedges. We were not alone – behind and in front of us knots of chattering people carried picnic hampers and folding chairs, all heading for the gates of Hilltop Cottage.

'Cottage' is a bit of a misnomer. Hilltop is a large house with an extensive walled garden blessed with perfect acoustics. A canvas gazebo had been set up to offer the musicians cover if it rained. There was no such luxury for the audience, but it was unlikely to be a problem that evening: the sky above was magically blue straight up to heaven overhead, shading towards golden marmalade on the western horizon.

I waved to Elizabeth and Olly who were getting their tickets checked at the gate. I'd forgotten they were coming. I hadn't seen Elizabeth for a day or two, she'd been doing extra hours at the surgery and hadn't been in to man the shop. She and Olly share a house. He's fifteen and everyone except me believes that she's his aunt. Their relationship is actually more complicated than that.

We joined forces and spread our rugs on the grass

together. We had far more food than we needed. Olly had baked a quiche and made three different salads, with a summer pudding for dessert. It was a pity in my view that he'd gone off the idea of becoming a chef. At the moment he favoured becoming a jazz musician, or possibly a vet, but at his age he was likely to keep changing his mind.

'When do you break up for the summer, Oll?' I asked. 'Do you fancy a holiday job?'

'I've promised Pat I'll help out at Honeysuckle Farm.' He already volunteered at the animal sanctuary on Saturdays and loved working with animals.

'But they won't be expecting you all day, every day. Adam could use some help at the cafe. Just a couple of hours a day. He'd pay you. He can't afford much but . . .'

Olly's pale blue eyes lit with enthusiasm. 'Could I do the cooking?'

'I don't know about that, but he could certainly use a hand with clearing tables and washing up.' His little face fell. 'Maybe,' I suggested, 'you could be the barista.'

He grinned. 'Make all them fancy coffees with that big machine?' This obviously appealed a lot more. 'I'll think about it,' he promised.

Elizabeth surveyed the picnic spread. 'This should keep us busy all evening.'

'I'm sure we'll manage.' It is an unwritten rule that no concert in Ashburton begins on time. I reckoned we could fit in a good hour's scoffing and drinking before the string quartet arrived to tune up.

CHAPTER FIVE

Next morning the phone rang much too early. The first muzzy thoughts that clouded my brain as I fought to struggle out of the pit of unconsciousness was that I'd overslept and there was an irate dog owner on the phone demanding to know why I hadn't arrived to walk their pooch. Then I realised it was Saturday, not a dog-walking day, and that last night Sophie and I had drunk too much at the concert and taken a long time finding our giggling way back into town by the light of our wavering torches. Rather than me attempt to drive her home we decided she should sleep on my sofa. The phone was only a few feet from where she lay but, like me, she seemed to be struggling with returning to consciousness. She'd pulled the blanket up over her head and lay softly groaning. I fumbled for the receiver and picked up. 'What?' I demanded grumpily, squinting at the slice of bright light piercing the gap between the curtains.

'Miss Browne, is it?' A man's voice, unfamiliar.

'Yes. Who is this?'

'Mr Thorncroft gave me your number. He said you were the local contact.'

I rubbed my face and tried not to yawn. 'What for?'

'The caravan. We're delivering it this morning. You'll need to sign for it.'

I groped around inside my brain. 'But it's not being delivered until next week.'

'That's not what it says on the sheet here.'

'There must be some mistake.'

'I can't help that. We're almost at the site. We'll be there in a few minutes.'

'Oh, bloody hell,' I muttered. 'All right, you'll have to wait for me. I'll be there as soon as I can.'

I disconnected and began shaking Sophie on the shoulder. 'Wake up, Soph! We've got to get up. Sodding Daniel has landed me with taking delivery of his caravan.'

She dragged the blanket down her face and stared at me with one eye open. 'Caravan?' Her voice was croaky. 'What caravan?'

'Daniel's. Up at Moorview Farm. I can drop you home on the way, if you want.'

She yawned and struggled on to one elbow, dislodging Bill who had spent the night curled up on her tummy. 'No, I'll come.' She smiled sleepily. 'I've always wanted to take a look at that place.'

We bounced our way up the hill in Van Blanc about twenty minutes later. We had flung on our clothes, stopping only to down some aspirin with a quick coffee. I don't know what I looked like, but Sophie's usually neat black hair was standing up in spikes like a badly mown lawn. She gazed around her at the empty grassland of Halshanger Common opening up around us, the wild grasses bleached to the colour of straw by the dry summer heat. 'Bloody hell, it's a bit remote, isn't it?'

'It's not exactly in the centre of things.'

She nodded in the direction of a distant hill crowned by some impressive slabs of granite. 'Isn't that Rippon Tor over there?'

As we crested the brow of the hill, we saw that the track leading to the farmhouse was blocked by a flatbed lorry on which sat a pale green caravan. I braked and we both stared.

It was a very small caravan with rounded corners, bug-like in shape, reminiscent of an alien spacecraft from a 1950s B movie.

Sophie's voice trembled with laughter. 'Is that it?'

It certainly didn't look like anything Daniel could consider living in. I wasn't even sure he could get in through the door. 'No, it can't be,' I agreed. Not only was it being delivered on the wrong day, this must be the wrong caravan.

Not according to the man wielding the clipboard. He pointed with an aggressive finger to what was written on his paper. 'This is a vintage 1960s Sprite,' he assured me, finger repeatedly jabbing.

'But it was bought on the Internet,' I responded, 'sight-unseen. I don't think this is what Mr Thorncroft had in mind.'

Clipboard sniffed unsympathetically. 'I can't help that. It's been bought and paid for.'

'Are you sure you've got the right address? We weren't expecting it till next week. Could you ring your office and check?'

Clipboard huffed impatiently but did get as far as digging in his pocket for his mobile. He wandered away from us so that we couldn't hear him, and a muttered conversation took place. Meanwhile I tried to contact Daniel on his phone, but he wasn't picking up.

Clipboard came back to us with a triumphant swagger. 'Paperwork all checks out. This is the caravan that was purchased by Mr Thorncroft.'

'But I'm sure it's wrong.'

'There's nothing I can do about that.' He raised his arm to signal to his mate in the cab.

Groaning, the space-bug took flight, lifted up on chains and swung out from the flatbed to hover perilously in the air before being deposited on an area of level ground about fifty yards from the farmhouse door.

Clipboard was deaf to all persuasion. I refused to sign his paperwork so he dropped the keys at my feet and drove away in his lorry, leaving the caravan staring at us with an injured and slightly reproachful air. Sophie considered it, her head on one side. 'I think it's rather sweet.'

I picked up the keys from the grass. 'Shall we?' I asked.

'I think we'd better.'

I opened the door of the caravan, ducking instinctively as I entered. I have to say in its defence the interior was scrupulously clean, its lino floor and polished surfaces gleaming, the paintwork and matching soft furnishings the same shade of gloomy fish-tank green. But whilst Sophie could stand up easily, I could feel my curls brushing the ceiling.

She gazed up at me. 'Daniel's even taller than you. How is he supposed to stand up in here?' She looked around her, frowning. 'Where's the bed?'

I pointed at the narrow, padded couchette along one wall. 'I think that's it. There's probably a drawer that pulls out from underneath that turns it into a double.' I stooped to demonstrate.

Even as a double it made a very small bed, but it effectively blocked the means of getting from one end of the caravan to the other. Sophie grinned. 'And the two of you are supposed to cuddle up and get passionate on that?'

I didn't comment. I inspected the tiny hotplate and sink in the corner and experimented with opening and closing the windows and drawing the little curtains.

'Isn't there a loo?' Sophie asked.

'It doesn't look like it.'

She opened a narrow cupboard door. 'Ah, here's one. You can just about back into it if you keep your elbows in close to you.' She giggled. 'It's a good job neither of you are fat. Is this really what Daniel intended to buy, do you think?'

'Well, he's used to roughing it, but this is so small.' I took out my phone. 'I'll take some photos. I can send them to him later and see what he says. I don't see how he could possibly live here for any length of time, especially with Lottie.'

Sophie's eyes widened. 'I'd forgotten the dog.'

We went outside and I locked the caravan door. It turned out there was a knack to this and I had to have several attempts. Meanwhile Sophie had wandered up the path towards the farmhouse. She stood looking up, one hand shading her eyes as she surveyed the straggly plant growing from the cracked chimney pot, the sagging roof, missing slates and the upstairs window hidden by a tarpaulin. 'It needs a lot of work, by the look of it.'

'It would probably be easier to knock it down and start again.'

'I don't suppose we can get inside?'

I shook my head. 'Sorry, I don't have the keys.'

'I'm not trying to be nosy. I just wondered if there was a loo. The one in the caravan's no good. There's no water yet.'

'I think there's an outside loo here somewhere.'

I took her on a tour around the outside of the building and through the gate into the old garden. Its high stone walls protected it from moorland winds, but it was long neglected and grown wild, flower beds gone to seed and invaded by brambles, overgrown shrubs strangled lovingly by the twining stems of rampant bindweed, its white trumpet flowers blaring from among elegantly pointed leaves. Sophie rattled every external door in the house, discovering a tool shed and a broom cupboard. Then one door opened and we found ourselves gazing at an ancient white lavatory with no seat. It wasn't exactly what you could call a mod con. We stared at the trapped flies in the thick grey webs that festooned the ceiling. 'I hope you're not afraid of spiders.'

'Actually,' she said, eyeing them uneasily. 'I'm not that desperate after all.'

'Probably just as well, I'm not sure about the drains. In the meantime,' I said, glancing at my watch. 'I need to get moving. I've got to open the shop in twenty minutes.' It was Saturday. My turn.

'Do you mind dropping me off at home?' Sophie asked. 'I think I'll just go back to bed.'

I grunted. It was all right for some.

Daniel phoned that evening, a response to the photos I'd sent him of the caravan.

'Did you really mean to buy it?' I asked.

'Certainly, I meant to buy it. It has a great deal of antique charm. I thought you of all people would appreciate that, Miss B.'

'Oh, I do,' I assured him. 'But it's so small and the bed is tiny. But you really need to see it for yourself.'

'I can't wait. I'll be down next Friday. I'm really looking forward to seeing you, Miss B,' he added softly.

'Me too,' I murmured and we said goodbye.

I yawned. I'd been up too late the night before, too early this morning, spent all day in the shop and I was ready for my bed. I looked out of the window. The last light of the long summer evening had glimmered away and moths fluttered in the gloom. The garden below lay in darkness. It was definitely bedtime. I was already in my pyjamas when the phone rang again. I thought it might be Daniel, perhaps he'd forgotten to tell me something. But it was Sophie.

'Sorry, Juno,' was the first thing she said.

'That's all right. What's up?'

'It's my inhaler. I think I left it up at the caravan.'

'Have you only just noticed?'

'Well, no,' she admitted awkwardly. 'I noticed it hours ago. I didn't want to bother you, only . . .'

'You can't stop worrying about it.'

'I am sorry.'

'Are you sure it's in the caravan?'

'I hope it is. I put my bag down on the floor in there while we were in there poking around and it must have slipped out.'

I hoped so too. If she'd dropped it on the grass outside, we didn't have a cat in hell's chance of finding it, especially in the dark. The sensible thing, of course, would be to wait till morning, but that would leave Sophie stressing about it all night: just the sort of thing to bring on an attack. I sighed. 'All right. I'll go up there and see if I can find it.'

'No, pick me up on the way. It's my inhaler. I must come and look for it too.'

'There's no need,' I began.

'No, it'll be better with both of us,' she insisted. 'Two heads are better than one.'

Not necessarily. I put the phone down. I dragged my jeans and a fleece jacket on over my pyjamas, picked up my keys and headed for the door.

Halshanger Common lay in blackness all around us, the lights from distant houses reduced to golden pinpricks. It would have been easy to miss the farmhouse in the dark and I trundled the van along slowly. When my headlights picked out the standing granite slab that marked the gatepost I drew to a halt. I decided we'd walk the short distance to the caravan from there, rather than risk a puncture on the stony track up to the farmhouse.

The air felt thick and warm. All around us, a rasping orchestra of crickets fiddled in the long dry grass. We trod across the ground by torchlight, stepping around the scattered stones that glowed white in its beam. The light washed over the face of the caravan, its chrome fittings glinting, and we reached its door.

'You'll have to hold the torch while I fiddle around with this key,' I told Sophie. But as I turned it in the lock, she laid a warning hand on my arm. 'Look,' she hissed in my ear. 'There's a light on in the barn.'

I turned. A dull yellow glow was shining from under the ragged planks of the barn door. 'Is someone in there?' she murmured nervously.

I switched off the torch. If someone was in the barn, I wasn't sure I wanted to advertise our arrival. We stood in the dark, ears straining above the chorus of insects. There came a sound like the scrape of metal on metal, a soft clang, and I thought I caught a man's voice. I opened the door of the caravan as quietly as I could.

'Wait inside,' I whispered. 'Bolt the door after you.'

'What are you going to do?' she breathed, as I zipped up my jacket and began stuffing my hair inside my hood.

I couldn't imagine what anyone might be doing in an abandoned barn in the middle of the night; probably no good. 'I'm going to take a look.'

'No!' She screamed faintly, then clapped a hand over her mouth. 'They might be dangerous.'

'Then lock the door.'

'I'm coming with you.'

'Stay in there until I've had a look.' Her breath was already coming in little snatches, I didn't want fright to start her off on one. 'Look, it might be perfectly innocent. Go inside, have a fumble around and see if you can find that inhaler.'

'Right.' She agreed so readily I knew she didn't really want to come with me.

The feeble glow coming from under the barn door was enough to light my way without using the torch, the murmur of voices growing louder as I crept across the grass.

I peered in through a crack. An ancient tractor took up most of the barn. Two men were standing on the far side of it, peering inside at the engine, their faces shielded by the cover they had raised in the rusty bonnet. Were they trying to start the tractor up? It didn't look as if it was in a condition to go anywhere, it probably hadn't moved an inch in years. Something within the engine rustled and one man gave a satisfied grunt as he began to pull it out. It was a white plastic carrier bag.

The door to the barn was ajar, the old bulb-shaped light switch hanging on a twisted brown flex within reach of my fingers. Warily, I inched my hand through the gap, my fingers closing silently around the bulb. Then I flicked the switch, plunging the barn into blackness. There was a lot of swearing from the men inside. Metal clanged. I swung the door open, flipping on the torch.

They froze, startled, dazzled by the beam, instinctively raising their hands to shield their faces from the inquiring light, showing me palms and outspread fingers, their faces shocked and pale in the glare. I knew they couldn't see me behind the torchlight, I was just a dark, hooded figure. I didn't speak. After a few moments of silence one of them called nervously. 'Who are you?' I didn't answer. I was sweating beneath my jacket, my fearful heart walloping in my chest but they didn't know that. They glanced at one another, then rushed for the only way of escape. They charged towards me.

If the door had an outside bolt, I could have slammed it shut, trapping them both. As it was, I was forced to leap out of their way to avoid being trampled on. One of them gave me a hefty shove in passing, knocking me off my feet, sending the torch flying. It rolled in the grass, lighting up the white soles of their fleeing trainers. I grabbed it and aimed it at their backs as they raced into the dark. Sophie was standing open-mouthed on the steps of the caravan. 'Are you all right?' she yelled. As she hurried over the grass towards me, I heard the kick-starting of a motorbike somewhere in the blackness, then a roar as it sped away.

I switched the light on in the barn, picking up the fallen carrier bag and peered inside. 'They took this out of the tractor,' I told Soph as she drew close. 'They knew what they were looking for, it was hidden in the engine.'

'What's in it?' she breathed.

'Looks like little packets of white sugar.' I looked at her and grinned. 'Do you think they run a cafe?'

CHAPTER SIX

Detective Constable Dean Collins roared with laughter when we shone the torch around the inside of the caravan, his bulky frame taking up most of it. We'd already shown him the tractor and right now two uniformed police and an enthusiastic spaniel were searching the rest of the barn for drugs.

'But why hide them in there?' Sophie had asked.

'It's an excellent place to hide your stash,' Dean told her. 'They've probably been using it for years – the place has been deserted that long. It's dry and a lot safer than a hollow tree. I reckon it must have given them a shock to see this caravan had appeared. They obviously don't know that there's a new owner who has plans to move in.' He took out his notebook. 'I don't suppose you ladies managed to get a good look at either of them?' he asked, more in hope than expectation.

'They both wore dark clothes and had their heads covered,' I told him. 'One wore a hoodie, the other a beanie hat, pulled right down. He had some kind of scarf over the lower half of his face. The one in the hoodie had a thin face and one of those scruffy little beards.'

'How old was he, do you think?'

I shrugged. 'Mid-twenties? Sorry, it's not much of a description.'

'The one wearing the beanie hat had a white logo across the back of his jacket,' Sophie added.

Dean glanced at her. 'You don't remember what?'

She frowned. 'Like a big triangle. There was a letter A, and something else in small writing beneath it but I couldn't see what.'

Dean nodded. 'OK. Well, if you think of anything else . . .' His lips twitched in a smile. 'Whoever they are, they've lost quite a stash tonight, worth a lot of money. If I were you, Juno, I'd go home.' He frowned. Dean and I were mates and he knew enough about me to be suspicious of my activities. 'What were you two doing up here at this time of night, anyway?'

Sophie held up her inhaler in triumph. 'Looking for this.'

By the time I'd taken Sophie home and got back to the flat I was wide awake and buzzing with too much adrenalin from the night's events to think about crawling into bed. I sat up drinking coffee as the sky lightened outside and the sun came up on another fine day.

I knew I ought to phone Daniel, let him know what

had happened on his property, but he was probably still asleep. I decided to leave it till later. To be honest, I wasn't too keen on telling him what had happened. I'd promised him I would try to keep out of trouble and I knew he'd think that I should have waited till morning, not gone up to the isolated farmhouse in the dark with only a cowardly asthmatic midget for company.

I looked at my watch. It was Sunday and there would be a car boot sale on at Newton Abbot Racccourse. I'd go and have a look around for stock. After taking a nice hot shower, I decided gleefully. I'd get breakfast when I got there.

I lugged all my finds in through the door of the shop next morning. I'd had a good day at the boot sale: I came away with a printer's tray, a military overcoat with brass buttons, which I wore despite the heat as it was easier than carrying it, a pair of brass bath taps, which I could sell to a dealer in architectural salvage and a small Victorian footstool with most of its padding missing. This last item was part of my latest project to teach myself to upholster. I have a chaise longue desperately in need of recovering, which will cost a fortune to have upholstered professionally. Someday, I plan to have a go at it myself, but I've decided in the meantime I had better find something less intimidating to learn on. The footstool looked about my size.

I'd also picked up an old toffee tin full of cigarette cards bundled into rubber bands. As I opened the tin I was assailed by the whiff of old tobacco. There were hundreds of them, dating from the late 1890s when they were first introduced to help stiffen cardboard cigarette packets, up to the 1960s, printed with pictures of everything from famous film stars to football teams, aircraft and butterflies, each one a potential collector's item, a little work of art. Someone must have been collecting them for years.

But my prize find was the printer's tray. I'd been looking out for one. It was a shallow, wooden tray measuring about two feet by three, divided up into different sections. When printers used to set type by hand, it would have been used to store letters, to keep all the different blocks of type separate. I've seen some painted and hung on walls as display cabinets for small ornaments, but I had a different use in mind for this one. I placed it on her worktable in front of a frowning Pat. 'This is for you.'

'What is it?' she asked, always suspicious.

'It's to keep your beads in,' I explained, tearing off the military greatcoat before I died of heatstroke. 'My cousin Cordelia used to have one in her shop. It'll save you pouring them out into all those saucers.'

Sophie left her worktable to come over for a look. 'You can keep different types of beads in each of these little sections,' she explained, just in case Pat hadn't got the point.

Her face lit up with pleasure. 'Oh, that's lovely. I can have 'em all laid out in front of me when I'm making earrings. I'll be able to see what I've got.'

'I bet it looks lovely when it's filled up,' Sophie added.

‘You’ll sell more earrings too.’

I left the two of them poring over it while I carted the things I’d bought back to my unit in the storeroom. Despite the masses of fussy, frilly things I sell on commission for Ricky and Morris, vintage clothes too delicate to hire out and rejected from their theatrical wardrobe, the room still looks bare. I never seem to have enough stock to fill it. I nipped upstairs to wash my hands and said hello to Frank. He was busy with a book repair as I walked in, shoving some kind of orange stiffening material down the spine of an old leather-bound volume.

‘Is everything OK, Frank?’ I asked. ‘Do you feel you’ve settled in?’ He’d certainly filled the room up. Rows of old books in various states of disrepair lined his shelves and sheets of beautifully marbled paper were laid out flat to dry on pasting tables. The air smelt of damp paper and ink.

‘Yes, thank you,’ Frank smiled putting down his work. ‘I hear you met my wife the other day.’

‘She said she’d be glad to see the back of all this stuff.’ I couldn’t really stop to chat. I had a client to get to, a house to clean. I was just about to make my excuses when there was a clattering of heels on the stairs and a young woman burst into the room.

She faltered at the sight of me, obviously expecting Frank to be alone. She looked flustered, a pretty girl, probably in her late teens, wearing torn jeans, high heels and too much vanilla-scented perfume. ‘Oh.’ She flicked a glance from me to Frank and back again.

‘Ah, Millie!’ he said, standing up. ‘You’ve come to

collect that book, haven't you?'

He picked up a leather-bound volume from one of his shelves. 'Be sure to tell your customer that I've replaced the endpapers as he requested, but I've also had to reinforce the spine.' He spoke very slowly and deliberately, as if she was a bit thick.

She flicked another glance at me before she took the book he was holding out, reaching out for it nervously as if she feared it might explode. The wrists protruding from her sleeves were bony and too thin. There was something waif-like about her, a touch of the Victorian workhouse. 'OK,' she muttered.

'You will be sure to tell him, won't you?'

'Yes.' She stood clutching the book to her chest. She looked desperate to leave, to be released, like a greyhound in the traps.

'And have you got something for me?' Frank asked patiently.

'Oh, yes, sorry.' Dangling from one of her skinny wrists was a carrier bag that seemed to contain several small packages. She thrust it at him, turned on her heel and left as abruptly as she'd come, a lady of few words, obviously. She didn't strike me as someone who might be involved in the antiquarian book trade, but what do I know?

By the time I came back downstairs, Sophie and Pat were happily decanting beads into the tray. I'd done the same thing for my cousin Cordelia when I was growing up: filling different sections of the tray with glass beads to make earrings for her shop. For a moment my heart squeezed at the memory. She had taught me how to make earrings, but she was dead, too many years ago. I had passed on the knowledge to Pat and it was she who made them now.

When I came back at the end of the afternoon, the printer's tray was full and Pat had gone home. We'd had a few small sales, Sophie told me, including some cards for Frank. I popped upstairs with his money. He was painstakingly trimming some marbled paper to fit the endpapers of a book and I didn't want to ruin his concentration as he frowned over his work. I placed the money on the corner of his table. 'We'll be off in a minute,' I told him. 'I'm shutting the shop.'

'I'll be here a little while longer,' he said, without looking up. 'I'll let myself out.'

When I got back downstairs, I found Sophie had concocted a scheme for the two of us to go into Exeter and see the latest summer blockbuster at the cinema. 'I was going to go with Mum,' she explained, 'but she's had to work this evening.'

Which meant Sophie didn't have the car. 'You only want me for a chauffeur,' I accused her.

'I do not!' Her dark eyes flashed in indignation. 'Well, all right, I do,' she admitted. 'But you treated me to that concert the other night, I thought I'd treat you to the pictures.'

'A good film wouldn't do me any harm,' I conceded grudgingly. 'I don't get out much.'

During the evening I wondered if Cordelia's theory was right: that Capricorns are born old and get progressively younger. In which case I wondered how young I was going to have to get before I could enjoy a film like the one Sophie took me to see. Superheroes are not really my thing. I endured two hours of ear-achingly loud music and eyeball-searing special effects without very much idea of what they were fighting for or who they were fighting against. There didn't seem to be any real plot, just an unending series of battles and explosions. Possibly I failed to understand the finer points because it turned out to be episode four of a saga and I hadn't seen the previous three. It turned out that Sophie hadn't either. 'It was a bit confusing, wasn't it?' she admitted when we escaped into the warm, evening air.

I dropped her off on the way home. It was dark by now and quiet, no one much about on the streets of Ashburton, except a group of youngsters gathered on the pavement outside the Chinese takeaway, their faces illuminated by the bright lights inside. I recognised Frank's nephew Scott among them, and the skinny girl Millie, looking a lot happier than when I'd seen her in Frank's room earlier. They were all laughing.

Out of habit I took a shortcut down Shadow Lane. Above *Old Nick's* a light was shining from an upstairs room. I cursed, thinking I must have forgotten to turn it off when I locked up. Then I remembered. It was only Frank up in his workshop, burning the midnight oil.

CHAPTER SEVEN

Eventually, I filled Daniel in on the events at Moorview Farm.

'I can't turn my back on you for five minutes,' he'd complained bitterly, 'without you doing something dangerous, Miss B.'

That's the problem with Daniel. He's overprotective. His first wife Claire died when she was young and he worries that something might happen to me. To be fair, I'm only alive and breathing now because of his intervention, so I suppose it's understandable. I pointed out it was hardly my fault that drug dealers had used his barn to stow their stash in.

'Point taken, Miss B, but you didn't have to creep up on them,' he said severely. 'You should have phoned the police and stayed in the caravan with Sophie, cowering in a maidenly manner until they arrived.'

'Then they'd have got away with the drugs,' I argued. 'The sooner you get some work started on that farmhouse the better, Mr Thorncroft,' I told him sternly. 'It might deter people from stashing their drugs in the place.'

On Wednesday afternoon I had some hours free. It was another gloriously bright blue day, but threatening to be hot. The cool breezes of the moor beckoned. But I'd promised to help Ricky and Morris with packing some costumes for a forthcoming show, so I forgot about the moor and drove up to Druid Lodge. As I folded dresses for *Hello, Dolly!* into the big wicker hamper that stood waiting for them, I asked if there had been any further word from Gabriel Dark.

'He's coming here on Friday,' Ricky moaned, an enormous Edwardian hat, complete with curling ostrich feathers, balanced on each hand. 'He's bringing his car this time.'

'We've found him a place to stay in East Street,' Morris added, relieving him of a hat and sheathing it in a plastic bag before placing it carefully in a hamper. 'All the hotels and guesthouses are booked up for the summer and none of them could offer him an uninterrupted stay for six weeks. So, I talked to Mary. She's been trying to sell that flat above her shop for over a year. It's a lovely place but not a sniff of a buyer. She's agreed to rent it out to him, short-term.'

'Oh, hell's teeth!' My stomach sank inside me. 'I've just realised. Daniel will be here this weekend and the auditions are on Sunday.'

'Oh, don't worry about them, Juno,' Morris said soothingly, taking the other hat from Ricky. 'We can manage without you.'

'No, I've said I'll help and I will.' I just hoped they didn't go on for too long. I didn't want to waste a whole day when I could be spending it in the arms of my lover.

Dolly's costumes, hats and shoes took all day to pack. They had to be ready for the carrier to collect in the morning to take them to Southampton. I had to refuse the invitation to stay to dinner. Adam and Kate were opening *Sunflowers* for one of their occasional musical evenings and I'd promised to waitress, along with Soph.

I came home late to an ominous winking from the little red eye of the answering machine. I'd been busy taking orders for veggie curry and spicy bean casserole while a folk duo entertained the diners all evening and I'd had my mobile switched off. It was Daniel, asking me to phone back.

'I bet he can't come this weekend,' I moaned to Bill who was greeting me by winding himself in a furry figure of eight around my ankles.

'Certainly, I'm coming,' he assured me. 'But my direct flight to Exeter's been cancelled, so I'll have to fly to Bristol and travel the rest of the way by train. The good thing is that it's an earlier flight, so I should get to Newton Abbot at around the same time.'

'Get off the train a stop earlier,' I told him, 'at Teignmouth. I'll pick you up there.'

'Excellent thinking, Miss B.'

'Lottie can have a run on the beach.'

'I'm not bringing the dog on this occasion.'

'Oh, poor Lottie!' She'd hate being left behind, but she'd hate the plane and train a lot more.

Next morning, I arrived at the shop to find Pat and Sophie poring over the latest edition of the *Dartmoor Gazette*. Sandy Thomas had been at it again. Pat was tutting at a photo on the front page. 'He's only a young feller. It's a shame, that's what it is.'

'What's up?' I tried to peer over her shoulder.

'Suicide. He jumped off Tavistock Viaduct, the police are appealing for witnesses. It says here his body was found lying in Drake Road, the main road out of town for Lydford.' She pulled a face. 'It's a good job there weren't any cars coming, he might've taken someone else with him.' She squinted as she read the caption beneath a photograph of the man in question. 'Josh Naylor, his name was. He was only twenty-two.'

'But look, Juno,' Sophie tapped the picture with her finger, her dark eyes troubled. 'Look at his picture.' The face staring back from the page was of a young man, his chin partly covered by a scruffy, dark beard. 'It is him, isn't it?' she said as I snatched the paper up for a closer look. 'He was one of those two men in the barn on Saturday night.'

I nodded as I read the article again. 'Yes. Yes, it is.'

At the police station I asked for Detective Constable Collins and showed him the picture.

'This is one of the men you saw up at Moorview Farm?' he asked.

'I'm as certain as I can be. Sophie recognised him too.'

Dean was nodding. 'It makes sense. Josh Naylor has been caught dealing in Ashburton more than once. In fact, his name sprung to mind when you gave me the description of those two you saw the other night. I paid him a visit but his girlfriend insisted she didn't know where he was. I was still on the lookout when his death was reported in Tavistock. Though why he wanted to go throwing himself off Tavistock Viaduct . . .'

I eyed him with suspicion. 'You don't seriously think this was suicide?'

'Well, it could have been an accident,' he answered evasively.

'No, it couldn't. I've walked over Tavistock Viaduct. The walls are chest height, with a safety railing on top. No one could fall off accidentally.'

He cleared his throat. 'He could have been drunk or drugged to the eyeballs. He might have climbed up on the wall, messing about. We won't know for sure till the pathologist has finished with him.' He was thoughtful for a moment, passing a hand across the back of his bristly hair. 'In the meantime, don't go talking to all and sundry about having seen him on Saturday night, OK?'

I shrugged. 'All right.' But I wasn't convinced by the notion of accident or suicide. How likely was it, I asked myself as I walked back to the shop, that the death of Josh Naylor was not connected to him losing the stash of cocaine he'd been hiding in Daniel's barn? I decided that it wasn't very likely, in fact, not likely at all.

* * *

I knew I had some pictures of Tavistock Viaduct somewhere. At lunchtime I dug out a box of old photographs, hundreds that Cordelia and I had taken on our tramps around the moor when I was a kid. I used to come down from boarding school and spend all the holidays with her. Apart from my cousin Brian, who's a diplomat and has lived abroad for most of my life, she was my only family. Cordelia, an astrologer with a tiny shop in Totnes selling jewellery and New Age tat.

In the photograph I was holding she looked a bit wonky, probably because I was about nine when I took it. She was standing on a slight slant, her hands in the pockets of her dungarees, the cuffs turned up above red woolly socks and leather walking boots. She was laughing, her mess of curly hair whipped up by the wind. It was Tavistock Viaduct she was standing on. It used to carry the railway track across the valley above the town. The line is defunct now. And this was where Josh Naylor was supposed to have jumped to his death.

'I don't believe it,' I told her photograph. What's more I knew Dean Collins didn't believe it either.

I must confess to a sneaking affection for Tavistock. It's a market town on the western edge of Dartmoor and has a population roughly three times the size of Ashburton. It also has World Heritage Status and a definite sense of being grand. This is partly because of chunks of ruined historic abbey lying about the place but mostly due to activities of the Seventh Duke of Bedford who built fine stone cottages for all his mine workers as well as the Guildhall and the famous pannier market. Where it gets above itself in my opinion, is in laying claim to be the Home of the Cream Tea. Just because some bishop back in the dark ages dished out bread, jam and cream to the local peasantry, does not give the town the right to make such an extravagant assertion. But despite such audacious cheek it's a pretty place with interesting shops and I really like it. Elizabeth was in charge of *Old Nick's* that afternoon and would close up for me, so I escaped, trundling across the moor in bright sunshine and arriving in the town just as all the shops were getting ready to close. This was probably just as well: shopping wasn't part of my mission.

The viaduct sits at the edge of the town, casting its shadow over Drake Road and Banwell Street, the houses dwarfed by the massive stone arches straddling their rooftops. I stood at the foot of one, looking up. It was about twenty metres to the top. The thought of Jake Naylor's body being flung off and hitting the hard road beneath was not a comfortable one. I only hoped he was too drugged up to know what was happening to him.

The way to the top of the viaduct took me up a steep and winding road, bringing me abruptly upon the old railway station, converted now into desirable residences. There was no sign of where the railway line had been until I rounded another corner and found myself at one end of the viaduct, staring straight across it. A warning sign urged anyone feeling depressed to phone the Samaritans.

I peered over the parapet, down on to the rooftops of the houses below and an untidy patchwork of garages, yards and gardens, then up to the hills beyond the town. The old railway line that had crossed the structure was marked out now by a tarmac path running down its centre, grass and gravelly mud on either side. The spot from which Naylor was supposed to have jumped was clearly marked, not by police tape cordoning it off, but by a solitary bunch of rusty chrysanthemums, slightly wilted and sad. There was no card or message attached and I wondered who had put them there. Someone who knew Josh Naylor and mourned for him? There had been other suicides from this viaduct over the years. Did some compassionate soul mark each tragic death with an anonymous tribute, as some folk do at the site of roadside crashes?

There were other signs of activity too, footprints in the muddy soil. Which prints belonged to Josh wasn't clear. It seemed he had not been here alone that night. Were these footprints in the gravelly mud made by friends, drunk, roaring encouragement to him in his daring as he climbed up on to the parapet? Or did those prints belong to whoever had picked him up bodily and flung him over the high precipice to break to death on the road beneath?

The police must have wondered the same thing. The area might no longer be cordoned off, but I could tell that at some time during their investigation they had considered this a crime scene. I squatted down to look at one of the footprints and fingered the specks of white residue embedded in the tread. It was plaster of Paris, left from casts taken of these shoeprints. Would police have taken casts if they'd really believed Josh Naylor was a suicide?

I got that itchy feeling between the shoulder blades, the feeling you get when you're being watched, and turned to see a man leaning against the far wall. He was staring at me, hands in his pockets, a tall man in jeans and t-shirt, with the well-defined muscular torso and arms that spoke of serious time spent in the gym. His hair was a closely shaven pelt, like suede, so short that it was impossible to determine whether it was silver or blonde, just a glistening stubble on his skull. There was an intensity about his stare that I found unnerving, a deliberate air of purpose. I stood up. To go back the same way I'd come, I would have to pass close by him and instinct told me that I didn't want to do that. I carried on across the viaduct until I reached the other side.

Cordelia and I had often followed the footpath where the old line used to run, but I had never walked it alone. The trains are long gone. It's tree-shaded now, gnarled roots clinging to the embankment that rises high on either side, carved from the solid rock. It's a quiet place of tiny waterfalls and dripping stone, of shadowy ferns and still dark water in shallow ditches. I walked, evening sunshine slanting through the trees, dappling the shadows, gilding clouds of midges that danced in its light. I watched a grey wagtail bobbing at the edge of a tiny stream. The scene should have been magical, but I was conscious of how quiet and lonely the track was and kept glancing over my shoulder to see if my watcher on the viaduct was following.

The embankment gave way to fields, glimpses of sunlit grass just visible through the screen of trees on either side. I felt as if I'd left the town of Tavistock behind. But it was an illusion, only a short walk before I found myself at the end of the footpath, at the edge of the road that swept down the hill into town. Here there were houses, traffic, safety. I could follow this road to reach Van Blanc. But it would be quicker to retrace my steps. I stood at the end of the path and waited to see if the watcher on the viaduct might emerge. Minutes ticked by but there was no sign of him. Then three joggers came down the hill and turned along the path that led back to the viaduct and, emboldened by their company, I followed.

I met with no one more alarming coming the other way than a girl walking a pug, and put all thoughts of sinister, staring men behind me. Until I got back on to the viaduct and saw that the flowers that had marked Josh's memory had gone. Someone had stolen them from the foot of the wall.

I peered over the edge, and I could just see them, rusty petals torn to fragments and scattered on the road below. And I knew it was not the joggers who had mangled the flowers and thrown them off the viaduct, not the girl with the dog, not kids messing about. It was the man with the closely shaven head. I knew it.

CHAPTER EIGHT

I wasn't expecting to see Elizabeth. She'd locked up the night before and wasn't due in again for a few days but she walked into *Old Nick's* late the following afternoon. I was in the back room, studying the footstool I'd bought, working out how to take it apart. I hadn't got very far. My mind kept straying back to the previous afternoon, to Tavistock Viaduct and that intently staring man.

I was still thinking about him when Elizabeth appeared. 'Juno, could I have a word?' She leant in close to me and I caught the delicate fragrance of her face powder as she dropped her voice to a whisper. 'Is Frank upstairs?'

I nodded.

'In that case, perhaps we should go for a little walk.'

'Elizabeth, what . . . ?'

She laid a finger against her lips and I followed her

out through the shop, goggling with curiosity.

'Just off for a cup of tea,' I told Sophie as we passed.

'Oh, nice!' she said without looking up from her painting. She shoved her specs up the bridge of her tiny nose. 'It's all right for some people.'

'I'll bring you back some cake,' I promised.

We thought we might as well make good my words and went to 'Taylors' tea room, Elizabeth refusing to say any more until we were sitting at a table and had ordered. The starched, white tablecloths and the pretty, old-fashioned china seemed the correct setting for Elizabeth with her elegant upswept hair, her immaculate blouse and neat gold earrings. She always looked perfectly groomed, like a racehorse. It was almost impossible to believe that when I first met her, she was living in her car. I envied her elegance. I don't know a curry comb from a dandy brush myself.

'Something curious happened last night,' she told me calmly. 'I thought you ought to know about it.' She gave a little sigh as if choosing where to start. 'I shut up shop at the usual time. Frank was still working upstairs so I called goodnight to him before I locked up. I hadn't got as far as the car before I realised that I'd left my reading glasses behind. I'd put them down when I was serving a customer. I knew exactly where I'd left them, on a table in your back room. So, I went back and let myself into the shop, fetched my spectacles and was about to leave when I heard Frank come down the stairs and pick up the phone . . .'

She paused to let the waitress bring our tray of tea

and smiled her thanks before she carried on. 'I realised he hadn't seen me. I don't know why I didn't call out to him, tell him why I'd returned . . . but I heard him dial a number and then he said, "It's safe. They've all gone. You can come now." Well, that made me prick up my ears, I can tell you!'

'You're sure that's what he said?'

'Perfectly sure,' she responded with a touch of asperity. 'I've just had my hearing tested. Then he said, "It's no good crying to me. It's your own fault. I told you to have nothing to do with him." Well, then I was in a dilemma. I couldn't leave without announcing my presence and Frank would know I had been eavesdropping. Besides, I was curious to hear what else he might say. All I could do was stay absolutely still and quiet.'

'And did he say anything?' I poured tea through the strainer and slid a cup toward her across the tablecloth. The waitress returned with freshly baked, warm scones and there was another brief pause while she set them on the table with a pot of strawberry jam and a bowl of yellowy clotted cream.

'He said – and these were his exact words – "You'd better come now. Come to the side door."' Elizabeth leant forward slightly, her voice dropping to a confidential whisper. 'Then he added, "Just make sure you're not followed."'

'Followed?' I echoed. 'But he didn't say a name? You don't know who he was talking to?'

She frowned. 'No, he didn't mention a name, but I assumed he was talking to a woman.'

'Why?'

'Why would he worry about whoever it was being followed? I leapt to the conclusion – wrongly as it turned out – that he might be carrying on a clandestine affair, probably with a married woman, and he was worried about their being found out.'

'Frank?' I said, incredulous.

Elizabeth raised an eyebrow. 'Look, it may not be the raging passion of youth, but sex doesn't automatically stop after sixty, you know.'

'No, I know,' I agreed. 'Look at you and Tom Carter!'

She cast me a warning look. 'Tom and I are friends,' she said gravely. 'Our relationship is strictly platonic.'

'Of course,' I agreed, until Tom has his hip operation and then you'll be at it like polecats.

'What happened then?' I asked.

'Frank put down the phone. Just for a moment he hovered in the hallway and I held my breath. I thought perhaps he'd sensed that I was there. But then he climbed up the stairs and I crept out through the shop as fast as I could and locked the door behind me. I had to reach up and hold on to the little bell so that it wouldn't jangle.' She stopped to slice her scone into two precise halves. 'You know, what I found disturbing wasn't what Frank had said,' she went on, 'it was his tone of voice. He didn't sound like quiet, courteous Frank at all. He sounded most unpleasant.' She laid down her knife. Elizabeth, always so calm, seemed almost perturbed.

'You didn't see who came to the side door?

'I did. I waited outside of the shop windows until

I heard footsteps coming along the alley from the Sun Street end. When I heard a knocking at the side door, I risked a peep around the corner. It wasn't a woman. A man was standing there with his back to me. I couldn't see his face, but I got the impression that he was young. And he was fidgety, he seemed ill at ease.'

'I suppose this could all be perfectly innocent,' I said, dropping a dollop of cream from the spoon and slathering it on my scone, 'but it's Frank telling him to make sure that he wasn't followed that makes it sound as if something dodgy is going on.'

'Precisely.' Elizabeth passed me the jam. 'And if something dodgy is happening on your premises I think you have a right to know about it.'

'You didn't hear this man speak?'

'No. But when Frank opened the door to him, he said, "the best thing you can do is to lie low." Then the door was shut very quickly.'

'This does sound odd.'

'It certainly sounds as if Frank's visitor had been up to something he shouldn't.'

'Such a pity you didn't see his face. I wonder if it could have been his nephew, the one who helped Frank move in.'

'I wasn't in the shop on that day so I wouldn't know. All I can tell you is that he was wearing jeans, trainers and a dark jacket, pretty much a uniform for young men these days, and one of those soft hats they all wear.'

'You mean a beanie hat?'

She nodded.

'This jacket didn't have a white triangle on the back by any chance?'

Elizabeth raised a delicate eyebrow in surprise. 'Yes, now you mention it,' she said, dropping a spoonful of jam on to her scone, 'it did.'

'It's no good getting excited about white triangles, Juno,' Dean told me later.

I'd quickly filled Elizabeth in on the events up at Moorview Farm, the death of Josh Naylor and the search for his companion, a young man wearing a beanie hat and black jacket with a white triangle on the back. I also mentioned my visit to Tavistock, the footprints, the man lurking on the viaduct and the strange affair of the flowers. Then I'd rushed home to phone Dean, and I must say I thought his low-key reaction to my news was dispiriting.

I had the phone clutched in one hand while I applied blusher with the other. I'd already made myself late for picking Daniel up and was trying to multi-task. 'They're everywhere,' he went on. 'That white triangle is the logo for the alpine sports supplier on the trading estate, Ashburton Alpine Sports, it's called. Lots of kids around here wear clothes with it on. It doesn't mean there's any connection with whoever was with Naylor that night.'

'And talking of Naylor,' I said, 'don't think I believe that nonsense about his death being an accident or suicide. I've been up on that viaduct and you lot have been there taking plaster—'

'Why?' Dean interrupted.

'Why what?'

'Why were you up on Tavistock Viaduct? Not poking your nose into a police investigation, I hope.'

'Oh, come on, Dean! Josh Naylor wasn't alone on that viaduct. He was murdered. You know it and so do I.'

'We don't *know* anything,' he insisted. 'We're still waiting for his toxicology reports to come back and they take a bloody age.'

'Oh, bugger,' I muttered.

'What was that?'

'Me trying to get my lippy on. Anyway, someone was interested in what I was doing.' I described the man who'd been watching me.

'But he didn't follow you?'

'Well, no,' I admitted.

'He might just have been a weirdo, and throwing a few flowers off a viaduct might be a strange thing to do but it isn't a crime. Look, Juno, going back to Frank's visitor, all you know is what Elizabeth told you, which was one half of an overheard telephone conversation. It's not really anything I can do something about.'

'Thanks,' I snapped, 'a fat lot of good you are.'

CHAPTER NINE

Daniel perched on the wall of the railway station car park, a tall dark figure sitting with shoulders slightly hunched, a backpack at his feet and a large bouquet of flowers clutched in one hand. I reckoned he couldn't have been there more than ten minutes.

'Did you think I'd forgotten you?' I called out as I swung the van to a stop in front of him.

'A man of my charisma?' He unfolded his long limbs and stood up. 'Impossible!' Then he grinned. 'Although I did wonder if I'd made a mistake about you picking me up in Teignmouth.'

He put the flowers down on the wall and I slid into his enfolding hug. He is possibly the only man alive who makes me feel small in a good way, something about the fact I can put my head on his shoulder without having to stoop, something about the way he thrusts his long fingers through my curls and cradles my head. 'God, you feel good!' he murmured, his lips brushing my ear. 'How are you, Miss Browne with an "e"?'

'All the better for seeing you, Mr Thorncroft.'

We drew back to study each other. I thought he looked tired, dark shadows under his grey eyes. All this travelling was something he could probably do without.

'I'm sorry about last weekend, Miss B.' He presented me with the bunch of flowers. 'Please accept my humblest apologies for missing the concert and burdening you with my caravan.'

'These are lovely, but you don't need to apologise.'

'I'd have brought them anyway.'

'I'm glad to hear it. But I have to apologise too.' I told him about the auditions on Sunday.

He shrugged. 'It can't be helped. I was supposed to be here last weekend.'

'Why don't we put these flowers in the van with your bag,' I suggested, 'and go for a walk on the beach?'

He thrust his arm through mine. 'Sea air and thou, Miss B, what more could man desire?'

Five minutes later we were walking the long stretch of Teignmouth's sandy beach, tasting the salt wind on our lips. The tide was coming in, closing off the beach behind us as an incoming wave slapped a foamy frill against the foot of the sea wall, splashing up spray and forcing us to get a move on. We hurried towards the Ness, the red cliff that juts into the sea on the far side of the estuary, pausing to watch a rust-speckled cargo boat pass safely through the narrow channel in front of us. It carved a wake that sent the tiny pleasure boats at anchor in the harbour bobbing like toys in a bath. Teignmouth is a working port, exporting ball clay for generations and receiving cargo from all over the world. 'A few years ago, a Russian vessel refused the pilot,' I told Daniel as we watched it pass. 'It was stuck on that sandbank for weeks. It became quite an attraction.'

The cargo boat slid safely by and we turned the point beneath the lighthouse on to the landward side, what locals call the back beach, the strip of sand between a line of beach huts and the water's edge, where dinghies and cabin cruisers haul up and the sand is latticed with mooring ropes just waiting to trip the unwary. We were safe from the incoming tide here, but the salt spray was replaced by the rank smell of dried seaweed washed up on the tideline and a definite niffiness wafting from the fish quay nearby.

'I spy a hostelry,' Daniel cried happily as we picked our way cautiously along gritty sand littered with fragments of shell and lumps of bladderwrack. We headed for The Ship, an old sailors' inn famous for real ale, and sat at a wooden picnic table with a view due-west up the River Teign to Shaldon Bridge and beyond, and ate freshly caught prawns while a sinking sun set the clouds on fire above the distant moor.

I asked Daniel about his work in Ireland. I knew peat bogs and wetlands were as important as forests in fighting climate change. 'But what can you do if the peat has already been eroded?' I asked. 'It takes thousands of years to form. You can't just put it back.'

'No,' he admitted, 'but you can slow the erosion down. We've been building a system of leaky dams – basically, barriers of tree trunks laid down the hillsides. They slow the water that washes the exposed peat off the moor. Also, we're planting millions of plugs of sphagnum moss for the future. We were really making progress until some idiot with one of those instant barbecues started a fire.' He scowled. 'Bloody things ought to be banned.'

I nodded. Wildfire during a dry summer was always a danger on the moor and it only took a spark from a barbecue or campfire to start one off. 'A lot of shops around here have stopped selling them.'

'Anyway, we lost hectares of land, which meant we've had to start all over again. And that's meant finding a fresh lot of funding.'

'God, that's awful! I'm so sorry.' I considered him for a moment, reached out and touched the lock of dark hair falling over his forehead.

He shook his head. 'Let's not talk about it, it's too depressing. Tell me what happened with that night at the farm. They've got a bloody nerve, these people, storing their drugs on my property.' He grinned suddenly. 'You and Sophie must have given them a shock, though.'

'I think we did.'

'The police didn't find any more during their search?'

I hesitated. I hadn't mentioned Josh Naylor's death and I decided not to just now. I didn't want to spoil the evening. 'No,' I said.

'I really want to go and see my caravan.'

I leant across the table and threaded my fishy fingers

through his. 'Why don't we leave it until morning? It isn't going anywhere. And there are far more interesting things we could do this evening.'

'I can't imagine what you mean, Miss B,' he said and grinned.

In the sunlight the caravan looked even smaller than I remembered, as if it had shrunk in the last few days.

'It's magnificent,' Daniel pronounced, striding towards it.

'You don't think it's rather small?' I bet when he bought it, he never even looked at the measurements.

'Silence, Miss B!' he commanded as he wrenched open the door and poked his head inside. It was a moment before he spoke. 'Ah!'

'You could always use it for a henhouse,' I suggested.

'Shut up.' He stepped inside, tried to straighten up and failed. 'Ah!' he said again.

I stepped in after him as he pulled out the bed from beneath the couchette. 'Seriously, you'll get a permanent crick in the neck if you try to live in here.'

He ignored me and attempted to lie down on the bed. 'But this is wonderful. It offers such flexibility. I can hang my head and shoulders off this end. Alternatively,' he went on, 'I can hang my legs off the other end, or,' he stretched himself out fully, 'I can do both at the same time.' He grinned at me. 'Not much room for you, Miss B.'

'Or Lottie,' I pointed out practically.

From where he lay, he was able to flip open the door

of the loo. ‘A trifle compact,’ he commented and flipped it shut again. He turned his head. ‘Miss Browne, you’re blocking the view of my kitchen.’ He waved me aside with one hand and I stepped out of the caravan, out of his way. A few moments later, he joined me outside.

‘So, what do you think, Mr Thorncroft?’ I asked.

‘I admit that the situation requires a degree of thought,’ he responded.

I laughed and he thrust his arm through mine. ‘Onward, Miss B. To the farmhouse. Let’s see if the death-watch beetle has finally triumphed.’ As we approached the front door, he began to rummage in his pocket for the keys. As it turned out, he didn’t need them. The door was already open.

We stood in the kitchen, stunned into silence by the shattered window frame, the doors of the old dresser wrenched off, drawers ripped out and smashed, logs for the wood-burning stove tipped from their basket and scattered across the stone-flagged floor, the splintered glass glinting, the stuffing of Lottie’s old armchair torn out and lying around in fistfuls. Daniel bent silently to pick up a dented coffee percolator and place it on the stove. His footsteps crunched on glass. ‘Be careful where you step,’ he warned softly. ‘You’re sure this place was locked up the other night?’

‘Sophie and I walked around the outside of the house in the morning,’ I remembered.

‘I didn’t check the house in the evening. But the police were here. I’m sure someone would have noticed if the door was open. I think whoever broke in has done it since then.'

'It's a good thing the rest of the house is empty,' Daniel said grimly, 'there isn't any more furniture they could wreck.'

To me, it didn't look like the random work of vandals. It looked as if someone had been searching for something. They had even started ripping off wallpaper in frustration, revealing the older layers of years gone by underneath.

'I'm going to check upstairs,' he told me. 'You stay here and don't touch anything.'

Naturally I ignored what he said and followed close behind him, but there was nothing to see in the unfurnished rooms above except for a few empty cupboards, their doors flung wide. I phoned the police. Normally a random break-in to an empty property where nothing was stolen would not have aroused much response, but because of the drugs haul from the barn and the death of Josh Naylor, they arrived within minutes – *they* being Dean Collins, and, unfortunately, Detective Sergeant Christine deVille, otherwise known as Cruella. She and I never seem to get along. Let's put it another way, she hates me.

'You haven't touched anything?' she demanded by way of a greeting, her strange violet gaze sweeping around the room.

We assured her that we hadn't. 'Except the coffee percolator,' I added. 'Daniel picked that up off the floor.'

'Let's hope they've left a few prints behind them,

whoever they are.' She looked at us coldly. 'We'll need to take your prints for elimination purposes.'

'You've already got mine on record,' I reminded her.

She gave a little tug of her mouth, smile or sneer it was impossible to tell.

'And mine,' Daniel added, 'from the Verbena Clarke case.'

Meanwhile, Dean was looking around him. 'There's a partial footprint on that window frame, and I think someone cut himself on the way in.' He indicated one of the shards of glass twinkling by his shoe. 'That looks like blood.' He straightened up, holding the bloodied shard of glass with tweezers and depositing it in a ziplock bag. It's amazing the equipment policemen carry in their pockets. 'Whoever did this was searching for something. I wonder if one of our friends from the other night paid a return visit?'

'They can't have hidden anything in here,' Daniel objected, 'not unless they've broken in on a previous occasion.'

'That's not impossible, Mr Thorncroft.' Cruella looked around the damp-stained walls with obvious distain. 'This place isn't even weatherproof, let alone secure. I take it you weren't keeping any valuables here yourself?'

'No, I wasn't.'

'At least we know it can't have been Josh Naylor responsible for this,' Dean grinned, 'because he's dead.'

Daniel frowned, suddenly intent. 'Who's dead?'

I groaned inwardly. Dean and his big mouth.

'One of the suspects from the other night, sir,' Dean went on, 'Josh Naylor. He fell from a great height. Very unfortunate.'

'Was it an accident?'

Dean gave a slight shrug. 'At this stage we don't know.'

Daniel turned his fierce gaze on me. 'Juno, you were going to tell me about this?'

'Of course,' I answered. Sometime or other.

Cruella meanwhile was involved in discussion on her radio with someone speaking in Cockroach. I made out the word *fingerprints* and sighed.

'We may as well get out of here,' I told Dean. 'Your fingerprint people will be in here for ages and you won't want us in the way. Can we go?'

'I think we've finished with you for the moment,' Cruella cut in before Dean could open his mouth, making it clear that the decision was hers, not his.

'When will I be able to board up that window?' Daniel asked.

She gave her tiny smile. 'Not until the fingerprint people have finished.'

He turned to Dean. 'Will you let me know when that is?'

Dean grinned. ''Course I will.'

We had lunch in *Rust and the Wolf*, a restaurant whose dimly lit and discreet entrance leads to the nearest thing Ashburton has to an American diner. Western and biker artefacts decorate the interior, burgers, burritos and tequila are on the menu and cartoons of Wylie Coyote play on its back wall. Food is good and it's not only popular with the young.

'I see Cruella's manners haven't improved,' Daniel commented. He'd been dangerously quiet since learning of Josh Naylor's death. Apart from ordering from the menu, this was the first time he'd spoken.

I shook my head. 'She doesn't like me at all.'

For a moment he smiled. 'She's jealous.'

'Of what?'

'That beautiful wide mouth,' he whispered, kissing me. He might be right. Cruella was a stunning-looking young woman with black hair and icy violet eyes. But her mouth was like a line of stitches, a bit deficient in the lip department.

'But seriously, Miss B,' he added. 'Why didn't you tell me this man Naylor had been killed?'

'I knew it would worry you. I wanted to choose my moment. And we don't know it was murder,' I lied. 'It could have been an accident.'

He considered me for a moment, a deep frown between his dark brows. 'Juno, you're not planning on involving yourself in this investigation?'

'Of course not!' I decided not to mention my trip to Tavistock Viaduct. 'It's nothing to do with me.'

'You won't do anything dangerous?'

'I'm not totally irresponsible.'

He laughed in a way that made me want to hit him.

'Look,' I hissed. 'I never knew this man Naylor, and I might add, I would never even have laid eyes on him or his drugs if it wasn't for you and your bloody caravan.'

That gave him a moment's pause. 'Touché, Miss B.' He sighed. 'You're right, I'm sorry.'

I was silent and he added, 'I just don't want you getting hurt. We know whoever broke into the farmhouse didn't find what they were looking for. They might try again. I don't want you there if they do. So, no more going up there without me. Promise?'

'I've got no intention of involving myself in anything dangerous,' I told him piously.

He smiled ironically. 'Forgive me, Miss B, but I've heard that before.'

I gave an exasperated sigh and he put a hand on my cheek, staring at me from worried, storm grey eyes. 'You have no idea how it tears me up when I learn you've been putting yourself in danger.'

Before I could speak, his phone rang and he took the call.

'That was your friend Collins,' he told me. 'They've finished up at the farmhouse.'

'That didn't take long.' Whenever the dreaded fingerprint men came anywhere near my place, they seemed to take hours.

'They lifted a few smudged prints but there was nothing much to find, apparently. I can go and board up that window.'

'After dessert,' I protested.

He grinned. 'On the blackboard it says there's a choice of banoffee pie or chocolate brownies. What are you having?'

CHAPTER TEN

Flyers about the auditions had been posted up all around Ashburton. A large turnout was anticipated so Ricky and Morris had booked a room upstairs in the Arts Centre, a spacious room regularly used for exercise classes. By the time I arrived, about twenty minutes before the auditions were due to start, there was already a crowd of hopefuls milling about in the forecourt outside, a lot of them mothers who wanted their infant daughters to be fairies, the last people I imagined Gabriel Dark would want to see.

'We've been told to wait out here,' a woman told me sharply as I walked past the queue.

'I'm not auditioning,' I explained as I opened the door, 'just helping out.'

Upstairs there was no sign of the great man, just Ricky and Morris setting up a table for the director to sit at and arranging the chairs against the walls where people could sit and wait their turn.

I had armed myself with my trusty clipboard and a goodly chunk of paper, each sheet ruled into columns headed with contact details and roles being auditioned for. I also had a handful of pens, which I was certain to lose.

With about a minute to go, Gabriel arrived looking pale, heavy-eyed and more than a little hungover. He also looked appalled. 'I had to fight my way through hordes of kids outside,' he complained, 'what the hell are they doing here?'

'They're here to audition,' Morris explained.

'What do they think this is,' he demanded crossly, 'a school nativity play?'

'The mothers want their little ones to be fairies.'

'Well, they bloody can't!' he snapped. 'It says quite clearly on the flyer that the minimum age is twelve.'

'We get the same trouble at the panto auditions,' Ricky told him, grinning. 'They think that just one glimpse of their adorable child will make you change the rules.'

Gabriel pinched the bridge of his nose as if he was already very tired. 'Juno, just get rid of them.'

'Sorry?' I was there to take names, not do his dirty work.

'Don't worry, Juno,' Morris said hastily, 'I'll go down and have a word.' He turned to Gabriel. 'Is it all right if I let the others come up now?'

'Yes, yes.' Gabriel waved the question away as if it was an irritating fly, then pulled out his mobile phone and disappeared into the adjoining kitchen.

Ricky was grinning out of the windows that looked down over the forecourt as we heard Morris's voice floating up from below. 'Now, would all the under twelves like to come over here to me for a moment?'

'Good luck, mate,' he chuckled.

I sat at the table with my clipboard, ready for the hopefuls I could already hear clumping up the stairs. To my surprise the first person in through the door was Sophie.

'You didn't tell me you were going to audition,' I protested as she scribbled down her name.

'Well, I wasn't really sure whether I would until the last minute,' she confessed, rolling her dark eyes at me. 'I thought I might try for Hermia. She's supposed to be small and dark, like me. What do you think?'

It hadn't occurred to me before but she'd be perfect. 'Go for it.'

'I'm ever so nervous,' she confided as Ricky came to scribble his name.

'You'll be fine,' he told her.

'Are you auditioning?' I asked him.

'Depends who else turns up,' he said. 'I might have a go at Egeus if Gabriel's short of men.'

'Egeus?' I repeated, frowning.

'That's Hermia's father,' Sophie put in.

'Yes, I know.' But Ricky had the height, looks and commanding voice that were perfect for Theseus, Duke of Athens. The problem was, of course, that Theseus gets married at the end of the play, and Ricky was about a quarter of a century too old to be considered a likely bridegroom. I was busy taking details for a while, surprised to see Ron from *Keepsakes* antique shop. I didn't know he was into amateur dramatics.

'Oh, I do the odd bit now and again,' he told me, 'I thought this could be fun.'

Olly arrived then with Elizabeth. She'd offered her help behind the scenes, but Olly announced he'd come to audition. I smiled at him in surprise. When I'd first met him, a year ago, he'd never have done anything to draw attention to himself.

'What part are you auditioning for?' Sophie asked him. 'Puck?' It was a reasonable assumption. Olly's small for his age with a pixie-like appearance.

'Puck?' he repeated in disgust. 'I'm not playing no fairy.'

'Who then?'

'I want to play Flute the Bellows-mender. He's one of the comics.'

'Isn't he the one who plays Thisbe when the comics put on their play for the Duke's wedding?' she asked.

'That's right.'

'So you don't want to play a fairy,' I said, 'but you don't mind playing a man who dresses up as a woman?'

'S'different,' he insisted.

Morris came puffing up the stairs, red-faced after dealing with disappointed little 'uns and outraged mums. Sophie nudged me as a tall, fair-haired young man walked in. 'Isn't that Scott?' she whispered, 'Frank's nephew, the one who helped him move into the shop. I wonder what part he's auditioning for.'

I wondered too. He certainly looked good and was surrounded by a twittering flutter of hopeful fairies as soon as he appeared. 'I'll find out.' I glided towards him with my clipboard, squinting over his shoulder as he filled in his details. I heard him tell the fairies that he'd been forced to study the play at school, thought it was a load of rubbish but wanted to gain some acting experience because it was his ambition to be in films.

'What's he doing here?' Olly muttered, scowling.

'Do you know him?'

'He used to go to my school. He left a few years ago but he was a right tosser. Oh, this is Marcus.' He introduced a boy who stood hovering next to him, looking nervous. 'He wants to play Wall.' Marcus beamed at me from behind owlish glasses. He was around Olly's age and probably looked the same now as he did at five years old and would grow up to look the same at forty-five, although possibly with less hair. He was a very solid-looking boy and I thought he would make an excellent Wall.

Ricky clapped his hands to bring the room to order. We were already late starting, and with not enough chairs for everyone to sit down, the crowd was growing restless. Gabriel was still deep in conversation on his phone, talking to someone called Darling.

'Right then, boys and girls,' Ricky began amiably, 'I'd just like to begin by thanking you all for coming. It's great to see such a large turnout. Now, I'd like to introduce . . .' he went on, backing towards the kitchen door and raising his voice, 'Gabriel Dark, who we're all very honoured to welcome as our director—'

There came a muffled curse from the kitchen and Gabriel shot into the room, pocketing his phone. The assembled throng, feeling it was required of them, politely applauded his entrance. After a moment's surprise he remembered to smile becomingly and took a modest bow.

'I'm sure Gabriel would like to begin by saying a few words,' Ricky concluded.

'Yes, right, um . . .' his eyes swept around the room. 'Goodness, there are a lot of you, aren't there?' He laughed and his audience joined in. 'Well, the first thing to understand is that if you're lucky enough to be cast in this play – and I'm afraid some of you will be disappointed,' he warned solemnly, 'I expect absolute commitment from everyone involved. We're working to professional standards here. I don't care about your brother's wedding or your dental appointments, I expect you to put this production first and be at every rehearsal. OK?' He clapped his hands in the slightly stunned silence that followed and rubbed them together. 'Good. The second thing is that we must consider what this play is really about. *A Midsummer Night's Dream* is not just a pretty comedy about fairies and lovers getting lost in the woods. At its *core*,' he made a fist as if to emphasise the word, 'it is a play about misogyny, patriarchy and male power.'

'Oh God,' Ricky muttered, eyes closing in despair.

For the next ten minutes Gabriel banged on. I could feel the excited atmosphere deflating like air from a leaky balloon. Whilst Scott was nodding wisely as if he agreed with every word Gabriel was saying, confusion and disappointment were writ large on the faces of many in the room. At last, he decided to shut up. He sat down next to me at the table and covered his mouth as he spoke. 'Everyone here is either too young or too old,' he muttered. 'And where are all the men?'

Ricky, who was standing behind us, leant over and patted him on the shoulder. 'Welcome to the world of amateur theatre, mate.'

'So, how's it going?' Daniel asked as I slid into my seat outside of the Old Library Cafe where we'd arranged to meet during the lunch break. He'd dropped me off in my van earlier and spent the morning at the farmhouse. He wanted the builders to start soon and there was a lot for him to think about.

It had been quite a trying morning. Gabriel, after a cursory glance at it, had taken little notice of my list. He'd simply pointed at people and told them which characters he wanted them to audition for. Fortunately, Ricky and Morris had whisked him off to the wine bar for lunch, so I could bitch about him as much as I liked.

'We had far too many girls and not enough men,' I told him. At least six girls had auditioned for Titania, Queen of the Fairies, despite the unfairy-like shape of some of them, with probably more to come in the afternoon. Daniel announced his intention to come and watch.

'Be careful, you might end up playing a part.'

He shook his head in mock sorrow. 'Alas, I have to return to Ireland.'

'So you do.'

'But seriously, weren't there any men?'

'There was Scott. I suppose he wasn't bad.' He was certainly full of self-assurance. He hadn't handled the verse well, but he was a suitable age and handsome enough to make a convincing Demetrius, one of the two rivals for Hermia's hand in marriage. He had the right arrogant swagger about him. He'd been asked to return in the afternoon to read with more of the girls. I wondered what Olly had meant when he'd said Scott was a tosser. I couldn't help noticing, as we left for lunch, that he shrugged on a black jacket with the white Ashburton Alpine triangle on the back. I looked around for Sophie but she was busy chatting with some fairies and hadn't noticed. I glanced at Elizabeth. His jacket hadn't escaped her attention. 'I've been watching our young friend there,' she murmured. His back was to us as he stood in a group with the others. 'The back of his head, the way he stands and moves,' Elizabeth went on, 'I'm certain that's him.'

'The man you saw visiting Frank?'

She nodded, 'Our Demetrius had been up to something.'

If it was Scott she'd seen at the side door of the shop, was he also the man I'd seen running away into the darkness with Josh Naylor? But this was not a good subject to muse about in Daniel's company, so I kept quiet.

Gabriel Dark came back from lunch smelling of wine and looking depressed. Ricky, who we'd met as he was finishing a crafty fag in the courtyard, said that he'd done nothing all through lunch but bellyache about the shortage of men. When he'd told him they'd probably have to put girls into some of the male roles, he'd been horrified.

No sooner had Gabriel slumped into the seat next to mine than he spotted Daniel and shook me by the arm. 'Who's that?' he hissed. 'What part's he here for?'

'I'm afraid he's not auditioning.'

'Why not?' he demanded furiously. 'Look at him,' he hissed as Daniel stood up to let Elizabeth sit down. 'He's so tall! He'd make a marvellous Theseus, or Oberon.'

'That's Daniel, he doesn't live around here.' I explained. 'He's just here with me.'

Gabriel glanced at me in surprise and then muttered something I couldn't catch.

Suddenly the room was filled by a voice as mellifluous as honey dripping from a spoon.

'I'm so very sorry we're late.'

Everyone turned to look at the doorway where Amanda Waft stood smiling in all her glory, her long wavy hair loose about her shoulders, wearing a floaty white dress that would have looked charming on a woman half her age.

'Who the fuck is that?' Gabriel whispered, as she began her stately and erratic progress across the room, her husband Digby trailing in her wake.

'Amanda Waft,' I whispered back, 'And Digby Jerkin. They're professionals, man and wife, used to have a series on television.'

'Oh, dear God,' he groaned, as if recognising some

ghostly apparition from the past, 'so it is. What are they doing here?'

'They live here,' I told him. They'd been months searching for their perfect home and finally seemed to have found it in the village of Landscove, two miles up the road.

He watched in horror as Amanda minced towards him. 'Is she pissed?' he whispered.

'She always walks like that,' I whispered back. She was also always slightly pissed but I didn't tell him that.

'I hope you don't mind my coming,' she said, stopping in front of the table. 'Digby is going to audition, of course, but I'm only here for fun. I do realise I am much too old to play Titania,' she paused, her eyebrows faintly raised, as if waiting for Gabriel to disagree. But he just stared at her, slack-jawed in wonder.

It was Ricky who spoke up. ''Course you're too old, Mandy, you silly tart! Come and sit down here next to me and behave.'

'Oh, Rickeeee!' she cooed joyously. 'But I would like to read a little,' she added to Gabriel, 'just for fun!'

'Right!' Gabriel rallied manfully. 'Well, in that case why don't you and er . . .' he pointed vaguely in Digby's direction. Digby thrust out his hand and shook Gabriel's heartily. 'I'm Digby Jerkin. Hello!'

'. . . you and Digby read right now?' Gabriel continued.' Digby, what part are you . . . er?'

'I thought I might have a try at Bottom,' he responded modestly, '. . . unless, of course, you've cast it already?'

Gabriel gave a rather hollow laugh. 'No such luck, old man.' He waved an arm at the empty space in the middle of the room as if it no longer mattered to him what went on. 'Please, carry on!'

Amanda looked anxiously at the wooden floor. 'Are there any cushions?'

A few people gave up the ones they were sitting on to create a pile onto which she gracefully sank, feigning sleep. She and Digby then proceeded to perform the most famous scene in the play. Titania the fairy queen, bewitched by a love potion, wakes to see the humble weaver Nick Bottom, on whom the fairy Puck has placed the head of an ass, and instantly falls in love.

Amanda's knees creaked as she rose from her bed of cushions, her descent again was too slow and stiff, but she was a powerful and expressive actress with a beautiful voice. There is something to be said for a lifetime's experience in the theatre, and whilst the scene wasn't perhaps as physical as it could have been, it was funny and, in its own way, strangely touching. She and Digby were so perfectly in tune with each other and with every nuance of the text, they moved their audience to a round of applause and took a bow.

Gabriel, who had shown his appreciation of Digby and Amanda by thumping lazily with one hand on the table, suddenly stopped, his eyebrows raised in surprise. While Digby and Amanda were performing, a stranger had slipped into the room, a young black man with film-star good looks. He caused a definite ripple and not just among the female population. Ricky began fanning himself as if he was having a hot flush. Gabriel prodded me on the arm. 'Find out who he is,' he hissed as the young man leant his shoulders against the wall. 'Find out what part he's auditioning for.'

I glided over to him with my clipboard, smiling a hello as I asked him to fill in his name and details. On my way back to my seat I glanced at what he'd put. Well, Matthew Prince, I told him silently, if you can walk and talk at the same time, I'm sure the part is yours.

Lysander, I mouthed to Gabriel as I sat down. Gabriel decided to try out Sophie as Hermia next. She'd been waiting all morning, getting increasingly nervous, and he asked the newcomer to read for Lysander, the man she loves. He tried to hand him a copy of the script, but it seemed Matthew had played the part before and knew the lines. Not only did he look good, he had a deep, rich voice and was obviously at ease with lyrical verse. He was tender and funny with Sophie's Hermia, and I think he helped to set her at her ease. The physical contrast between his dark good looks and fair-haired Scott as Demetrius, rival for Hermia's love, was striking. By the time he'd reached the end of the scene where Hermia's father accuses Lysander of stealing his daughter, Gabriel was beaming from ear to ear. Lysander's lines, as he argues he's a worthier man than Demetrius, took on new meaning. *I am, my lord, as well derived as he, As well possessed; my love is more than his . . .* Suddenly, the production had the edge that Gabriel had been looking for. Not only was *A Midsummer Night's Dream* a play about misogyny, patriarchy and male power, it was now about racism as well.

CHAPTER ELEVEN

I decided to try and be subtle with Frank. Next day I knocked on his door and asked him if he'd like a cup of coffee. 'I'm making one for myself.'

'Well, how kind,' he said, smiling, 'but I'm fine, thank you.'

'Goodness,' I cried, slipping into the room, 'you're writing your Christmas cards early.'

The table he was sitting at was covered in rows of neat, white envelopes, each one with a first-class stamp in the top right corner. There were also rows of small, marbled greeting cards in abstract patterns and colours, predominantly orange.

'No, no,' he laughed. 'One of the things I do in my spare time is . . .' he indicated a chair, 'please sit down, Juno. I run a little charity. I write to men in prison.'

'Oh, that's nice,' I responded inanely, not really sure if it was.

'I send inspirational messages,' he continued, warming to his theme, 'something positive and uplifting. Not always religious, you understand,' he added with a smile. 'I have to cater for all faiths. You see, what people don't realise is how much men in prison rely on contact with the outside. I always include a few stamped addressed envelopes in case they wish to correspond. Writing paper, envelopes, and especially stamps, are quite expensive. Prisoners can't earn much money so the gift of a few stamped envelopes is much appreciated.'

'Well, that's great, Frank, that's a really kind thing to do.' It occurred to me that my friend Henry, currently on remand in Dartmoor and facing a charge of murder, might appreciate some stamped envelopes too. But that was not what I'd come in to discuss and I changed the subject.

'Your nephew auditioned well yesterday,' I told him. 'He was most impressive.'

Frank's puzzled frown revealed he had no idea what I was talking about.

'Your nephew,' I repeated, 'Scott. He auditioned for a part in *A Midsummer Night's Dream*.'

'Did he?' Frank raised his eyebrows. 'I had no idea he had talents in that direction. He's not really my nephew,' he went on to explain, 'he's the son of a neighbour. I've known him since he was a small boy and he's always called me Uncle Frank . . . Good, was he?'

'Oh very,' I assured him. 'I'm sure he'll get a part.'

Frank nodded slowly as if digesting this information. 'Good-looking boy, of course,' he mused and then tailed off into thoughtful silence. I got the impression he wasn't too pleased. The conversation really wasn't going anywhere and I was wondering how I was going to bring it round to whether or not it was Scott who had been Frank's visitor the other day. I was on the point of asking if he was related to the Tinklers of Cuddyford after all, when I heard Sophie calling my name from the shop downstairs.

Frank smiled. 'It sounds as if you're wanted, Juno.'

I didn't really have an excuse not to answer her, so I took my leave in a rather lame fashion, my little chat having accomplished nothing at all.

'Sorry,' Sophie said, as soon as I reached the bottom of the stairs. 'I thought you were up in the kitchen. I didn't realise you were talking to Frank.'

'It doesn't matter. What's up?'

She looked at me from anxious dark eyes. 'Have you heard anything about the auditions yet?'

'No. Gabriel is going to email the cast list to Ricky and Morris first for their approval.'

I stifled a yawn. I'd got up very early to take Daniel to Newton Abbot Station. I wouldn't see him again now until he'd finished with the Irish project. After our goodbye, I'd come back to walk the Tribe. I yawned again. Suddenly a cup of coffee seemed like a genuinely good idea. 'It'll probably take Gabriel days to make up his mind.'

'I wonder if I'll get Hermia.' She stared at me hopefully.

'Do you think I was all right?'

'More than all right,' I told her. 'You were really good.' I'd always suspected Sophie could act. It had a lot to do with those long-lashed, orphaned-seal eyes of hers that she could employ with such devastating effect whenever she wanted something. They'd been working overtime at the auditions, turned first on Hermia's cruel father and then on her lover, Lysander, in the very comely form of Matthew. And Sophie is a Pisces and according to Cordelia, no sign of the zodiac is better at shape-shifting identities than they are.

A thought occurred to me. 'There was a girl who came in the shop the other day. She came to see Frank, a thin, dark-haired girl. Her name's Millie. Did you see her?'

Sophie nodded. 'She comes in a lot.'

'Really?'

'Yes, she brings stuff in for Frank and collects books from him.'

'She seemed nervous, that's all. It just struck me as a bit . . .' I was about to say *odd*, when the phone rang. I picked it up to find Ricky hissing at me from the other end.

'There you are, Princess!' He sounded agitated. 'Can you come up to the house?'

I looked at my watch. I had clients to get to. 'I'm going to be busy for an hour or two. What's up?'

'It's that bloody Gabriel Dark. He's emailed us his cast list.'

I slid a glance at Sophie who, fortunately, had gone away to get on with some painting.

'I can't get to you before lunchtime.'

'That'll do!' Ricky sounded relieved.

'If you're sure you really need me.' I couldn't really see what the cast list had to do with me, other than to try to pacify Sophie and Olly if they hadn't got the parts they wanted.

'Yes,' Ricky replied ominously, 'We need to have a little talk with you.'

Whilst I was whizzing around trying to get Maisie's shopping done before lunchtime, I happened upon Dean Collins coming out of the Co-op. I assumed he was off duty as my god-daughter, Alice, was dangling in a sling on his front, her chubby legs hanging down in a very stylish pair of rainbow-striped leggings I had bought her. After I had paid due godmotherly attention to her squidgy cherub cheeks and quiff of duckling yellow hair, I asked if there was any news on Josh Naylor.

He smiled grimly. 'Toxicology's back. He was pumped full of drugs when he died.' He paused and added reluctantly, 'But we don't think he could have fallen off that viaduct without help, if you know what I mean.'

'There must be a less public way of making a murder look like suicide.'

'Naylor was small fry. Most likely, those drugs he tried to collect weren't his and someone higher up the food chain wasn't happy when he couldn't deliver. Throwing him off the viaduct was a way of sending a message to anyone else who might be involved. This is what happens if you mess us about.'

'No news about his friend in the black jacket?'

Dean shrugged his broad shoulders. ‘Not a clue. We’re continuing our enquiries.’ Alice had quickly grown bored with our conversation and began to grizzle. Dean and I were about to go our separate ways when I remembered something. ‘You don’t know anything about Frank’s accident, I suppose?’

He stared at me blankly. ‘You mean Frank Tinkler?’

‘He was knocked down in a hit-and-run accident about a year ago. He wasn’t hurt, but according to Sandy Thomas, a witness who saw it happen was convinced the driver had aimed at Frank deliberately. You don’t know anything about it?’

He shook his head. ‘No. And if you think I’ve got the time to go digging up old witness statements, you’re mistaken.’

I pulled a face. ‘You’re no fun anymore.’

‘Do you remember the old cigarette cards?’ I asked Maisie as I put her shopping away. At ninety-six she could always remember things from long ago, if not what day of the week it was and what she’d had for breakfast.

‘Oh, I do!’ she cried. ‘My old Bob used to collect ’em, God rest him.’ She chuckled. ‘I did, too, when I was at school. I was always after my dad when he’d bought a new packet of cigarettes, wanting the card. They used to come in the packets of tea as well. And the Co-op, they used to do ’em too.’

‘I bought a tin full of them the other day, at the car boot sale.’

'What do you want them old things for?'

'They're collectors' items these days, Maisie. Some of them are valuable.'

She tutted and shook her head. 'Some folks got more money than sense. Mind you, we were always trying to swap 'em at school,' she admitted. 'Trade the ones we had more than one of for ones we hadn't got. I remember Bob used to keep his in an album. Sets of 'em, he had.'

'Do you remember what they were?' I asked, sitting on a stool by her feet.

'Trains, mostly and motor cars . . .' She held up a knotty forefinger as she remembered, 'and racing greyhounds, I remember, but then he'd collect anything to do with sport.'

'And what did you collect?'

'Oh, film stars, we used to like them at school. And birds of paradise and things from round the world like people in funny headdresses.'

'Shall I bring over the ones I've got? We could sort through them and see if any of them are the same ones you and Bob had?'

'If you like.'

'Next time,' I promised. Right now, I had to get up to Druid Lodge and find out what was the matter.

'So, what's up?' I asked as soon as Ricky let me in through the door.

'Bloody Gabriel!' he shuddered, leading the way to the breakfast room where Morris was already presiding over the teapot. 'There are twenty named parts in *A*

Midsummer Night's Dream, not counting attendants and extra fairies, and he's only cast half of them.'

'But we must have seen fifty people yesterday.'

'Well, they're not good enough, he says. He wants to hold more auditions on Wednesday.'

'But you're supposed to start rehearsals on Thursday, aren't you?'

'That's what we told him,' Morris interjected, pouring me a cup of tea.

'I had a long argument with him this morning,' Ricky went on. 'I told him, this isn't the West End, this is Ashburton. You haven't got unemployed actors queueing round the block, desperate for a job. We've got to make use of who we've got.'

'Besides, it is a community production,' Morris added, putting a plate of chocolate biscuits down in front of me. 'It's not about perfection, it's about including anyone who wants to be involved – well, as much as we can. He's turned away all those youngsters and they could have been fairies and attendants and things.'

I paused to select a chocolate biscuit. 'So, what parts has he cast?'

'Well, he has made some sensible decisions,' Ricky admitted.

'Little Sophie's playing Hermia,' Morris beamed.

'And of course,' Ricky went on, 'Scott and that gorgeous young man . . .'

'Matthew?' I suggested.

'Matthew,' Ricky nodded, 'are Demetrius and Lysander.'

'He's given Helena to Marian,' Morris added. Marian had come from Okehampton, a tall, athletic-looking girl, not pretty, but with a winning smile. And she'd been good too. She'd play Hermia's best friend, the girl Demetrius had fallen out of love with.

'Did you know she plays rugby for Dartmoor Damzels?'

'No, I didn't.' I was envious. Girls didn't play rugby when I went to school. I'd have loved it, but it was a bit late for me to start playing now.

'Of course, *Maurice* has got a part,' Ricky interrupted, rolling his eyes in Morris's direction. 'He's playing Snug.'

'Snug the Joiner,' Morris explained. 'And Olly's playing Flute. I must say, it is lovely to see how that boy's come out of himself since his aunt Elizabeth moved in with him . . .'

I smiled. Elizabeth was homeless when I met her, on the run from the complications of her old life, and Olly needed a responsible adult to live with him before someone found out he'd been living alone since the death of his nan, and alerted social services. Putting the two of them together seemed like the perfect solution and so far, it had worked very well.

Ricky snatched the list from him. 'You'll take all bloody day, reading it,' he snapped as Morris tutted in protest. 'Digby's playing Bottom. Needless to say, Gabriel hasn't cast Amanda. And your friend Ron from the antique shop is playing Quince.'

'And what about Titania?' After the number of girls who'd auditioned, I hoped he'd cast at least one of them as Queen of the Fairies.

Ricky sighed. 'Emily.' She had been the prettiest of the girls, and the most fairy-like, slender, with a swan-like neck and long, thick fair hair. She studied dance and she'd acted with great sensitivity, but she was also very softly spoken.

'You could hardly hear what she was saying in the rehearsal room,' I objected. 'How is she going to be heard out in the garden?'

'That's what I asked Gabriel.' Ricky lit up a cigarette. 'He said we would have to work on her voice projection.'

'And what about you?' I asked. 'What part have you got?'

He took a long drag and exhaled. 'Philostrate,' he answered, enunciating very precisely. I couldn't even remember who that was. 'He's on for about a page.'

I grabbed the cast list he held out and studied it, trying to get my head around things.

There were three important male characters missing – Oberon, King of the Fairies, Duke Theseus and Hermia's father, Egeus. 'And Gabriel casts you in a tiny part like Philostrate? What's the matter with him?'

Ricky gave me a wolfish grin. 'That's just his little way of showing me how unimportant I am.'

'The man's an idiot.'

'You said it.'

'The thing is, Princess,' Morris added slyly, 'we're missing a woman as well.'

I frowned. 'Who?'

'Hippolyta, Duke Theseus's bride. It's a very small

part,' he began in a wheedling voice.

I glanced from him to Ricky, immediately suspicious. They were both staring at me in a way I didn't like. 'She's only got a few lines at the beginning, and again towards the end.'

'No,' I said firmly. 'Absolutely not!'

'Oh, go on!' Ricky nudged me. 'She's the Queen of the Amazons. Suit you down to the ground.'

'Thanks.'

'We'll make you a fab costume.'

'I don't care!' The thought appalled me. Hippolyta might only have a few lines at the beginning but she and Theseus opened the play. She was almost the first person who spoke. 'I've told you. I don't like performing. Surely, one of those other girls . . .'

Ricky was shaking his head. 'Gabriel didn't like 'em. And this part needs someone with a bit of, you know . . . presence.'

'Why don't I go and see Gabriel?' I offered, thinking frantically. 'I might be able to talk some sense into him.'

Morris blinked at me uncertainly. 'Well, if you think it would do any good . . .'

I glanced at my watch. 'I've got another client this afternoon. But I'll get him to meet me later for a drink, tell him I've got a few ideas.'

Ricky smiled. 'And have you?'

I hesitated. 'Not at the moment,' I admitted. But to avoid the spectre of having to perform myself, I'd damn well think of something.

CHAPTER TWELVE

I slipped back to *Old Nick's* after my final client of the day. Pat had been minding the shop and I passed her in the doorway as she was about to lock up. A quiet day, she told me, apart from Sophie yacking the whole afternoon about the auditions and stressing about whether she'd got her part. 'Oh, and a man came in and put in an offer for that oak dresser you've got in your back room,' she told me. 'He offered half the price on the ticket. I told him he was a cheeky beggar but I wrote his telephone number down, said you'd get back to him. I thought you might want to get rid of it, seeing as you've had it hanging around a while. I stuck the number on your table.'

'Thanks, Pat.'

'By the way, Frank's still upstairs.' She frowned, mystified. 'I think he must like it here.'

I laughed. 'It's probably quieter than at home now he's got his grandchildren living with him.' She nodded a goodbye, the bell jangling as she closed the shop door. I slipped to the back room to pick up this phone number. I suppose letting the dresser go cheap was better than it not going at all. Pat was right, it had been hanging around.

Frank must have been listening for the shop bell as Pat went out because as soon as I'd picked up the number, I heard his footsteps on the stairs. I assumed he was on his way home and I would have called out to wish him goodbye but before I could speak there came a soft knocking on the door that led into the alley. I was pretty sure Frank didn't know I'd slipped in as Pat was leaving, so I slid quietly behind an old dressing screen and waited.

Before he reached the foot of the stairs the knocking came again. Through a slit in the screen, I saw Frank stop in the passageway and poke his head into the shop, looking left and right, checking that no one else was around. Then he opened the door to his visitor, a slim, attractive woman, somewhere in her forties, with shoulder-length brown hair. She was smartly dressed in a dark business suit and carried a slim briefcase.

'Ah, Susan! How very punctual you are,' he said pleasantly and stood back to let her into the hall. For a moment I wondered if Elizabeth had been right to wonder about the possibility of Frank having an affair. Certainly, his visitor was a younger and more attractive option than the rather colourless Jean.

But Susan did not look as if she was in the mood for pleasantries. ‘What on earth made you set up here, Frank?’ Her voice was strained, as if it was an effort for her to speak.

‘I needed a new space to move into,’ he replied. ‘Now the grandchildren are at home there are too many prying eyes about, too many interfering little fingers. And recently some of the more inquisitive members of Neighbourhood Watch have been noticing the comings and goings of our little band of helpers. Here, there are no neighbours and there is no CCTV. Once the shop has shut, this lane is deserted and any comings and goings are unobserved. And it amuses me to be here in the home, so to speak, of Ashburton’s famous amateur detective. I appreciate the irony of the situation.’

‘Don’t be too amused, Frank,’ Susan responded bitterly. ‘She might find you out.’

Frank chuckled indulgently and pointed the way. She pushed past him and I heard the brisk click of her heels as she climbed the wooden stairs.

I kicked off my trainers and tip-toed along the corridor. The two of them were in Frank’s room by now. He didn’t bother to shut the door, he thought that he and Susan were alone.

‘So, to what do I owe the pleasure of this visit?’ he asked. ‘Why did you want to see me?’

‘You know why I’m here.’ Her voice was tense and she paused to clear her throat. ‘I want you to release me from our arrangement.’

Frank laughed softly. ‘Impossible.’

'It's too risky.'

'You are only being asked to do one small thing.' Whatever it was, this thing, he made it sound reasonable.

Susan's voice was trembling as if she was losing the struggle between anger and fear. 'Some of these people of yours aren't even represented by the firm.'

Frank's voice remained calm. 'Are your employers suspicious? Have any questions been raised so far?'

'No, but what you're asking me to do is illegal. If I get caught, I'll lose my job—'

'You seem to forget, dear Susan,' Frank cut in, 'that Jonathon's continued good health depends upon our arrangement, at least for the next two years. If you were to lose your job then you would no longer be of any use to me, and once our arrangement is null and void, I'm afraid I could no longer guarantee Jonathon's safety.'

'Frank, I'm begging you—'

'So, you'd better make sure,' he carried on over her pleading, 'that there are no slip-ups, that you don't lose your job. Or shall I arrange for my friend to make another little film on his phone with your son in the starring role?'

'Dear God, no!'

'Well, then. I don't think there's anything left to talk about, is there?'

I could hear Susan sobbing. 'You bastard.'

'There is no need to upset yourself, my dear,' he told her smoothly. 'Things will continue just as they are for the present. Everything will be fine, you'll see.'

Her voice came back at him, ragged and raw with

emotion. 'If anything happens to Jonathon,' she vowed, 'I'll kill you, Frank. I swear I will.'

He laughed. In the face of her desperation, his silky calm was chilling.

Suddenly she was racing from the room. I barely had a moment to draw back, retreat down the corridor before her heels were clattering on the stairs. As she wrenched open the door to leave, still sobbing, she turned to look back for a moment, dark mascara tears running down her white cheeks. Our eyes met and for a fraction of a second hers widened in shock. Her lips parted on a sharp intake of breath. I raised my finger, warning her not to speak and she gave the briefest of nods. Then she fled, slamming the door after her.

I quickly slipped behind the screen and into my shoes. I wanted to race after her, to find out who she was, to talk. But Frank was still moving about upstairs and he mustn't know that I'd overheard.

He began to whistle a jaunty tune as he switched off the light. I held my breath, standing rigid behind the screen, my fists clenched tight. I listened to him locking his door, rattling the padlock. He seemed to take an age. Then he was down the stairs and out, pulling the outer door to with a soft click, still whistling as he walked down the alley.

I let out my breath, struggling to make sense of what I'd heard. The pleasant, gentlemanly Frank I knew was blackmailing this poor woman, forcing her to break the law. And he'd threatened something terrible would happen to her son if she ceased to co-operate. How could Frank have any power over what happened to him? He'd talked about making a film. Was he involved in pornography, in some kind of paedophile ring? And who were his band of helpers he'd talked about, for God's sake? I thought briefly about calling Dean Collins, telling him what I'd heard, but I hadn't a clue who Susan was or where she came from. And while Dean knew me well enough to know I wouldn't make things up, it would only be my word against Frank's that the conversation had taken place, that Susan had been here at all. I had to find out more. I wanted to know what was going on. A few streets away the bells of St Andrew's chimed and I glanced at my watch. I cursed, already late for the appointment I'd made to meet dratted Gabriel Dark.

He was on the phone when I arrived and didn't see me come into the wine bar. He was talking to Darling again, and seemed agitated. From what I could make out of the voice screaming at the other end, so was she.

'Well, don't let them in, for God's sake!' he hissed at her. 'Tell them they'll have to get a warrant . . .' He became aware of me suddenly, standing by the table. 'Just tell them I'm not there,' he muttered and ended the call. He put on his boyish smile and stood up, greeting me with a kiss on the cheek. I pulled his emailed cast list from my bag as I sat down and he ordered us both a glass of Pinot Grigio. 'How are you enjoying Ashburton?' I asked him.

'I don't know if "enjoy" is quite the right word,' he responded gloomily.

'Aren't your digs OK?'

'Oh, fine,' he responded, 'the flat is very comfortable. It's not that. Actually, I had a very pleasant afternoon, a long walk in the sunshine.'

I wondered what he was expected to do with himself when he wasn't rehearsing the play. He surely didn't get a six-week jolly, all expenses paid, in the beautiful Devon countryside in return for working two hours each evening? No, he informed me, his time was not completely his own. Part of his Arts Council brief was Theatre in Education. 'School workshops.' A shudder passed through him. 'Never work with children or animals.'

I smiled. 'You don't enjoy that kind of thing?'

'Trying to get a bunch of teenage delinquents to appreciate the finer points of *Julius Caesar*?' He grimaced. 'Not my idea of fun.'

What he needed at this moment, I decided, was empathy. I smoothed out the folds of the cast list on the table and laid a hand upon his arm. 'I can see what terrible difficulties you've been having with this.'

He sighed hopelessly. 'I don't know what we do. There are just not enough men.'

'Ricky and Morris are hoping we might poach a few from Dartmoor Operatic,' I said optimistically. 'Of course, they'll be singers rather than actors and none of them young. We don't have the choice you might have in a city – I'm afraid we have to make use of who we've got.'

Gabriel sighed. 'That's what Ricky said.'

‘I hope you don’t mind,’ I went on, ‘but I’ve got one or two suggestions.’

He swept his arm wide in a hopeless gesture. ‘Please, Juno, right now I’m willing to listen to any ideas.’

‘Well, I notice, for example, that you haven’t cast Amanda Waft?’

He looked genuinely stunned. ‘That old hag? What do you think I’m going to cast her as?’

‘She’s a very experienced actress with a wonderful voice. It seems a pity to throw her away completely.’

He frowned. ‘How do you think I could use her?’

‘At the moment, you have no one to play Hippolyta. It’s only a small part,’ I began repeating Morris’s words before Gabriel could open his mouth to object, ‘she’s only on at the very beginning and a bit towards the end.’

He shook his head. ‘She’s too old.’

‘Only if you cast a young Theseus,’ I insisted. ‘But what if they were both more mature? After all, isn’t this essentially a political marriage?’

He nodded reluctantly. ‘Well, yes.’

‘If you cast . . . say . . . Ricky . . . as Theseus, their ages would be roughly the same. They both look younger than they really are and the other thing to remember,’ I added, smiling, ‘is that in the garden the audience is a long way away.’

‘It could work, I suppose,’ he admitted grudgingly. ‘But I’ve cast Ricky as Philostrate.’

‘He’s the Master of the Revels, isn’t he? The one who presents the entertainments for the Duke’s wedding? Couldn’t it just as easily be a Mistress of the Revels? The character is only on for a page. I see from this list that you've cast a girl as Puck . . .so perhaps one of those girls who didn't make it as Titania could play Philostrate.' I sipped my wine, leaving the idea a few moments to brew.

Half an hour later we had filled in most of the gaps in the cast list. I had persuaded him to cast Ricky and Amanda as Theseus and Hippolyta and fill in the other fairies and attendants with the girls he'd rejected out of hand. This only left us with gaps for Egeus and Oberon.

It struck me that Gabriel was not so much short of actors as short of imagination. Perhaps he just felt out of his depth. Or perhaps his mind was really on his domestic worries. He certainly sounded fraught on the phone. Perhaps The Valkyries had been getting at him again.

Despite his obvious desire to linger over another glass of wine, I left with the newly scribbled cast list. I felt guilty leaving him. He didn't know anyone in Ashburton and he might be lonely. 'I've got the morning free tomorrow. D'you fancy a drive up on to the moor? I could show you around a bit and we could have lunch in a pub?'

'That'd be really kind of you, Juno,' he responded, 'but I'm busy in the morning. I'm running a workshop at Exeter College.'

'OK. Another time perhaps.' I promised him I'd be at the first rehearsal to help in whatever way I could, and headed up to Druid Lodge to deliver the good news.

'So, I've got to marry the old trout, have I?' Ricky asked, running an eye down the cast list. 'Thanks, Juno.'

'I'm sure you can stick with Philostrate, if you prefer.'

The phone rang and Morris jumped up to answer it.

'You got yourself out of playing Hippolyta, I see,' Ricky sniffed.

'As long as Amanda's prepared to play the part.'

'Oh, she'll jump at the chance,' he assured me. 'The problem's going to be keeping her sober.'

Morris came bustling back in, shaking his head.

'Who was that?' Ricky demanded.

'Sally Frost,' he answered, plumping down in an armchair. 'From Dartmoor Operatic,' he added for my benefit.

'Any good?' Ricky asked. 'Any volunteers?'

Morris began polishing his specs. 'Just one.'

Ricky closed his eyes and gave a long-suffering sigh. 'Don't tell me.'

'I'm afraid so.' Morris perched his specs back on his nose.

'Not bloody Eric?'

'Who's Bloody Eric?' He sounded like a marauding Viking.

'He's keen, is Eric,' Ricky explained. 'He likes to be in everything. Problem is, he just can't learn his lines.'

'Is he suitable for any of the parts?'

'He'll make an Egeus, I suppose, although he'll look more like Sophie's grandfather than her dad.'

'The problem with Eric is,' Morris continued solemnly, 'that he seems to think line-learning is some kind of competition. He always congratulates himself on being the first person at rehearsal to get his book down.'

Ricky grinned, 'But he never learns 'em properly.

We waste hours of rehearsal time while Eric struggles to remember his words. He began to laugh. 'Gabriel is going to love him! In fact. It'll be worth having Eric involved, just to wind him up.'

I didn't linger at Druid Lodge. I decided I'd have to ring Dean Collins. I repeated the conversation I'd overheard between Frank and Susan but he said pretty much what I thought he'd say. Until we could identify Susan, or she complained to the police about Frank, there wasn't anything he could do. 'In the meantime, I'll have a root around,' he promised, 'see if I can dig up anything on Tinkler. But Juno, that's strictly between ourselves, all right?'

Afterwards I phoned Elizabeth. 'I couldn't believe that it was Frank I was listening to,' I told her. 'The things he was saying to this poor woman. He sounded as if he was enjoying tormenting her. I don't know how I'm going to look him in the eye again.'

'We'll have to be careful,' she warned me. 'He mustn't suspect that we know he's up to something.'

'I've been wondering if Susan might work for a firm of accountants and Frank's blackmailing her into cooking the books.'

'Sounds plausible.'

I felt I ought to warn Pat and Sophie to be careful of Frank, but I didn't know what to tell them. And I didn't want them to alter their behaviour around him, to make him suspicious. I decided I wouldn't say anything just yet.

* * *

Next morning, as I didn't have to show Gabriel the delights of Dartmoor, I buzzed into Newton Abbot for a tour of the charity shops, something I do regularly in my search for stock as I can't afford to go to proper auctions. But I'd only worked my way halfway along Queen Street, having netted nothing more exciting than a Sheffield-plate sweet dish, when I spotted him across the road. Gabriel was a long way from Exeter College. He was standing on the pavement, seemingly oblivious of the people milling around him, muttering to himself, his gaze fixed firmly on the ground in front of him like someone about to throw himself under a bus. His face was white. Either he was ill or he'd just had a nasty shock. I called his name, but he didn't hear me, my voice deadened by the roar of a passing motorbike. I was about to cross the road to him, when he suddenly turned and strode away. It was only then that I noticed that the establishment he'd been standing outside of, and had probably just emerged from, was a bookmaker. Gabriel had just lost money.

I couldn't help myself, I started to follow him, keeping a few yards back. He walked along Queen Street and through the pedestrian precinct. There were flower and food stalls here, buskers playing, shoppers sitting around on benches enjoying the sun, charity fundraisers with clipboards waiting to mug passers-by, but Gabriel looked neither to right nor left. I'd worked out where he was heading. There was another betting shop at the top of the town, tucked up a side street near the clock tower. He led me straight to it. I hung back and watched him disappear inside. Either Gabriel had an unerring nose for bookmakers or he must have visited this one before. 'Hell's teeth,' I muttered. It seemed he had problems a lot bigger than who he was going to cast as Oberon.

I called in at *Old Nick's* with my meagre spoils. Sophie was at her table, waiting to shut up shop. Instead of working on her latest watercolour of Dartmoor ponies grazing among the heather, she was going through the script of *A Midsummer Night's Dream*, highlighting her lines. She was excited about the first rehearsal and, I suspected, equally delighted that the handsome Matthew was going to play her lover. If I knew anything about her, she'd be half in love with him already.

'Is Frank upstairs?' I asked.

'Oh yes, he's up there,' she said sunnily. 'Marbling away.'

Somehow, I couldn't face the thought of going up to say hello, of putting a bright, false face to mask how I was really feeling about him. 'Have we done any business today?' Sophie didn't answer, her head down in her script, her brain in fairyland. I headed for the ledger where we recorded our sales each day: a knitted poodle and two pairs of earrings for Pat, three greeting cards for Frank, two small watercolours for Sophie and nothing for me. Typical day, really.

A little dispirited, I left Sophie to lock up. I walked down Shadow Lane to the far end where I had parked the van, passing the launderette, the only other business along that sunless passage except for the funeral directors.

I stopped. Scott was sitting in the launderette reading the *Dartmoor Gazette*. I popped my head around the door. 'Congratulations!' I called out to him. 'On getting your part,' I added as he glanced up, staring at me as if I was insane, 'Demetrius?'

'Oh . . . oh yeah,' he answered gracelessly and went back to his newspaper.

I looked around the launderette. Apart from Scott, the place was deserted. 'Waiting for your washing?' I asked stupidly.

He didn't bother to look up. 'That's right.'

'Bye, then,' I said cheerily. 'See you at rehearsal.'

'Yeah.'

Outside I glanced back in the window at Scott studying his newspaper. It was completely silent in that launderette, no washing machine sloshing or spin dryer whizzing. All the machines were empty, their doors open. Scott wasn't waiting for his washing to dry. He was waiting for Sophie to shut up shop, so that he could go to the side door and visit his Uncle Frank.

CHAPTER THIRTEEN

'Who is it?' Maisie squawked down the phone like a parrot. I could just imagine her wizened old claw gripping the receiver. The theme tune for *Emmerdale* was blaring in the background. I knew she kept the phone on the table right next to her chair or I wouldn't have bothered her.

'It's Juno. I'm sorry to bother you,' I began.

She tutted. 'I'm watching my programme.' There was muttered cursing as the volume of the television was turned down. 'What d'you want?'

'I'll be very quick,' I assured her. I'd been trawling through the *Dartmoor Gazette*'s website looking for the account of the hit-and run incident involving Frank. After an hour I'd found it. The incident had been witnessed by a Mr Edward Mole. 'Isn't Teddy Mole your friend Nelly's husband?' I asked.

'No. Ted's her brother.'

'You don't know where he lives?'

'Poundsgate. What d'you want to know for?'

'I just wanted to ask him about something he saw. He was a witness when Frank Tinkler nearly got run over in a hit-and-run.'

She tutted. 'I told you them Tinklers were a bad lot.'

I wasn't sure how nearly getting mown down by a car qualified but I didn't say anything. She chuckled. 'I'll tell you one thing, if you want to get anything out of Teddy Mole, it'll cost you a pint.'

She was right as it turned out. I borrowed Kate's phonebook and looked up the name Mole. There are an awful lot of them in Devon, but only one, thankfully, in Poundsgate. I dialled and explained who I was to the man who picked up.

'Oh, you're *her*!' he wheezed. 'I've heard about you from Nelly.'

I bet. And Nelly had heard about me from Maisie. I didn't like to think how often I was the subject of discussion at church coffee mornings. I explained what I wanted.

'What d'you want to know about that for?'

Because I'm growing more and more suspicious about the man I've just rented space to in my shop. I didn't say that. 'I just wanted to . . . er . . . check the facts. I won't take up more than a few minutes of your time.'

He seemed to be considering for a moment, making a low growl like a bear coming out of hibernation. 'I don't mind having a chat about it,' he wheezed eventually.

'D'you know the Tavistock Inn?'

'I do,' I assured him.

The Tavistock Inn is nowhere near Tavistock. It's on the way there, on a bend in the road at the tiny village of Poundsgate. It's a pretty road, wooded with oaks, the River Dart rushing alongside, its foaming water visible through the trees for much of the journey, roadside stones green and cushioned with moss. It crosses the river at Newbridge, a crowded spot in the summer. There's a car park where visitors can queue up for ice cream. As I passed it that morning, two wild ponies were loitering near the van in the hope of a snack. They obviously hadn't read the sign that says *Do Not Feed*.

These days, the village of Poundsgate is no more than the pub and a few clustering cottages, the post office and shop long gone. But the pub itself is a place of legend. Conan Doyle is said to have stayed there when he was writing *The Hound of the Baskervilles,* although to be truthful if he'd stayed in all of the hostelries that make that claim he would have had to have written a much longer book. A less verifiable legend is that the Devil himself popped in for a pint on his way to snatch the soul of Jan Reynolds, a gambler with whom he'd made a pact. The deal was that Satan could take his soul if he ever caught Jan in church. On hearing that Jan was at worship in nearby Widecombe, Old Nick is said to have slammed down his pint, his sizzling tankard leaving a scorch mark on the bar, and ridden off on his black horse. He then tethered his steed to the steeple, smote the church with a bolt of lightning and galloped away with the soul of the unfortunate Jan and three of his gambler cronies. This is a picturesque way of explaining how in the great storm of 1638 the church of St Pancras in Widecombe-in-the-Moor was struck by rare ball lightning, killing four parishioners and injuring many more. I don't suppose the thought of the Almighty smiting his congregation while they were in there worshipping Him would have gone down too well. The Devil was a far more acceptable culprit. Anyway, it only goes to show what trouble gamblers can get into. Gabriel Dark take note.

I parked across the road from the pub, its white frontage fussied up with the trailing pink flowers of hanging baskets, and separated from the carriageway by a fenced beer garden. I hoped I might spot Ted Mole sitting there. It was warm with a gentle breeze and a perfect day for enjoying a drink outside. But it seemed the warmth had driven him into the dimmer surroundings of the quaint oak-beamed bar. Nelly Mole is a shrivelled little crone of a woman, bent and beady-eyed. Her younger brother Teddy looked nothing like her, at least not if he was the one person sitting inside, a red-faced man-mountain with a double chin bulging over his collar and a wok stuffed up his shirt. He would have made three of his sister.

'Mr Mole?' I enquired.

His chin wobbled as he nodded. Wherever his neck muscles were, they were well hidden. 'Mine's a pint of Doom Bar.'

'Certainly.'

‘And a packet of crisps,’ he gasped. He was a noisy breather. I’d noticed that on the phone.

I took out my purse and dumped my bag on the seat opposite him. ‘Just the one?’

‘What?’

‘Sorry. What flavour?’

He decided on cheese and onion and after I’d bought his pint and half a cider for myself, I settled down at his table. ‘Thanks for agreeing to talk to me.’

‘No problem.’ His pale blue eyes rested on me. ‘What do you want to know?’

‘You were a witness when Frank Tinkler nearly got run down by a car last year. Can you describe what happened?’

‘I was in Ashburton, visiting our Nelly.’ He rocked his vast bulk forward slightly so that he could pick up his pint. I had to stifle the urge to pick it up for him. ‘Bumped into a chap I knew on Eastern Road.’ He seemed puffed by the exertion and took a sip of ale, cogitating. ‘I suppose we were chatting there about ten minutes. I’d noticed this car parked at the end of Balland Lane, idling its engine. I thought the driver must be waiting for someone.’ He took another sip and rocked forward again so he could replace the glass on the table. ‘Then your man comes along . . . Mr Tinkler . . .’

I had to wait while Teddy went through another rocking procedure to pick up his packet of crisps. ‘He started to cross the road . . . as if he was going up Balland himself. He lives up that way, he told me . . .’

Balland Lane, near the cricket ground, on the way

to Cuddyford Cross, perhaps Maisie had been right and Frank was related to her bad lot, after all. Ted withdrew a crisp and nibbled. Even his hands were plump, his knuckles just dimples in his soft flesh, but for such a huge man he was a remarkably delicate eater. 'Well, the driver of this car accelerated away from the kerb, see, engine roaring, aimed straight at him . . .'

'You're sure it wasn't a case of just not seeing him?'

'No. In any case, it's not a place you'd put your foot down, not going in that direction.' He nibbled thoughtfully. 'If you were heading the other way . . . out towards the A38 . . . well, maybe. Anyway, this 'ere driver nearly clipped him. If he hadn't leapt back towards the pavement, he'd have come off badly, I reckon. As it was, he just rolled in the gutter, got a bit bruised . . .' he laughed like the last wheeze of a dying accordion, '. . . bruised his dignity mostly. We rushed over to pick him up, like, me and this chap . . .'

I nodded but couldn't imagine Teddy rushing somehow.

'He was all right, just needed dusting off. We thought he might've been a bit shocked and we were right there by the hospital, but he wouldn't go in and get himself checked over.'

'And you didn't get a chance to take the car's registration number?'

He rocked forward to reclaim his pint, gasping with the exertion. 'All happened so fast. Course, I wished I'd taken more notice when it was idling at the kerb. It was a dark green estate, I remember that.'

‘What did Frank think? Did he think it had been deliberate?’

Teddy chuckled, sending a ripple through his neck. ‘If he did, he didn’t say so. He cursed that driver for a fool. But I reckon she lost her bottle, she swerved just at the last moment.’

‘She?’

‘Oh, ah!’ Teddy nodded wisely. ‘It was a woman driving, for sure. Didn’t I mention that?’

An image of Susan flashed into my mind. She’d threatened she would kill Frank; perhaps she’d tried once already. ‘You don’t remember what she looked like?’

‘Only got a glimpse of her in passing. Long blonde hair, dark glasses.’

Not Susan, unless she was wearing a disguise; which meant there must be another woman out there with as strong a motive for killing Frank as she had.

Bloody Eric turned out to be a cheery little man and I thought he read for the role of Sophie’s father very well. I whispered as much to Morris, who was sitting by me at the time. We were back in the room where auditions had been held. This was to be our rehearsal space on weeknights. On Sunday afternoons, weather permitting, we would rehearse in the garden.

‘Oh, he’s lovely so long as he’s got the script in his hand,’ he agreed in a low voice. ‘It’s when he puts it down that the trouble starts.’

I was there to wield my trusty tape measure so that we could make a start on costumes, although Gabriel still hadn't made up his mind what he wanted. Ricky and Morris were threatening to go ahead without consulting him if he didn't decide soon, go for classical Greek. As Ricky put it, they didn't have time to mess about.

Elizabeth was there in her role as prompt. Her services wouldn't be needed while the cast still had scripts in their hands, but she was typically conscientious and wanted to familiarise herself with the text. She was there for rehearsals only. Gabriel had given the cast fair warning that they would not have a prompt to rely on in performance. 'This is Shakespeare, for God's sake,' he'd told them. 'You can't take prompts in Shakespeare.'

'He doesn't know Eric yet,' Ricky murmured.

We'd started the rehearsal late because Gabriel was in the kitchen on his phone, engaged in another whispered, urgent conversation. Then he suddenly swept into the room, clapping his hands and yelling, 'Come on everyone!' as if we'd been the ones keeping him waiting.

We got going at last, but progress was painfully slow. He kept interrupting the cast with irrelevant observations. It seemed to me that he wasn't so much directing the play as playing the director, as if his role was a performance in itself.

Shortly before nine a voice piped up from the corner. 'Excuse me.' A sturdily built woman who, up until that moment, I don't think Gabriel had even noticed, raised her hand. 'Excuse me,' she said again.

'Yes, what is it?' Gabriel frowned at her. 'Who are you exactly?'

I recognised her. She was April Hardiman, Olly's

next-door neighbour. 'I'm the registered chaperone for the production,' she informed him, 'for the under-sixteens.'

'Yes, and?'

'They have to go home at nine o'clock,' she told him steadily, 'it's in the rules.'

Gabriel glanced at the cast members sitting around the edges of the room, some still waiting to say a word. 'Well, we haven't got any fairies here tonight, so I don't think that applies, does it?'

Olly raised his hand a little nervously. 'I'm only fifteen,' he told him, grinning. 'Sorry.'

Marcus raised his hand too. Gabriel ignored him. 'Look, Mrs er . . .' he began.

'Hardiman.'

'Look, Mrs Hardiman, we haven't got to the comics' scene. Olly hasn't done anything yet.'

April was unimpressed. 'Perhaps if you'd started on time.'

Gabriel let out a frustrated sigh. 'Yes . . . well . . . perhaps on this occasion we could bend the rule a little?'

She was already shaking her head. Laws protecting minors appearing in theatrical productions, professional or amateur, are most rigorously enforced, and no one was more determined to enforce them than April. 'He has to finish at nine. He's got school in the morning.'

'You're absolutely right, April,' Elizabeth put in. 'But perhaps, as I'm here, we might make an exception? After all, the rules allow children to be chaperoned by a family member.'

'Only if that family member is not otherwise involved

in the production,' April insisted, 'onstage or off.'

'But I'm not really prompting tonight,' Elizabeth smiled. 'The actors are still reading from their scripts. I'm just observing.'

April was silent for a moment, thinking this over. She looked a bit like a cow, chewing the cud.

'So perhaps, just on this one occasion, Olly could stay a little longer,' Elizabeth suggested. She cast a warning glance in Gabriel's direction. 'I'm sure we won't be going on much later, will we?'

'No, no, of course not!' he agreed hastily.

'Very well,' April conceded after a little more thought, 'just this once.' She got up heavily from her chair. 'I'll bid you good evening, then.'

'Good night,' we all called out to her.

'And thank you, April,' Morris added.

'Yes, thank you,' Gabriel put in. Then he let out a long sigh. 'Bloody hell! Is she going to be here every night?'

'I'm afraid she has to be,' Morris told him, 'every night whenever a minor is involved.'

'And that's every night,' Ricky told him frankly, 'what with the fairies. And Emily's not sixteen yet, either.'

Gabriel scowled at Sophie. 'How old are you?'

'Actually, I'm twenty-five,' Sophie told him, rolling her dark eyes, resigned to being challenged about her age in every pub she went into.

'So, you're telling me I can't rehearse Titania or Puck or any of the fairies, or half the comics, later than nine o'clock?' He threw up his arms in despair. 'How am I supposed to work in these conditions?' He thrust back his chair and stood up. 'Right, five minutes break everyone. I need a fag. Juno,' he called back over his shoulder as he left the room, 'make me a coffee, will you?'

Morris scrabbled to his feet. 'I'll put the kettle on,' he volunteered, scuttling into the kitchen.

'I could do with a fag an' all.' Ricky got up and lazily followed Gabriel downstairs to the forecourt, probably with the aim of placating him. Everyone else congregated in the kitchen, including Digby and Olly and the other actors who hadn't said a word yet.

'You take some measurements while we've got a minute, Juno love,' Morris said. 'I'll see to the coffees.'

I wandered away with my tape measure, ready to add Amanda's measurements to the list I'd already got. She was in the corner, slyly slipping a hipflask out of her handbag. She jumped when I said her name and slipped it back again, then smiled and submitted graciously to being measured. Tall and willowy, she was more or less a tube. I moved on.

'So, what position d'you play, then?' Scott asked Marian, grinning, as I measured across her rather broad shoulders. 'You should be a full back with shoulders like that.'

'Fly half,' she told him.

He sniggered. 'Blimey, if you're only a half I wouldn't like to see a full one.'

'Piss off,' she recommended.

He moved away, seeming highly pleased with himself. I was inclined to fall in with Olly's estimation that he was a tosser. He smirked as I put the tape measure around his chest and I felt him puff himself out. 'Pity about Josh Naylor, isn't it?' I said casually and glanced at his face. Alarm flickered in his eyes for a moment, then he shrugged. 'I don't know any Josh Naylor.'

I slid the tape around his waist, keeping him close. 'Sorry, I thought you did. He committed suicide you know, threw himself off Tavistock Viaduct.' I pulled it tighter. I could feel him fighting with the impulse to thrust me out of the way, but he could do nothing but submit to the tyranny of my tape measure, his jaw clenched. 'You didn't know him?' I raised his arm to measure from his shoulder to his wrist. 'I thought the two of you were friends.'

'I don't know where you got that idea.' He stared resolutely ahead of him, blanking my gaze. 'I've never heard of the bloke.'

'Oh?' I shrugged. 'My mistake. I thought I heard . . .'

He shot a glance at me. 'Heard what?'

I gazed at him innocently. 'That you and he were friends.'

He thrust my tape aside, his endurance at an end. 'I never knew him. All right?' And he stomped off to join the others.

The rehearsal went on. But despite the comic antics of Digby, Olly and company, my mind was still on Scott. He'd been with Josh Naylor at Moorview Farm, I was convinced of that. Whether he'd been up on that viaduct when Josh fell to his death was a different question.

The rehearsal didn't finish until a quarter to eleven, and by then Elizabeth wasn't the only one concerned about the time. The majority of us had to be up early for work next morning, something that Gabriel himself didn't need to worry about. Before everyone left, he consulted the rehearsal timetable. 'Right, as we've got Titania tomorrow and she'll have to finish at nine, I'd like us all to start half an hour earlier. So be here, ready to start at seven. Juno, could you send out an email, make sure everyone knows—'

'Sorry, Gabriel,' Morris interrupted him. 'I'm afraid we can't have this room before seven-thirty.'

Gabriel scowled, 'Why not?'

'It's in use.'

'Yoga,' Ricky added. 'They don't finish unknotting themselves before half past.'

'Oh my God!' Gabriel moaned, clapping a hand to his brow. 'All right, seven-thirty it is. But no messing about, you lot,' he told us all piously. 'I want to start on time.'

Olly raised a nervous hand. 'I can't come tomorrow. Sorry. I've got an orchestra rehearsal.'

Gabriel heaved a long-suffering sigh and closed his eyes in an affectation of despair. 'What?'

'I can't help it. We've got a concert next week.'

He shook his head. 'Very well.'

'Excuse me,' Marian asked, tactfully moving the conversation on. 'But what are we doing about finding an Oberon?'

'Yes, good question,' Gabriel agreed. 'We'll manage tomorrow, I'll just have to read him in myself.'

'I could ask around the campus,' Matthew volunteered. He worked at Exeter University. 'A lot of students stay in town over the holidays. There might be someone who could do it.'

'And we've still got the word out,' Ricky assured him.

'I'll ask around as well,' Marian volunteered.

'Well, let's hope between us we can come up with someone, otherwise . . .' Gabriel sighed as the Valkyries began riding in his pocket. He took out his phone and switched it off.

'Otherwise, I'm afraid, we're stuffed.'

CHAPTER FOURTEEN

The streets of Ashburton were packed, as they were on the third Saturday in July every year, the pavements crowded with onlookers waiting in the sunshine for the procession of the annual Ale-Tasting and Bread-Weighing Ceremony to pass. This ritual has been taking place every year since before the Domesday Book, there being no Office of Fair Trading back then. Maisie wanted to see the procession as she's only seen it seventy or eighty times before. There was no one else to take her so I volunteered. It's too far for her to walk from her cottage to the centre of town, and she can't stand for long. I knew the town hall car park would be full, so I picked her up in the van and parked in Shadow Lane outside *Old Nick's* where I decanted her into a wheelchair, having made sure before we left her place that she had sunglasses, sun hat, handbag, walking stick and anything else she might need. The sun was bright and fierce and I was wearing a wide-brimmed straw hat myself.

'You look like a great big sunflower,' she informed me.

I didn't know if it was a compliment or not, but took a chance. 'Thanks, Maisie.' I'd also slathered myself in factor thirty; we redheads burn. It's not easy steering a wheelchair over cobbles, or along narrow, bumpy pavements full of people, despite Maisie holding her walking stick out in front of her and waving it from side to side to clear the way. It generally did the trick, people happy to give way graciously after the first clout on the shin or elbow. I began to wish I'd worn dark glasses as well.

I parked us both by the bakery on West Street where we knew that the procession was bound to stop, manoeuvring us into a tiny slice of purple shade cast by an awning. The distant sound of the brass band and a rousing cheer signalled that the procession had set out from St Lawrence Chapel. As the band went trumpeting by, a voice sounded loudly in my ear. 'What on earth's going on?' Gabriel Dark had appeared next to me on the pavement. He looked tired and hungover, pretty much his default position. I explained to him about our ancient local custom.

'I could see the mayor and a lot of people in fancy dress gathered outside that odd tower I can see from my flat.'

'That's St Lawrence Chapel,' I told him. 'And that's not the mayor, it's the Portreeve.' I went on to bore him some more with the fact that Ashburton is the only town in the country to retain this ancient office, which dates back to Saxon times. He, or she, is responsible for visiting every alehouse and baker in the town once a year to ensure that the ale is of good quality and bread the correct weight. This was a ritual that used to take all day, back when Ashburton boasted an inn or tavern every few yards; now, sadly, it only takes a couple of hours.

Maisie was oblivious of our conversation, rapt by the procession of jugglers, stilt-walkers and musicians merry-making their way along the street in an assortment of medieval costumes. I spotted a few of our fairies twirling amongst a troupe of dancing girls, flowers in their hair. I also noticed Scott and Millie among the crowd, his arm around her shoulder. I pointed him out to Gabriel. 'There's our Demetrius.' He was whispering in Millie's ear and she was smiling. They kissed briefly. They looked like an item. Some of the fairies would not be pleased. Further down the street, the Portreeve and Master Bailiff had stopped to bang their poles ceremonially on the door of the nearest pub. It was a bit like Black Rod banging on the door of Parliament but more fun.

'Are you the master of this inn?' A booming voice demanded of the landlord when he opened it.

'I am,' he replied.

'Then I command you to produce two tankards of good ale.'

I happened to glance across the street and saw

Digby and Amanda watching as the Portreeve drank the ale before declaring it to be of fine quality. Amanda was hidden behind dark glasses, but from the way she was clinging on to Digby's arm I think she'd tested a few tankards already. Gabriel had pulled his phone from his pocket and was taking photographs as the procession approached the bakery and went through the same ritual, this time demanding two loaves, which they weighed on a brass scale, the bailiff declaring that 'the master baker do sell wholesome bread of good weight'.

'What happens to all this bread?' Gabriel asked as the loaves were taken away and the Portreeve headed for the Exeter Inn.

'They get auctioned afterwards.'

'I think I've seen enough,' he told me as the procession gave way to general revelry. 'I might go and sample some of that ale myself.' He watched the procession go. 'Somewhere quiet,' he added and turned in the opposite direction.

I was hoping Maisie might have had enough. It was a lovely day for the procession but it was hot, the sun shining bright on the white walls of surrounding buildings, heat bouncing up from the pavement. I felt sorry for the Portreeve and officials in their velvet robes. I was about to suggest wheeling her back to the shop for a drink when a voice hailed us from across the street.

'Hello, Maisie!' Ricky was crossing the road towards us, weaving his way between revellers determined to revel at all costs. He leant forward to take her hand. 'I haven't seen you in ages. How are you, you wicked old crone?' Maisie screeched with laughter. If anyone else had greeted her that way she'd have whacked them with her walking stick.

'I saw you with wonder-boy,' Ricky said to me. 'All right, is he?'

I shrugged. 'It's difficult to tell with Gabriel.'

'He'll cheer up once we've found an Oberon.'

I wasn't so sure, unless the King of the Fairies could cast a spell and give him better luck on the horses. 'Where's Morris?' I asked.

'Round at the deli, which is where I'm heading. I'll see you tomorrow, darlin'.' He kissed me on the cheek, said goodbye to Maisie and loped off around the corner.

Two of Maisie's friends from church had spotted us meanwhile, and I resigned myself to a few more minutes standing around in the heat while they caught up with all the gossip. I watched the end of the procession, a flute and tabor playing as dancers with coloured ribbons twirled and a jester with bells on his hat capered and turned cartwheels. I caught sight of Scott across the road. There was no sign of Millie this time. He wasn't alone though. Someone was walking with him, a tall man wearing shades, his arm draped around Scott's shoulders as if they were the best of mates. I didn't get a sense of matiness. I thought Scott looked uneasy, more than that, afraid. The sun glinted on the fair stubble on the man's head. I knew I'd seen him before. I continued to watch as the two of them headed towards the inn, the man in shades gesturing, talking vociferously. I realised: he was the watcher from the viaduct.

CHAPTER FIFTEEN

I wanted to follow them, but I couldn't abandon Maisie. I wheeled her back towards the shop. 'You've gone very quiet,' she commented as we trundled our way along the narrow pavement of Kingsbridge Lane.

'I'm just hot.' It was a relief to turn into the cool gloom of Shadow Lane. But if I was quiet, it was because my mind was racing. Josh Naylor's partner in crime, Scott, and the man I'd seen lurking at the spot where Josh had died – I'll call him Close-Shave – obviously knew each other. Were they involved in his death?

I struggled to wheel Maisie across the threshold of *Old Nick's*, Sophie leaping up to help hold the door open. She had volunteered to man the shop while I took Maisie to see all the medieval jiggery-pokery. She'd seen it before dozens of times and wasn't doing anything else, she'd sighed a little sadly, so she might as well get on with her painting.

‘You look a bit hot and bothered, Juno.’

I puffed out my cheeks. ‘I am a bit. I’m going up to get a cold drink. What about you, Maisie, cup of tea?’

‘Yes please. And, Sophie, help me to get out of this contraption!’ She waved her walking stick imperiously. ‘Now I’m here, I wanna look around.’

I realised Maisie probably hadn’t visited the shop since she came to our grand opening the year before. I climbed the stairs to the kitchen and was confronted by the door to Frank’s room, shut and padlocked. Where was he today? The avuncular figure that Scott had gone crying to when he was in trouble, the same man who was blackmailing Susan, how much did he know about what had happened to Josh Naylor? I pondered this as I boiled the kettle for Maisie’s tea. I had to find out what was going on. I wanted to know who Frank really was, what kind of man was renting space in my shop.

I carried down the tray with tea for Maisie, coke and lemonade for Sophie and me, and the few remaining biscuits in the tin. I could hear Maisie in the back room laughing at the rail of Ricky and Morris’s vintage clothes. ‘I used to have camiknickers just like them,’ she was telling Sophie, ‘back in the war. Crêpe de Chine, they were, with lace all around the edges.’

‘You must have looked very glamorous, Maisie.’

‘Oh, I kept ’em for best, I only wore ’em when Bob came home on leave.’

‘Tea up!’ I called and Maisie came tottering through into the main shop, clinging on to Sophie’s arm.

‘I’m going to have one of them funny pictures,’ she

informed me, as we settled her into Sophie's chair, 'one of them what Pat makes.' She pointed her walking stick at the display of country panoramas that hung on Pat's wall, pictures of country scenes made from felt and other fabrics, with peg dolls dressed as farmers or shepherds with tiny sheep. They sold very well to the tourists. 'I want her to make me one of my cottage, with the stream running outside.'

'She could put you in the picture,' Sophie laughed, 'with Jacko.'

'Ah,' Maisie cackled, nodding in agreement, 'that'd be good.'

'You seen Frank today, Soph?' I asked.

She shook her head. 'He's gone to a book fair, I think.'

We gossiped and ate broken biscuits. I watched Sophie and Maisie laughing together and felt a surge of affection for them both. And I thought about Frank. What did he do in that room he kept locked when he wasn't there? Just who was it I had introduced into our cosy little world? I had to find out.

Rehearsals at Druid Lodge are always a lot of fun. Ricky and Morris lay on a lavish tea. This was the first Sunday rehearsal and for many of the cast, the first time they had seen Druid Lodge, its gardens and the place where they were to perform. The excitement level rose. For the first half hour people were just wandering around, exploring the woodland and the lake, watching the ducks with their fluffy ducklings, or the dragonflies darting over the still water like daggers of emerald. There was a lot of joyful screaming as the fairies chased each other around under the trees. I glanced at Morris and saw him smiling.

Gabriel clapped his hands to bring us all together. 'Now then, before we start, I just want to run through how our performance space,' he waved an arm vaguely in the direction of the woodland, 'relates to what we've actually mapped out in the rehearsal room.' This took some explaining, as an entrance that had meant coming through the door in the rehearsal room now meant leaping out from behind a tree or bush, and some of our fairies are a bit thick. He'd just about got everyone sorted when April Hardiman raised a hand. 'Excuse me.'

'Oh Christ, what now?' Gabriel muttered. 'Yes, what is it?'

'I'm chaperoning the children.'

'I know.'

'So where am I to be?'

'Be?' Gabriel repeated, mystified.

'Well, if we were inside, in a proper theatre,' April explained steadily, 'I would wait in the wings as each child came off the stage and escort them to their dressing room. Children are not allowed to wait in the wings unaccompanied. They have to have a separate dressing room where I can keep an eye on them.' She indicated the garden with one hand. 'So, where will it be?'

'Well, er . . .'

'Don't worry, April,' Morris bustled into the breach.

'It'll all get sorted out. We'll put up a little marquee, especially for the children, hidden among the trees.'

'It'll have to be separate from the adults,' April insisted, 'and they have to have a separate toilet.'

'We know. We did the same thing for *The Tempest* a few years ago.' He took her by the arm. 'Would you like me to show you where we put it? Would that put your mind at rest?' he asked and nobly bore her off to the bottom of the garden.

If it wasn't already difficult enough rehearsing in the garden for the first time, and still having no Oberon, Bloody Eric had decided to complicate things further by putting his book down.

'No, no don't prompt me!' he cried every time Elizabeth tried. 'I know it. It's on the tip of my tongue. Just give me a moment.'

After a dozen such disruptions, Gabriel, who'd been simmering away since April's interference, finally rose to the boil. 'We can't grind to a bloody halt every time you've forgotten what comes next,' he yelled at Eric. 'Now pick your blasted book up and don't put it down again until you've learnt your lines properly.'

'But I have learnt them,' he protested indignantly. 'If you'll just give me a little moment to think . . .'

'No, I won't' Gabriel retorted. 'We're running out of moments. Where's your script?'

'It's at home,' Eric admitted, looking uncomfortable. 'I don't need it anymore.'

Gabriel gazed at him in disbelief. 'I'll decide when you don't need it anymore! You ever turn up to one of my rehearsals without your copy of the text again and I'll bloody sack you. Understand?'

I thought this was a bit reckless. We didn't have enough actors as it was, we couldn't afford to sack the ones we'd got. Eric goggled at him, speechless. It was Ron from *Keepsakes* who came to his rescue. 'Borrow my script,' he said. 'I'm not in this scene.'

But as the rehearsal carried on, I found the only person I was really watching was Scott. He didn't seem his usual swaggering self somehow and his performance lacked its usual energy. When he wasn't performing, he seemed quieter than usual, preoccupied. He didn't come into the house with the others when we broke for tea, but hung around outside, smoking a skinny roll-up.

'You all right, Scott?' I called out to him through the window. 'You don't want a drink?'

'No, I'm all right, ta.' he called back.

I fetched a drink for him anyway, an excuse to wander out and chat to him. Then I saw Millie. I hadn't noticed her before. Maybe she'd been hanging around, waiting for us to break, but now she and Scott were deep in conversation. I couldn't hear what they were saying, but the two of them looked serious, worried. At one moment Millie put her arms around Scott, a gesture not of romance, but of comfort. I found it touching, her skinny little arms around his broad shoulders. Then she kissed him on the cheek and hurried away.

I would love to have known what they were

talking about, just as I'd love to have overheard Scott's conversation with Close-Shave the day before. Perhaps it was that which made him look as if he had the weight of the world on his shoulders.

CHAPTER SIXTEEN

I was awake all night, plotting what I was going to do next. It was on my mind next morning, all the time I was walking the Tribe through the fields, lobbing balls for them to chase, then shopping and cleaning for Maisie and fetching prescriptions for Tom Carter. The problem was I had to put my plan into action while Sophie and Pat weren't in the shop, which meant I'd have to wait until I had a free evening. I didn't want to do it in the dead of night because putting lights on in *Old Nick's* might attract attention. And I'd have to do it on my own. I had thought about asking Elizabeth to help me, but what I was going to do wasn't strictly legal and getting caught could lead to awkward questions, which I knew she'd rather avoid. There was another rehearsal that evening.

I'm usually busy with Mrs York on a Monday afternoon, but she was away on holiday and didn't need me, so I gave the girls the afternoon off and took a turn minding the shop myself. Frank was upstairs, I learnt as I took over from Sophie at lunchtime. I popped up to say hello. I have to admit, I took a deep breath before I knocked on his door, the memory of his conversation with Susan still in my mind. Not that I felt afraid of him exactly, but I had to act naturally with him, not reveal my true feelings. I put on a smile. 'Fancy a tea, Frank?'

I could see he'd been busy. There were rows of greeting cards laid out on his worktable, all waiting to be touched up, it seemed, with drops of Sunset Orange. 'Thank you, Juno. That would be most kind.'

He was so pleasant, so polite. I wondered if I'd been hallucinating, if the conversation between him and Susan had ever taken place, that I'd dreamt the whole thing, that no one had ever tried to run him over in the street. As I placed his mug of tea carefully on to his table, I noticed a flyer pinned up on the rack of shelving behind him. *Antiques and Book Fair*, it proclaimed, at the new Butchers' Hall in Tavistock.

'When's that?' I asked, pointing. He reached out for the flyer and passed it to me.

'I've rented a stall there,' he told me. 'I'm taking along a few antiquarian books.'

I made a note of the date. 'I've not been to the Butchers' Hall since it's been refurbished.'

'There will be antiques stalls as well,' he said. 'Perhaps you should pay it a visit.'

'Yes, I might.' I handed the flyer back to him. 'Well, I can see you're busy. I'd better go down and mind the shop.'

I hurried down the stairs silently repeating the phone number I'd read on the flyer, and scribbled it down as soon as I'd grabbed a pen and paper. Then I softly picked up the phone and dialled. I hadn't yet visited the newly restored Butchers' Hall at Tavistock. I'd take a stall there myself. I was probably being stupid, as whatever else he was, Frank was a legitimate dealer in antiquarian books and was probably going to Tavistock to do no more than turn a profit. But if there was any connection between Frank and the place where Josh Naylor met his death, I wanted to know what it was. Up until now I'd wondered what he might have learnt from Scott about what had happened on that viaduct. For the first time I found myself wondering if he might have been involved.

But going to the fair was going to give me problems. It was being held on a Saturday, my regular day for minding *Old Nick's*. I didn't like to ask Pat to stand in for me, she was always busy at weekends at the animal sanctuary. I'd have to talk nicely to Soph. Another problem was what to take. The fair was strictly antiquarian books and antiques only, the man on the phone had told me, no crafts. That meant I couldn't take anything for Pat or Sophie. I'd have to rely entirely on my own stock to fill my stall and limit it to things that were small and transportable. To be honest, I didn't have much that would fit the bill. My valuables cabinet contained a few small pieces of silver but I'd need more than that. I had a pair of cloisonné vases, some cranberry glass, a few pieces of brass and some Beswick animal figures, but not enough to fill a table.

Then I remembered the cigarette cards. I'd put them back in the tin after I'd bought them, stored them temporarily in the bottom of the oak dresser. In fact, its cupboards contained a lot of old tat that was going to have to find a new home if someone was seriously interested in buying it. I retrieved the tin and set it down on a table, moving aside some plates, picked up a bundle and began to lay the cards out on the surface.

I picked up a full set of roses, pretty cards, probably pre-First World War. I'd have to look them up on the laptop later to see what they were worth. Sets of cigarette cards are usually displayed in sheets in clear plastic wallets, ring-punched to fit into albums. I'd order some sheets when I got home. But sometimes sets are broken up into smaller groups of six or twelve, then mounted and framed. I'd seen sets of cricketers and golfing cards presented in this way. I grabbed a pen and sorted through each bundle, writing a list of what each set was about. It might be worth breaking some sets up and getting them framed, if the framing wasn't too expensive.

I'd been so absorbed in the cards and my own musings that I hadn't heard Frank come down stairs. Suddenly he was tapping politely on the open stockroom door. I nearly jumped out of my skin.

'Sorry, I didn't mean to startle you,' he told me, smiling. 'I'm just off.'

I laughed foolishly, a hand to my thumping heart. I glanced at my watch. There was still an hour till closing time. 'You're off early, then?'

He was holding a thick sheaf of envelopes in the crook

of one arm. 'I want to get these in the post and then I thought I'd slip home.'

'OK, then. Goodnight.'

I heard him let himself out of the side door. Already my mind was racing. He wouldn't be back until tomorrow. I could put my plan into action right now, I wouldn't have to wait. I abandoned the cards, went into the main shop, turned the sign on the door to *closed* and locked it. No one had come in all afternoon, so I doubted if I'd be losing any customers by shutting early. I switched off the main lights and hurried upstairs to the kitchen.

From a cupboard under the counter, I heaved out my toolbox and extracted my little battery-powered drill. I keep it there in case we need to hang stuff on the shop walls and there isn't a screw in the right place. It's very compact and it fits in my hand like a revolver. Every girl should have one.

It was perhaps as well that the padlock hanging on Frank's door was not the sort that could be picked with a hairpin. I might have tried it and knowing my luck the damned thing would break off in the lock. No, if I wanted to break into Frank's room for a snoop around then the only thing to do it was to remove the entire metal plate from the door, with the padlock attached and the hasp on the door frame that it fitted into, something that would take ages with an ordinary screwdriver but would be no trouble at all for my little power drill.

I took a squint at the screws in the metal plate, selected the right drill-bit and fitted it. Then I switched the drill into reverse, so that it unscrewed, rather than screwed.

I paused. What possible excuse could I offer Frank for what I was doing if he came back and caught me? Better he didn't get in at all. I nipped downstairs to the side door and drew the bolts across.

I attacked the screws in the door frame first, thinking that they might be tricky. But they were no match for my whizzing little drill. I put each screw into my pocket so I wouldn't lose any. There were eight screws in the metal plate and they all came out with ease, although as I got to the last two, I had to support the plate with my free hand. I didn't want the weight of it to snap the last screw or pull it free leaving tell-tale splinters in the woodwork. I laid the plate down carefully, opened the door and stepped inside.

Frank was a remarkably tidy worker. His table was bare, no sign of the little orange greeting cards, the white, stamped envelopes or the marbled paper that had covered it earlier. All the inks were put neatly in boxes on a shelf. I looked through them. There was none of the expensive Sunset Orange, I noticed, the ink Frank hadn't allowed Sophie to use. He must have run out. On the shelf below, stacks of white paper were piled, their edges as perfectly aligned as if they'd been stacked by a machine. The trays he used for marbling were scrubbed clean and upended on the draining board in the corner. I opened the table drawer but there was nothing in it except some pencils, a few paper clips and a rubber stamp.

I picked it up. It was not an old-fashioned rubber stamp, the kind that needs a separate ink pad, but one of the modern ones with the ready-inked letters housed inside a plastic casing. Usually, the wording of the stamp is printed on top of the plastic case, so that you can make sure it's the right way up before you use it, but this one was blank. Curious, I looked around for a scrap of paper to stamp it on. But the waste-paper basket was empty and I didn't want to disturb any of the carefully aligned paper on the shelf. So, I pressed down and stamped myself on the back of the hand. It was a less than perfect surface for stamping but I could make out the message clearly enough, even though I'd stamped it upside down: *Rule 39 Letter.* What the hell did that mean? Shrugging, I put the stamp back where I had found it and turned my attention to the shelves. But apart from the inks and papers, some paintbrushes and a large quantity of elderly books in various states of disrepair, there was very little to see.

On the bottom shelf were two deep, reinforced cardboard boxes, the sort used for storing documents. I crouched down, lifting the lids carefully. The first one was full of receipts. I leafed through them but they were connected with ordinary business expenses and none of them seemed significant. The second box had a label on saying it contained one thousand business envelopes. I found myself looking down on exactly that, the top edges of a full box of white business envelopes. I stood up, sighing. Carefully, I withdrew a leather-bound volume from between its companions on the shelf and opened it, breathing in the dry library smell of its pages. The inside of the cover and endpapers were exquisitely marbled in shades of blue, veined in gold. It was a first edition, a biography of T.E. Lawrence. Was it rare, I wondered? Expensive? Perhaps it was stolen. Perhaps that was why Frank kept his door locked.

Something fell from between its pages and fluttered to the floor. It was an old-fashioned bookmark, decorated with pressed flowers, petals long faded to shades of brown, and a silk tassel hanging from one end. The name *Enid* was written in faded ink on the back. It must have been there years. How old was Enid, I wondered, and did she press those flowers herself? This kind of thing fascinates me. I turned to the flyleaf, looking for an inscription, but there was only a date. 1939. Had Enid left the bookmark in that page, never to return and finish the book? Or had Frank kept it there to mark a particular page so that if the bookmark wasn't returned correctly, he'd know someone had looked in it? I hadn't taken note of which page it had been marking. I'm getting paranoid, I decided. I slid the bookmark back in halfway through the book and returned it to the shelf.

This had been a complete waste of time. I'd found nothing that was in any way incriminating, just wasted a lot of effort doing something that I had no right to do. I tried the handle of the safe, in case by some miracle it might open. I didn't really expect it to and it didn't. On top of it I noticed a circular mark on the shiny black metal, as if someone had put a wet coffee cup down and the liquid had dried. Except this liquid was orange. Possibly, Sunset Orange. I nearly rubbed the mark with my finger but stopped myself in time. It wasn't a wise thing to do. Had Frank put that bottle of ink down on the way to putting it away in the safe? Was it that expensive? I looked at my watch. It was time to put the padlock back on the door and go home.

This turned out to be easier said than done. I screwed the plate back on the door first, so that it would support the weight of the lock whilst I put the screws back into the door frame.

I got four corner screws into the plate and felt it was safe enough to let the padlock hang. But as I put in the final four and turned my attention to the screws in the door frame, my trusty little drill began to slow down, its whizzing song stuttering and lowering in tone, a sure sign it was running out of battery power and needed recharging. By the time I reached the final two screws, it had sung its last. Drat, how had I let this happen?

I dug my old screwdriver from the toolbox and went back to tackle the final screws. After using the power drill, screwing them in by hand took forever. As I was fitting the last one into the hole, there was a noise at the side door. Someone was turning the key in the lock. Frank was back. The bolts rattled as he pushed against the door. I heard his exclamation of surprise as it refused to yield.

I turned to the last screw, fumbled in my haste and dropped the bloody thing on the floor. By now Frank, realising the door was bolted, was pressing on the doorbell, I looked around for the dropped screw, but I couldn't even see it. I knelt and groped around on the mat. Frank, meanwhile, had left the side door. He'd probably gone around to the main door of the shop to see if he could get in that way. As he was never responsible for opening or locking up, he didn't have a key to the shop door. It might have the closed sign on it, I thought as I grubbed around desperately, but it wasn't yet closing time and my old Van Blanc was parked across the lane. Frank would know I must be in here. I threw everything into the toolbox and flung it into the cupboard in the kitchen. Then I raced down into the shop to let a furious-looking Frank in by the shop door.

'I'm so sorry,' I cried before he could open his mouth. 'I could hear you banging on the side door but I was in the loo.'

He was all smiles in an instant. 'That's perfectly all right, Juno, I'm sorry to have bothered you but for some reason the side door was bolted.'

'My fault. I was just closing up and we always used to bolt that door at night before you came here and . . .' I was speaking in a rush and stopped to take a breath, '. . . old habits die hard, I'm afraid.'

I stood back to let him in. 'Of course,' he said amiably. 'It's just I realised I'd forgotten something.'

We both laughed. I had to resist the impulse to follow him up the stairs, to watch him let himself into the room. Would he notice a screw missing from the door frame? Would he step on it? There were tiny flakes of paint on the mat from where the screws came out, would they arouse his suspicion? I held my breath and waited.

Nothing about the door seemed to give him any pause, so once he'd gone in and closed it behind him, I rushed to the landing and shut myself in the loo, leaning against the door, my heart hammering. After a few deep breaths I recovered, went to the basin and ran water. It seemed Frank hadn't noticed anything about the door. As soon as he left, I would find the missing screw and replace it, and brush up the tiny flakes of paint from the mat. In the meantime, I just had to hope he hadn't noticed the *Rule 39 Letter* stamped on the back of my hand.

CHAPTER SEVENTEEN

It seems I am not destined to become an upholsterer after all. Or put it this way, I shall never re-cover my chaise longue because a woman came into the shop next day and actually bought the thing. It turned out she *was* an upholsterer, and, it seemed, always on the lookout for the odd chaise. We settled on a price and I threw in the footstool for free. I was relieved not to have the bother of it.

My customer, a smiley blonde called Jill, was impatient to get it back home to her workshop. 'I want to get going on it,' she explained. 'Once it's re-covered, I can sell this sort of thing three times over.' Her clientele was obviously different from mine.

'Problem is, I drove here in my little Renault. If I'd known, I'd have bought the Suburu.'

'It'll probably fit in my van,' I said recklessly. 'Where do you live?'

'Ilsington. It's not far.'

It was only a few miles away so we agreed on a few extra pounds for delivery and Jill gave me directions to her place. She was going straight home, she said, and I promised I'd deliver it that afternoon.

Sophie had been earwigging on our conversation. 'It's a bit heavy, isn't it? How are you going to manage?'

'I'll bring the van up to the front door. If you don't mind giving me a hand loading it in . . .'

'You could ask Frank,' Pat suggested. 'Shall I give him a shout?'

'No!' I blurted out. After my escapade of the previous evening, I felt more comfortable avoiding him. But I'd spoken too quickly. Pat and Soph gave me a curious stare. 'We don't need a man,' I laughed scornfully, 'we can do it.'

We dragged the chaise through the shop easily enough, but it was bloody heavy when it came to hoisting it into Van Blanc. Also, the end of it stuck out and I couldn't close the van doors. I had to tie the handles together securely with rope.

'That's safe, is it?' Sophie frowned. 'It's not going to slide out of the back when you go uphill?' She obviously did not have much faith in my knot-tying ability. 'I think I'd better come with you . . . just in case.' This was really an excuse to get out of the shop. I know she felt cooped up, on hot summer days like these, when she really wanted to be out in the fresh air, sketching and taking photographs of the countryside.

I looked at Pat. 'As long as you're happy being left in charge?'

She shrugged her shoulders. 'O'course.'

'Great!' Sophie beamed. 'I'll just get my camera.'

Ilsington is one of those pretty Devon villages that predates the conquest. It has its fair share of white-painted thatched cottages, a medieval church, and a village shop run by volunteers. It also boasts an impressive country house hotel and a real pub, The Carpenters Arms. We found Jill's place without difficulty, one of the aforesaid white-painted thatched houses, with a large garden, her workshop sitting in an old shed at the far end. After unloading the chaise, she gave us tea for our trouble and we spent a pleasant half hour sitting in the garden, sipping Earl Grey and enjoying the scent of the white rose that rambled riotously along the sun-warmed stones of her garden wall, watching the house martins swooping in and out from under the thatched eaves.

'On the whole, I'm envious,' I confessed to Sophie while Jill was inside fetching the tea.

'How about you?'

'On a scale of nought to ten,' she responded, batting her dark eyelashes, 'about eleven.'

'Of course, it's churlish to resent the good fortune of others,' I added piously.

'Especially when they're as nice as Jill,' she said as we watched her striding across the lawn to us with a loaded tea tray.

We left on a promise that if I ever came across any chaises, daybeds or drop-end sofas I would ring Jill immediately, and after Sophie had snapped her way around most of the village, gathering material for her watercolours, we got back in the van.

'Do you think we could go back the long way?' she asked. 'I'd like to take a few pictures of Rippon Tor.'

'Why not? We'll go back via Halshanger Common and I can take a look at Daniel's place, make sure no one else has broken in.'

I only meant it as a joke.

By the time Sophie had taken enough photographs of Rippon Tor and then demanded I stop the van, forcing me to screech to a halt so she could leap out and click off a few shots of purple foxgloves growing wild on top of a moss-covered stone wall, it was another hour before we drew up at Moorview Farm. We sat in the van and stared. The door of the caravan was wide open and hanging drunkenly from one of its hinges, the long cushions from the banquettes scattered outside, their covers ripped open, chunks of foam littering the grass.

I groaned. 'Oh, fuckity-fuck!'

'Someone's broken in,' Sophie added unnecessarily.

'It certainly looks like it.'

We trudged across the grass and poked our heads nervously inside. The poor little space-bug had been ripped to pieces, all its internal fittings torn apart. It looked as if someone had taken a sledgehammer to the walls and flooring, smashing through the panels in a search for secret hiding places. The little sink in the corner had been ripped out, left hanging from one of its pipes. The loo had been yanked off the wall.

Sophie picked up a length of torn curtain on a bent

curtain wire and dropped it again. 'Why would anyone do this?'

'For the same reason they broke into the farmhouse. Someone is looking for something.'

'Drugs?'

'I can't imagine what else they'd be looking for.'

'You don't think they might just be vandals?' she asked doubtfully.

'They're pretty thorough vandals if they are.'

'Poor Daniel's not going to be happy.'

'You can say that again.' I felt sick at having to break the news to him. 'I'm going to walk around the house, check it's all secure,' I told Sophie. 'You take a few pictures of all this. We can show them to the police on the way home.'

CHAPTER EIGHTEEN

We didn't make much progress at rehearsal that night. This was partly due to Gabriel's late arrival, smelling as if he'd just come from the pub, and partly due to the improvisation he made everyone perform before we were allowed to get started. The evening was half gone before we began working on the text. Then things really started to go downhill. We still had no one to play Oberon, so Gabriel decided to read it himself. Emily, obviously intimidated by the thought of acting with him, spoke more softly than ever.

'No! No! No!' he yelled, the moment she opened her mouth. 'How the hell are you ever going to be heard in the garden, eh? I can barely hear you in here. Project, for God's sake!'

In the silence that followed, Emily, who'd turned blood-red with embarrassment, stammered an apology.

'I thought we'd be wearing radio mics,' she explained, 'like when we did *Les Mis* at school.'

Gabriel, realising perhaps he'd been too fierce, reined back a little. 'Well, there will be some sound amplification, certainly. But I'm afraid personal radio microphones are not something the budget will stretch to. We are going to have to rely on skill. Now, darling, shall we try it again? Louder this time.'

Emily nodded, and managed to raise her volume slightly, but she was obviously struggling.

'Just try and relax, will you?' Gabriel interrupted her in a voice guaranteed to make her shut up like a clam. 'Breathe,' he added on a long sigh.

They staggered through the scene. Emily, released by her exit, fled to the protection of April Hardiman who murmured words of encouragement in her ear. Meanwhile there was a lot of behind-the-hand whispering and glance-flicking among the fairies. Peaseblossom, Cobweb, Mustardseed and Moth seemed to have become a gang, bonded together by jealousy.

We moved on to the next scene where Helena is bemoaning the fact that Demetrius has abandoned her because he now finds Hermia more beautiful.

'. . . *I am as ugly as a bear*,' she lamented.

'Yeh, right,' came a voice from the corner. It was Scott.

'Fuck off!' Marian recommended, all lovelorn woe deserting her.

Gabriel slammed his hand down on the table. 'Can we attempt to take this seriously?'

'Yeh, you're not on the rugby field now,' Scott grinned.

'I'd take you down if I was!'

'We haven't got the time for this, children,' Gabriel shouted. 'Scott, just put a sock in it, will you?'

But shutting his gob seemed to be something Scott found difficult. I'd felt sorry for him when I'd seen him with Millie on Sunday. Today he was acting like a prat. When Matthew and Sophie got up to take their places, he muttered something else, something loud enough for only those closest to him to hear. A second later Matthew grabbed him by the neck of his t-shirt and slammed him up against the wall, pinning him there, his forearm pressing hard against his throat. 'Don't you ever use that word in front of me,' he snarled, dark eyes blazing with fury. 'Let's get this straight, right now! I am not putting up with it, understand?'

Scott struggled, trying to yank his arm away, his face turning puce.

'Let him go, Matthew!' Gabriel yelled.

'He's a racist little shit,' Marian declared angrily. 'I heard what he said. He should apologise.'

'I'm sure he will, just take your arm off his neck.' Ricky's voice was steady and calm as he laid a gentle hand on Matthew's shoulder. 'We don't want any nasty accidents, do we?'

'Please . . . Matthew . . . don't fight . . .' Sophie gasped, suddenly turning pale. She began groping for her inhaler. She's useless with any kind of confrontation.

Slowly, Matthew released his hold, his burning gaze never leaving Scott's face. Scott collapsed forward, clutching his throat, then elbowed his way through the people surrounding him, head down, and fled. One of the fairies tried to catch his arm but he thrust her aside. 'Leave me alone!' he muttered hoarsely.

'I told you that bloke was a tosser,' Olly muttered as he passed.

'Scott!' Gabriel called out and hurried after him.

'Calm down, Soph,' I pushed her gently into a chair. 'Everything's OK. Take a few deep breaths.'

Ricky patted Matthew on the shoulder. 'Gits like him aren't worth it, mate.'

Matthew released his tension in a long breath. 'I'll punch him if he calls me that again.'

Ricky looked around at a room full of worried faces and grinned. 'Time to take five, I think, boys and girls.'

'I'll put the kettle on,' Elizabeth volunteered. 'Sophie needs a cup of tea.'

Eventually, Gabriel managed to coax Scott back into the room where he mumbled an almost inaudible apology to Matthew who accepted it with a curt nod. For a horrible moment I thought Gabriel might try to make them shake hands, but he avoided that embarrassment, instead launching into a little homily about mutual respect and the need for us all to bond for the sake of the production. The uncomfortable atmosphere continued while we drank our coffees, most people avoiding Scott except for the gang of worshipful fairies and Marian, who judging by the look on her face as she whispered into the ear of her onstage lover, was telling him exactly what she thought of him.

He pulled away from her. 'You ever thought about transitioning into a woman?' he demanded. He really could be obnoxious. Perhaps we should have let Matthew throttle him after all.

After everyone had gone home, Ricky, Morris and I were left washing up coffee cups and putting the room in order for the tai chi class the following morning. Sophie had accepted the offer of a lift from Matthew, which made Ricky raise his brows at me and grin. 'A little real-life romance going on, is there?'

'That would be nice.' Poor Sophie, she hadn't had a boyfriend for ages.

'I feel sorry for Emily,' Morris shook his head, his arms sunk in soapsuds. 'She's trying her best.'

'Gabriel bullying the poor kid isn't going to make her louder,' Ricky said. 'It's likely to have the opposite effect.'

'But she does need to speak louder,' I pointed out, 'she'll never be heard in the garden.'

Ricky frowned. 'You're right. And nothing turns an audience off quicker than someone who can't be heard.'

When I got home, I managed to get through to Daniel and gave him the bad news about his caravan. He listened in shocked silence.

'What the bloody hell is going on?' he demanded when he found his voice.

'Josh Naylor must have hidden more drugs up at the farm. Someone is still looking for them.'

'Let's hope they've run out of places to look. Perhaps they'll leave my house alone now.'

'I'm sorry about the poor little caravan,' I said. 'Shall I email you the photos?'

He gave a depressed sigh. 'I suppose I'd better face the worst.'

'It was too small, anyway,' I ventured.

'That's hardly the point.'

'I know. I'm sorry.'

'I'm shocked at your heartlessness, Miss B.'

'I'm sorry,' I repeated. 'Do you want me to get the bits taken away?'

'Of course not. We'll hold a proper funeral when I get back.'

I stifled a laugh. 'Right.'

'Seriously, though, Miss B,' he added. 'You will stay away from the place? No more going up there just to check on things. You promise?'

'I promise,' I said.

CHAPTER NINETEEN

There is something about the smell of wet earth. According to psychologists, the aroma of soil after rain triggers some kind of feel-good factor in the human brain. It does in mine. It had rained during the night, fat raindrops falling after deep, distant rumbles of thunder over the moor. The first rain after several dry weeks seemed like a blessing, cooling the air. The morning smelt fresh as I walked the Tribe, wet leaves dripping diamonds on to the woodland floor. The dogs shook sparkling raindrops as they plunged among ferns that had unrolled their tight fists and spread their fronds in damp ecstasy. They disappeared into the lush undergrowth, lost from view except for Dylan, whose plumy tail waved above it all like a flag.

I whistled to them, launching tennis balls as I trod the woodland path. They raced past me, Nookie and Dylan in the lead, followed by Boog, then E.B., who stopped to check on my trainers, his bushy eyebrows knitted in a worried frown, and Schnitzel bringing up the rear on his little legs. But when I reached the clearing where I expected to find them, there was no sign. The wood seemed suddenly empty, silent save for a woodpigeon's drowsy bubble of song cooing somewhere among the branches. Then I heard whining and whimpering, the excited yip of Schnitzel's bark, and followed my ears.

The dogs had gathered on a granite outcrop, a place where the woodland floor fell away sharply and an overhang of rock made it impossible to get any further without climbing. A jumble of tree trunks, brought down in ancient storms, littered the slope beneath, their gnarled roots clawing the sky. The dogs had found something. Dylan and Nookie were pacing restlessly, their wolf-like gazes fixed intently on something on the slope beneath them, while Schnitzel ran up and down, yapping, trying to find a way to reach whatever lay below. They were excited, but nervous. Whatever they'd found, they didn't know what to do about it. Perhaps a stray deer was trapped down there in the tangle of branches and tree trunks, perhaps it was a dead badger.

But this was no woodland animal. The body of a man, legs twisted oddly, one arm flung out like a broken doll, lay on the slope below. His face was turned away from me, but with a sickening jolt I realised who he was. I called his name, but I expected no response. There is a silence and a stillness that is nothing like unconsciousness, that is only like death. At the sound of my voice a blackbird fluttered from a branch nearby, chittering alarm. I picked my way along the rocks, trying to find a place where I could scrabble over the edge of the overhang. I sat down, stretching out to grab the twisted limb of a fallen oak, the only handhold within reaching distance. The bark felt slick and slippery after the rain, but I curled my hand around it tight, trusting it enough to slide my bum off the rock before I braced and dropped down on to the ground below, feeling the impact through the soles of both feet. I stumbled a little, getting my balance on the uneven slope, then stepped across the trunk of a fallen tree to take a closer look.

His eyes were half-closed as if the lids were heavy, but beneath them his blue stare was milky and lifeless. His clothes were stained with mud and blood and dampened by the rain, a ragged wound like a blood-red mouth gaped under his outstretched arm, staining his white t-shirt. His hair was wet, flattened by the rain, a glistening sheen on his skin. A tiny pool of raindrops had formed in the cup of his upturned palm. There was nothing I could do for him. Tears pricked my eyes. The dogs were whining, anxious to follow me. I yelled at them to be quiet and clambered back the way I'd come. I didn't want to disturb the crime scene.

It seemed to take for ever, hauling myself up over the edge of the rocks, hampered by Boog the boxer as she innocently snuffled at my hands and tried to lick my face in greeting. For a while I sat on the edge of the overhang, catching my breath, listening to the hammering of my heart. E.B. sat next to me, his eyebrows twitching and

I cuddled him, comforted by the warmth of his body, the rough softness of his wiry fur. When I felt steadier, I got up, still taking in deep breaths, put the dogs on their leads and walked them back to the point where the footpath through the woods emerged at the roadside. I checked my phone for a signal, made the necessary call and waited for the police to arrive. I couldn't help thinking about *A Midsummer Night's Dream*. Not only did we have no Oberon, now we would need a new Demetrius.

It was Dean Collins who reached me first and secured the crime scene. He was still there now, long after the inspector had examined the body and come away. I'd been allowed to take the dogs and deliver them to their various addresses. Then I went home to shower and change. I stood beneath those needles of hot water a long time, breathing in the steam, steadying my breathing, trying to feel calm. With my eyes closed, all I could see was Scott. The image that kept coming into my mind was not of him lying dead, but the memory of him and Millie together in the garden, Millie's skinny arms around him in a gesture of almost maternal comfort. Despite his boorish swagger, his insulting remarks, he was just a kid in trouble. And whatever it was, that trouble had stolen his young life. When I eventually got out of the shower, I phoned Sophie at the shop to warn her that I'd be later than expected, before making my way to the police station.

Detective Inspector Ford regarded me with an air of

weary resignation, as if we'd been through one of these interviews too many times before. I'd already explained to him how I knew Scott, how I was pretty sure he'd been with Josh Naylor that night in Daniel's barn and that this was what had got him murdered. I also told him about seeing Close-Shave on the viaduct and with Scott outside of the Exeter Inn. This drew no comment beyond a slight raise of his heavy brows, and a glance at Cruella who sat next to him, scribbling notes.

'When was the last time you saw Scott?' he asked. 'Alive, I mean.'

'At last night's rehearsal.' I thought I'd better tell him about the argument between Scott and Matthew. I hated myself for doing it, but they would find out as soon as they questioned any of the others.

'And do you know what caused this violent outburst?'

'I didn't hear what was said,' I admitted, 'some kind of racist insult. The people who were close enough to hear it didn't seem to think that Matthew reacted unreasonably.'

'But things had calmed down between them by the time they left?'

'As far as I could tell. If you're asking me if the incident was serious enough for Matthew to have murdered Scott afterwards, I'd have said no.'

The inspector didn't comment, just paused long enough for me to wish I hadn't volunteered my opinion. I saw Cruella smirk. 'And when the rehearsal ended,' he asked, 'what happened then? Everyone went their separate ways?'

'I don't know where Scott went. But I know he has a girlfriend, Millie.'

'You don't know where we might find her?'

'I'm afraid not. But she runs errands for Frank Tinkler, he would know how to get hold of her. But I do know that Matthew gave Sophie a lift home. He lives in Exeter and drives past her door.'

If I thought that would put Matthew in the clear I was to be disappointed. 'Dropping her off would only take him five minutes.' Cruella didn't even look up from her scribbling.

'Is there a rehearsal this evening?' the inspector enquired.

'Not until Sunday now.'

'In that case, Juno, it would be helpful if you could supply us with the names of everyone who was there last night. We need to speak to them all, find out if anyone knew where Scott was going when the rehearsal finished.' He glanced at Cruella. 'But first we need to find this Matthew . . .'

'Prince,' I supplied.

'Matthew Prince and talk to him.' He shot me a glance under his brows. 'You don't know where we can find him?'

'I don't, but I took contact details from everyone at auditions. Ricky and Morris have the list now. It'll be easy enough to get his phone number.'

'Thank you, Juno,' the inspector sighed. 'That would be helpful.'

* * *

'So, what did she ask you?' I asked Sophie the moment that Cruella left the shop later that afternoon.

'Same things the police asked you, I suppose,' she responded softly. Pat was dealing with a customer just a few feet away and we were speaking in hushed voices. 'She wanted to know what I knew about Scott, which is not much, and whether he'd mentioned where he was going after rehearsal.'

'He didn't, did he?'

She shrugged. 'Not to me. I just assumed he was going home, like the rest of us. Or to the pub.'

'But what about Matthew? She must have asked you about him.'

Sophie sat down at her worktable and picked up her paintbrush, as if she'd suddenly had enough of the conversation. 'She wanted to know what time he dropped me off.'

'Well?'

'Ten past ten,' she said reluctantly.

'As early as that?' I was disappointed. I'd hoped there might have been time for some snogging in the car.

Sophie rinsed her paintbrush with slightly more vigour than was needed. 'He just dropped me at my door and off he went. And as I told Cruella, if you want to know what time Matthew got home, then the person to ask is his partner. He lives with her.'

'Oh, bad luck, Soph,' I said sadly. 'I thought you were in there.'

'He's already taken, unfortunately,' she responded primly.

'Did he mention anything on the drive home,' I asked, 'about what happened with Scott?'

'Cruella wanted to know that too. But he didn't. Not a word. To be honest, I think he'd forgotten about it by then.' She frowned. 'But you don't really think that Matthew could have murdered Scott, do you?'

I shook my head. 'This is all about drugs. I think that whoever killed Josh Naylor killed Scott.' I'd already decided this was Close-Shave. 'It's just bad luck Matthew reacted violently to what Scott said, and in front of everyone else.'

Sophie's eyes widened. 'Do you think Frank knows? I mean, do you think he knows Scott is dead?'

I hadn't thought of that, I realised guiltily. 'Has he been in today? Have you seen him?'

She shook her head.

'The police will have informed Scott's parents by now. I'm sure Frank will find out soon.'

'Juno, are you OK?' she asked suddenly. 'You found Scott's body. It must have been horrible for you, and I haven't even asked you how you're feeling.'

'I'm fine,' I assured her. 'Really.' To be honest I wasn't sure how I felt, still a bit spaced out, as if nothing was quite real.

'How did he die?' she asked, tentatively.

'I think he was stabbed.' I sighed. 'If it was Scott who broke into Daniel's place, and he failed to find those drugs . . .'

'You think it was Scott who broke up the caravan, then? Could he have done all that damage on his own?'

'If he was desperate enough.'

'Poor Scott.' Sophie looked up from her painting, struck by a sudden thought. 'What's going to happen about the play now we've got no Demetrius? Will it still go on?'

'That'll be Ricky and Morris's decision,' I said. 'It's their production. I just wonder if they've told Gabriel.'

CHAPTER TWENTY

I spent the evening on my own, at home, pricing sets of cigarette cards. It may be the nerd in me but I enjoyed it. Perhaps it was just a relief to be doing something safe and unthreatening for a change. I'd already picked out half a dozen golfing cards from the 1940s and taken them to the local gallery to be framed. I put some sets into plastic display sheets, and set aside some others which looked as if they might be worth taking to auction. There was a particular set of American Beauties and another of Animals in Fancy Dress, both Victorian, which I needed to find out more about. It was helping to keep my mind off more gruesome subjects and in any case, I would need some cards priced ready for Saturday's fair at Tavistock.

I'd been up to Druid Lodge and had a long chat with Ricky and Morris earlier about what would happen to the play now Scott was dead. They had *the show must go on* written into their DNA, but they were as horrified as everyone else at his murder and understood that not everyone might feel willing to continue.

'God knows,' Ricky said, 'we don't want to cause his family any more suffering. We're going to call everyone together on Sunday, gauge their feelings.' He drew on a cigarette and exhaled with a deep sigh. 'Of course, if we do go on, the big question will be, where do we find another Demetrius? We still don't have an Oberon and the clock is ticking.'

'How did Gabriel take it?' I asked.

Apparently, he'd reacted to the news of Scott's death with understandable shock, followed by deep gloom. He'd been at Druid Lodge earlier but, despite an invitation to stay, had gone off to wallow in despair on his own.

'Do you think he'll be all right?' I asked. He already had enough troubles.

'His girlfriend is coming down to stay for the weekend,' Morris told me, 'so she should cheer him up.'

I remembered him standing shell-shocked outside of the betting shop in Newton Abbot. She'll have to go some, I thought.

I was just going to bed when my doorbell rang. I trudged downstairs in my dressing gown and bare feet, praying I was not going to find a depressed and drunken Gabriel on my doorstep. But it was Detective Constable Collins, stone cold sober.

'Any chance of a cup of tea?' he asked.

I stood back to let him in. 'Are you on duty, Officer?'

'I am or I'd be asking for beer.'

'You'd be out of luck,' I told him frankly as we ascended the stairs. 'Tea I can manage.'

He sank down on my sofa as soon as we got into the flat and closed his eyes. He'd had a very long day and wasn't sure it was over.

'How's it going?' I asked, putting down a mug of his favourite walnut-coloured brew with three sugars.

'Scott Pritchard died of a single stab wound under his arm,' he told me wearily, 'severed an artery. He probably bled out in a couple of minutes. We're looking for a long-bladed knife, probably a kitchen knife.'

'God, that's awful.' I shivered. 'Any idea who killed him?'

He sat up with a grunt, reaching for his mug of tea. 'Well, Pritchard has no criminal record, no history of drug abuse. His connection to Naylor is an obvious line of enquiry . . .'

'What about Close-Shave?'

'Who?'

'The man I saw talking to Scott on Saturday, the same man I saw on the viaduct?'

Dean pulled a face. 'It would be interesting to know what he and Pritchard talked about. But at the moment we've no reason to suppose he was involved in his murder. And anyway, we don't know who he is.'

I sighed, frustrated. Close-Shave was involved in all this somehow, I could feel it in my gut.

'We've talked to your friend, Matthew Prince. He says

a neighbour who was putting out his bins can confirm his time of arrival back in Exeter. They had a chat when he parked his car. If that's true, there was no time for him to have committed the crime.'

'Do we know what time Scott died?'

'Sometime around midnight is the pathologist's best guess. Prince says he was at home then, that he and another resident in his block were out on the landing, knocking someone up to complain about his music being too loud. We need to talk to these neighbours, but if what he says checks out, he's in the clear.'

'I hope so. I'd hate to think he was involved.'

'But the reason I've come,' Dean brightened slightly, 'is to tell you about Mr Frank Tinkler.'

I stared at him. 'What?'

'It'll cost you a biscuit.'

It would cost me a packet if I knew Dean. I hurried back from the kitchen with the Rich Tea. He pulled a face. 'Where are the chocolate digestives?'

'That's the best I can do.'

He picked up four. 'Right. Well, your friend Frank came into the station this afternoon to make a statement.'

I watched a biscuit disappear into Dean's mouth, whole. 'Really?'

'Really,' he nodded, crunching. 'He was very shocked to hear of Scott's death. He's like an uncle to him, apparently, or he was. He said Scott was more likely to confide in him than his mum or dad. He'd known about the lad's friendship with Naylor for months and had warned him to stay away from him. Apparently,

Naylor had been shooting his mouth off about making big money from dealing in street drugs. He also told us that after Naylor was killed, Scott had come round to see him in a panic, at your shop. He was scared. He and Josh had failed to deliver drugs to some nasty people. He was convinced they'd killed Josh and that he might be next,' he added, as another biscuit disappeared. 'Frank told him to go to the police. Which he didn't.'

'This more or less confirms what Elizabeth overheard.'

Dean nodded. 'I thought you'd want to know. Uncle Frank was only giving little Scottie some good advice. He's not quite the villain you supposed.'

'I might believe that if I hadn't overheard his conversation with Susan.'

'Well, until we can identify this Susan, there's nothing we can do about her.'

'You haven't managed to dig up anything about Frank?'

He shrugged. 'Clean as a whistle, so far.'

I decided not to tell him about my conversation with man-mountain Teddy Mole. He'd disapprove. 'Why do you think he came to see you today?'

'He was being a good citizen. Like you, he's convinced it was Scott's involvement with drugs that got him killed, something neither of his parents knew anything about. They'd never even heard of Josh Naylor, didn't know he and Scott were mates.'

'What about Millie?' I asked. 'Did you ask him about her?'

'Yup. He said she and Scott grew up in the same

street, went to the same school. Childhood sweethearts, by the sound of it. But Mr and Mrs Pritchard did not approve of the relationship. Millie's dad is in and out of prison, according to Frank, keeps getting done for drugs – possession, not dealing.'

I wondered if Millie's dad might be one of the prisoners that Frank sent his uplifting little cards to.

'Her mother ran off,' Dean went on, 'and the kid lives alone. That's why Frank tries to help her. She hasn't got a proper job. He likes to keep an eye on her, give her things to do so he can pay her a bit.'

I wasn't sure Frank's motives could be that pure.

'Thanks for the tea, Juno.' Dean drained the mug in one long gulp as he stood up. 'One more sugar next time.'

I sat thinking for a long time after he'd gone. A part of me longed to talk to Daniel, to hear the warmth in his voice. But I didn't want to tell him about Scott's murder. He already believed that it was impossible for me to refrain from poking my nose into police investigations. I didn't want him to know I'd found another body.

We all expressed our condolences to Frank when he next came into the shop, a couple of days later. He was subdued, but didn't appear to be suffering agonies of grief. He was sadly philosophical, as if Scott's end was inevitable once he had, as he put it, fallen in with the wrong crowd. He didn't stay long. He had just come to pack up some stock he was taking to Tavistock.

I packed my own stuff into the van so that I wouldn't have to get up too early next morning, went home and sat down with Bill to watch a film. It turned out to be a film about drug dealers. They were, I have to admit, marginally more attractive than the rather grubby cops who were trying to put a stop to their activities. The drug dealers were ingenious and had a sense of humour. The cops lived terrible home lives, ate a dreadful diet and seemed permanently depressed, possibly because they weren't earning the sort of money that the drug dealers were. I sat munching leftover flapjacks from *Sunflowers* and making critical comments to Bill about the implausibility of it all. There came a scene set in a gents' urinal, which seems to be obligatory with a certain sort of gritty cop thriller. This scene went further though, by allowing us to follow a drug dealer into a cubicle, where he locked the door behind him, stood up on the seat, and extricated a plastic-wrapped package from inside the cistern.

I prodded Bill gently. 'Are you thinking what I'm thinking?'

There was still light in the sky when I arrived at Moorview Farm. The soft indigo of dusk was pierced with a few bashful stars overhead but towards the west the sky was still pale aquamarine with feathery gold clouds receding towards the horizon. I know I'd promised Daniel I would stay away, but the drugs would either be there or not, and I reckoned I'd be in and out of the place in a few minutes. I parked in front of the remains of the caravan. A warm breeze rustled the dry grass and stirred a ragged curtain in its broken window. I bit my lip. Poor Daniel, he hadn't seen the damage yet.

I walked around the back of the dark and silent farmhouse, letting myself through the wooden door into the garden and caught the scent from an ancient honeysuckle that sprawled against a ruined wall. Something rustled furtively amongst the bushes, some small nocturnal creature that I'd disturbed in its foraging. I opened the door to the old loo, brandishing a long-handled broom I'd borrowed from Kate's kitchen. I was well armed. I'd taken the precaution of bringing a silk scarf an old client had given me. I never wear it because it's a lurid shade of pink, but it was perfect for covering my head. I am full of respect for spiders; they are wonderful creatures, but I don't want them in my hair, nor a lot of dead flies. I wafted the broom aloft, breaking through dusty ropes of cobwebs with its stiff bristles. The loo didn't have a seat, so I searched around until I found a piece of wood wide enough and laid it across the pan for me to stand on. I tested it cautiously, rocking slightly to test if it would bear my weight, before I straightened up and drew level with the old cistern. The lid was thick with dust, save for a few tell-tale smears. Someone had touched it recently. I lifted it and shone the torch, but there was so little space between the cistern and the ceiling that I couldn't aim the beam at the correct angle, couldn't see if there was anything inside. I gripped the torch between my teeth, trying not to gag, and pushed back my sleeve. There was nothing for it but to grope about. The water was cold enough to make me shiver but my fingers closed on something smooth, hard and rectangular that was definitely not a ballcock. I wangled it out of the cistern, scraping my knuckles on the ceiling as I pulled. It came out dripping, a block about the size of a brick, wrapped in thick plastic and bound around with gaffer tape. I squeezed the package between my fingers but there was no give in it at all. Whatever was inside was a solid block of something. Heroin, cocaine, cannabis? It could have been marzipan for all I knew.

I stepped down from my platform and closed the door behind me, returning the toilet to the silent realm of the eight-legged. I pocketed the torch and headed back across the garden, clutching the package in one hand and the broom in the other. I was planning to drive straight down to the police station with my booty and give everyone there a nice surprise. I'd look bloody silly if it was only marzipan, but generally confectionary items don't get hidden in cisterns.

I rounded the corner of the farmhouse and stopped. A tall figure in leathers and crash helmet was standing by my van. I dodged behind the corner of the building, then peered around for another look. As I watched, he laid a deliberate hand on the bonnet, testing if the engine was warm. Then he walked out of sight. I craned my neck to see where he had gone. I saw his bike then, a sleek, mean hunk of metal gleaming dully in the gloom. He took off his crash helmet and set it down on the pillion. I could see only his silhouette, outlined against a streak of pale sky but there was something too horribly familiar about that closely shaven head. Then his face, his pelt of silver blonde hair, was lit by the blue glare from his mobile. It was Close-Shave.

He was staring at the dark buildings around him, the silent farmhouse and the barn, the empty caravan. He spoke into his phone. I strained my ears to hear but couldn't catch his words. After a few seconds, he pocketed the phone again, the briefest of calls. What was he doing here?

He headed straight towards me and my heart lurched in panic. I ducked back behind the garden door and gently pulled it to. There was no lock, no bolt to keep him out. And there was no escape from the garden. Even the ruined walls were too high to climb in time. I searched the dimness for a hiding place and wriggled my way behind a thicket of bushes, squeezing between the branches and the rough stone wall and stayed still, my elbows close to my body, the broom clutched against my chest, its cobwebby bristles scraping my chin. The gate opened and I held my breath.

Close-Shave took a few steps into the garden and stopped. He stood still for several, long agonising moments, looking, listening. Then he flipped on a torch and shone it around. A moth fluttered blindly in its beam. He headed for the toilet door, then flung it open suddenly as if he expected to find someone cowering behind it. For a moment he stood motionless, staring at the impromptu platform that I hadn't had the sense to take away.

He stepped up on it. I could hear the dull clang as he lifted the lid of the cistern, see the glow as he shone the torch about inside. There was no doubt about what he was looking for. Was this one final search that he'd decided to make after everywhere else had been ransacked, a sudden inspiration that the place had been overlooked, or had he seen the same film that I had?

Then he came back into the garden, shining his torch around the walls. 'Come out, come out wherever you are!' It was the first time I'd heard him speak. He had a distinct West Country accent, but his voice was no less cold for that. I could feel sweat running down from under my scarf. The torch beam glinted on something he drew from his pocket, something he flicked open. Cold fear clutched my stomach. He was staring straight into the bushes where I was hiding, playing the light among its branches. My mouth was sucked dry and I swallowed. My heart was hammering so hard it was a wonder that the leaves around me weren't quivering in a frenzy. Inch by inch, I altered my grip on the handle of the broom.

I heard a low laugh. 'I see you.' And the light advanced towards me.

I had to let him get close enough. Then the business end of the broom shot out between the branches and chopped him across the throat, the bristles in his face. He staggered backward, snorting, tripped on a tussock of grass and landed on his back. He rolled over, and as he started to haul himself to his knees I crashed through the bushes and swung the broom like a croquet mallet, smashing him on the temple with its wooden head. He sprawled on the floor, the knife flying from his hand. I hesitated, brandishing the broom, ready to hit him again. But he lay still, apparently senseless and after a few moments I felt it was safe to lower my weapon. I picked up the torch and shone it over him. I could see dark blood in the silver of his hair. I wanted to find the knife, maybe the knife that killed Scott Pritchard. I cast around with the torch beam but couldn't see it. It must have fallen somewhere in the long grass. I wanted to rifle through his pockets, find out who he was, but I didn't dare. I wasn't hanging around for the moment when he woke up. I was all for buggering off, top speed. I ran, still clutching the broom, the brick of drugs I'd slid into my jacket pocket pounding against my thigh.

When I reached the van, my hands were shaking so much I could hardly get hold of my key.

I glanced at the motorbike. I didn't want Close-Shave astride that menacing machine chasing me in my little van. If only I'd found that knife, I could have slashed his tyres. I groped around until my fingers closed over a fragment of rock, about the size of a small potato. I placed it in the gleaming exhaust pipe, tore the scarf from my hair, screwed it into a wad and shoved it in afterwards, blocking the pipe. Then I used the handle of the broom to ram the bundle as far up inside as they would go, as if I was loading a cannon. All the time my hands were shaking, and I was straining to hear any sound from the garden above my own ragged breathing.

I tossed the broom into Van Blanc and slid into the driver's seat, taking a moment to draw in a breath before I turned the ignition. There was no sign of Close-Shave. As I pulled away, I glanced in the rear-view mirror at the motorbike. 'Let's see you roar away on that, you bastard.'

CHAPTER TWENTY-ONE

'So, after assaulting a complete stranger with a dangerous weapon, you then vandalised his motorbike.' Cruella fixed me with icy violet eyes. She was enjoying herself. I could tell.

'It wasn't a dangerous weapon. It was a broom. And he wasn't a stranger,' I retorted. 'He was the same man I saw hanging about on Tavistock Viaduct, at the spot where Josh Naylor was murdered, and the same man I saw talking to Scott Pritchard.'

'Are you sure it was the same man?' Cruella raised her eyebrows. 'It was dark. Did you get a proper look at him?'

'Yes,' I insisted. 'I had a torch. Don't you think it's too much of a coincidence that he turns up at the same place that Naylor and Scott came to search for drugs and goes to the one place they obviously didn't look?'

Cruella smirked. 'Too much of a coincidence altogether.'

'You think I'm making this up?'

'Well, he's not there now, is he?' She turned to the uniformed officer sitting beside her for confirmation. A squad car had been sent up to the farm when I'd arrived at the station, garbling my story, and thumped the block of drugs down in front of an astonished desk sergeant. They'd searched but there was no trace of Close-Shave or his knife. 'He wasn't there, and neither was his motorbike.'

I wasn't surprised he'd disappeared, but the bike was a puzzle. He couldn't have ridden it away, not unless he'd discovered what I'd done and I doubt that when he found his bike wouldn't work, a rock up the exhaust pipe was the first thing that came to his mind.

'He had a phone. He must have called for help.'

The uniformed officer shook her head. 'Pity you couldn't have got hold of that phone, Juno. That would have been useful.' Then she quailed under Cruella's withering stare.

'This knife you claim he was carrying . . .' Cruella went on.

'I'm not claiming anything. He had a knife, a flick knife.'

'Well, there's no sign of that either.'

'What about the drugs?' I asked pointedly.

'Ah yes!' Cruella gave her tiny smile. 'The package, which you say contains drugs, and which only you could find. And on your boyfriend's property.'

'Oh, for God's sake!' I cried, ready to thump the table with frustration, 'now what are you insinuating?'

At that moment the cavalry arrived in the form of Detective Inspector Ford, followed by Dean Collins. 'I'll take over from here, thank you, Sergeant,' he announced. He knew that Cruella and I have previous.

For a moment her little mouth worked furiously, like a rabbit chewing a dandelion. 'But sir!'

'Thank you, Sergeant,' he repeated firmly. 'And you too, Constable. Go and do something useful.'

The constable hid a smile as the inspector held the door open for them both to leave. 'Yes, sir,' she said softly. Cruella glowered at me as if her being ousted by her superior was my fault, and then marched out of the room. The inspector shut the door, then picked up my statement and studied it briefly before sitting down at the table. Dean sat next to him.

Inspector Ford raised his eyes and looked at me. 'Want to start again, Juno?' he asked.

He seemed to be in an unusually genial mood, so I plunged into the whole story over again, much to the amusement of Detective Constable Collins who seemed to find my sabotaging of the motorbike particularly hilarious. The inspector was frowning, his heavy brows lowered. 'I'm interested in how he got away so quickly, if you'd put his bike out of action.'

'He phoned someone before he came into the garden,' I told him. 'I couldn't hear what he was saying, but perhaps someone else was coming. Perhaps he was arranging for someone to meet him there.'

'Or he just phoned someone to come and get him when he realised the bike had a problem.' Dean suggested.

'Yes, they might have picked him up,' the inspector agreed, 'but what about the bike? He must have hidden it somewhere nearby. We'll resume our search in daylight.'

'With any luck, sir,' Dean grinned, 'he's intending to come back for it.'

'Do you think you could recognise this man?' the inspector asked me, 'if we showed you some photographs?'

I was about to answer when there was a soft knock on the door. The constable came back in and whispered something in the inspector's ear. He raised his eyebrows in surprise.

'What make?' he asked.

Another whisper.

'I see. Thank you.'

The constable disappeared and for a few moments the inspector seemed to be pondering silently. Then he spoke. 'We've just had that parcel of yours unwrapped. It wasn't drugs at all.'

Not marzipan, I prayed silently.

'It was a gun.'

'A gun?' I repeated, dumbfounded.

'In a box. A Smith and Wesson handgun with silencer.' He smiled. 'This could be a significant find. We're sending it to ballistics now for a firing test. You see, the marks a gun barrel makes on bullets are unique, like fingerprints. If this gun has ever been fired, we can trace it to any crime where bullets have been found at the scene.'

I nodded politely, although I knew all this already. Dean Collins had disappeared and returned with several sets of photographs. He laid six on the table in front of me. 'Is one of these our man?' he asked.

To my surprise, I found him straight away. I pointed to the second photo. 'That's him.'

He laid down three more sets of six photos, twenty-four in all. In the final set, I picked out Close-Shave again. The inspector gave a chuckle.

'Who is he?' I asked.

'He's a member of a Plymouth-based gang involved in drugs and organised crime,' he replied. 'Nasty character altogether. He's what you might call a foot-soldier – an enforcer, if you like.'

'You mean he beats people up?'

'Among other things. A few weeks ago, local police raided his flat, looking for drugs and weapons. They didn't find anything. Someone must have tipped him off and he'd either disposed of these things or hidden them elsewhere.'

'Or got someone to hide them for him,' I suggested.

The inspector nodded. 'This could be where friends Naylor and Pritchard came in.'

'And when they couldn't retrieve his stuff, he killed them. And now this charmer believes that I have his gun? Terrific!'

'Don't panic,' Dean said. 'We've got every copper in the county on the lookout for him.'

'And we'll get a press release put out about the gun.' the inspector added. 'We'll say it was found by a member of the public and handed in to the police. That should stop him hunting for it.'

'If he reads the local press.' I wasn't so sure he'd be a *Dartmoor Gazette* man myself.

'And let's find this bike. If he comes back for it, we can nab the bastard.'

A sudden thought struck me. 'Will you have to tell Daniel about this?'

'The gun was found on his property. He has to be asked if he can account for its being there,' the inspector explained. 'It's just a formality, of course, but we have to ask the question.'

'But you don't need to tell him it was me who found it, do you?' I could just imagine his reaction if he found out what I'd been up to. 'Couldn't you say you found it yourselves?'

'There's no need to give him any information on *who* found it,' he admitted after a moment. Then he smiled. 'We wouldn't want to get Miss Browne into trouble, would we, Collins?'

Dean grinned. 'No, sir. She can manage that on her own.'

I yawned all the way to Tavistock. After my sojourn at the police station, it was almost one o'clock and by then I was too wired to sleep. It's difficult running a stall all day if you're on your own. It's not so much that you need a helper to cope with customers, but it's useful to have someone to watch the thing when you need the loo, or to fetch all the calorific goodies you need to sustain you through a long and often boring day. But there was no one I could ask. Sophie was manning the shop. Olly helped Pat out with the animals at Honeysuckle Farm on Saturdays. I knew Ricky and Morris had their hands full making costumes, so that just left Elizabeth and she'd arranged to be with Tom Carter. So, I was stuffed.

After I'd arrived at the Butchers' Hall, I found my stall and made several trips back and forth to the van fetching my display stands and boxes of stock. Then I had to find somewhere to park. Luckily, I didn't have to search too hard and found a spot just around the corner from the market, near the river wall.

I set to, draping the stall with a chenille cloth I keep for the purpose and setting up the folding bookshelves for display. Then it was just a case of setting out my wares. I'd remembered to rescue the cigarette cards I'd had framed, just as the gallery was about to close the previous evening, and had borrowed a couple of Sophie's small easels to stand them up on. Most of the table would be taken up with the cigarette cards laid out flat in their display sheets, with the china and glass arranged on the bookshelves standing up behind. The tiny items, jewellery and silver, were in a glass-topped display box in the middle. It's satisfying, dressing a stall, and when I'd finished, I was happy that it offered a sufficient variety to make people want to stop and look. I organised my float, set up a chair to sit on, and stowed my bags and boxes under the table. The doors didn't open to the public for a while, so I had time to nip to the nearest cafe to fetch my first cup of coffee of the day. It might be high summer but inside the stone walls of the hall the air was cool and shivery. I fancied something to warm me up. I also bought some sandwiches and cinnamon rolls, just to keep me going.

'You'll spend a fortune on teas and coffees,' the man seated at the stall next to mine remarked. 'Julie and I always bring a thermos.' He and his wife were obviously well organised, their knees draped with tartan rugs as they sat sipping their tea and eating dinky breakfast sandwiches from a plastic lunchbox. I yawned, rubbing my hands together. If I'd got up an hour later or gone to bed an hour earlier, I might have thought about bringing a picnic as well.

I could see Frank, just. His stall was on the other side of the hall, set at a ninety-degree angle to mine, partly hidden by one of the pillars that held up the roof. He had filled his shelves with antique volumes, sample books of his marbling patterns spread out on the table along with his greeting cards and notebooks. At that particular moment he seemed to be counting change.

The glass doors of the Butchers' Hall opened and the public began to wander in. A group of women quickly gathered at my stall and I unlocked the display case for them. They wanted to give me money, a circumstance too rare not to be seized upon. One of them bought a Victorian pendant with a peridot drop, and another a pair of diamante dress-clips. If this keeps up, I thought happily as I wrapped their purchases in tissue paper, I'll pay for the hire of the stall in no time.

But it was just a flurry. I didn't sell anything else

for another two hours. During this time, I had only one potential customer, a morose individual in a mac who spent forever peering at the cigarette cards, before pointing to a single card in the middle of a set of cricketers and asking, 'Will you sell me that one? It's the only one of that set I haven't got.'

'But then I'll have a set with one missing. Hold on a moment, I'll look through my stock and see if I've got a spare.' I dragged out my toffee tin from under the stall and thumbed through all of the duplicate cards I had bundled together in a rubber band. No luck.

'And you won't sell me that one?' he scowled, pointing.

'I don't want to break up the set.' I didn't feel I was being unreasonable, but he tutted sulkily and moved away. I was free to watch Frank, happily chatting to a couple who were browsing through his books until I became aware of a man on the other side of my stall, waiting for me to notice him. 'Oh, I'm sorry,' I smiled. 'Did you want something?'

He pointed to the framed set of golfers' cards. 'May I have a closer look at those, my darlin'?' he asked.

I handed the picture to him. 'Do you collect cigarette cards?'

'No,' he replied, 'but I play golf and so does my wife. She'd love these.' He was a stocky individual, with wavy grey hair and a great air of feeling pleased with himself. It said more about him than his deep tan, the expensive logo on his yellow sweater and the heavy gold signet ring he wore. I could imagine him playing golf, him and his wife, probably on holiday in Portugal. He looked at the price tag on the frame and then shot me a glance. A knowing smile showed a glint of gold on a back tooth. 'What's your best?'

I still bridle at people who assume everything's negotiable. I know it's a sign of my immaturity as an antiques dealer but I wouldn't go into a greengrocers and haggle over the veg. I smiled too. 'It's there on the label.'

He laughed uncertainly. 'Now come on, love. That's not how we play the game, is it?'

'It's how I play it.'

'Oh, go on, indulge me. I like to bargain.'

I didn't like him. He was too sure of himself. I shrugged. 'Make me an offer.'

He did, a very low one, the cheeky bastard, and after that we haggled ferociously. It's true the cards had cost me pence but the cost of mounting and framing them was expensive. For him, I sensed, bartering was a game, but one he seemed determined to win. For his ego to be satisfied I had to come down to his price, he wouldn't come up to mine, even if there was just a farthing's difference in it. I nearly told him to get stuffed, but I wanted to sell and we struck a bargain in the end. I made a small profit, at least. I watched him glide away, the picture tucked under his arm. He stopped at the next stall. I wondered what kind of deal he might try to strike there.

My neighbour tapped my arm. 'You made Gerry pay more than he wanted to,' he nodded approvingly.

Wife Julie nodded. 'Well done, for not giving in to him.'

'Gerry? You know him?'

'That's Gerry Deal, that is.'

The knowledge was lost on me and I must have looked blank.

'He owns several antique shops down in Plymouth and in Cornwall – well, more like junk shops than real antiques,' my neighbour went on, 'anything second-hand, even electrical.'

'Doesn't he have a shop in Preston?' I remembered having driven past it on the long road that joins Torquay to Paignton. There's a rank of unlovely shops, and one of these has Gerry Deal's name writ large above the window. It's a big showroom with second-hand sofas and fridges outside on the forecourt, fine if that's what you're hunting for, but I'd never stopped to look.

'Oh, he's got them everywhere. Dodgy Deal, we call him, don't we, Dennis?'

'He's worth a fortune,' he added with a knowing nod.

'Why Dodgy?' I asked.

Julie was eager to gossip. 'Let's just say he doesn't enquire too closely into where things have come from.'

'And,' Dennis added, lowering his voice, 'he's been inside for er . . . tax irregularities.'

Unfortunately, we had to stop this fascinating conversation because I had another customer, a nerdy collector type. 'I'm interested in some cigarette cards made by Lambert and Butler,' he told me, staring at me earnestly, 'their motorcycle series from 1923. I don't suppose you have any?'

'Not here,' I admitted. 'But I have more cards back

at my shop.' I took his name and telephone number, together with a long list of other cards he was looking for and promised to get in touch.

I glanced back towards Frank's stall and felt myself stiffen. There was a woman talking to him. Her back was towards me, but her shoulder-length dark hair was familiar. 'Could you just keep an eye on my stall a moment?' I murmured to my neighbours, as I shimmied out from behind the table. 'I need the ladies. Would you mind?'

'Yes, love, any time,' Julie was saying but I'd already moved away. The fair was getting busy. I was forced to weave my way between knots of people looking around and moving slowly. The woman handed Frank a cardboard box. 'There you are.' She spoke softly but I could hear the loathing in her voice.

He smiled. 'Thank you, Susan.'

She turned away from him. By this time, I was standing directly behind her and she looked straight into my face. She took in a sharp breath, her lips parting in surprise, and then turned and marched swiftly away from me, heading for the door. I had to let her go. I couldn't run after her, call her name, not with Frank watching. I held back for a count of ten, until another customer distracted him, and then I hurried after her, through the glass door, out into the market courtyard.

It was busy in the cobbled space that surrounded the market, crowds of shoppers drawn by the summer sunshine, the cafes packed, not a seat free at any of their tables. No sign of Susan. She could have sneaked into the pannier market or escaped through one of the narrow passageways that led out on to the street. I walked around the market complex, searching in all the shops where she might have taken refuge, then came out beneath the stone arch of the old courthouse gate and stood in front of the Guildhall. I spotted her crossing Bedford Square. 'Susan!' I yelled. She looked back over her shoulder for a moment. 'Susan, please stop! I want to talk to you.'

She quickened her pace to a run, dashing over the crossing in front of two lines of traffic waiting with their engines throbbing as the last beeps sounded and the green man disappeared. By the time I teetered to a halt on the kerb, the traffic was back in full flow. I fretted at the pavement's edge, waiting for an opportunity to dodge across, but Susan was already disappearing down Plymouth Road. I was losing her. Next to me stood two children, a girl of about eight holding her little brother's hand. 'We have to wait for the green man,' he told me solemnly and put his other hand in mine. So much for risking life and limb dashing through the traffic.

By the time I'd made stately progress across the thoroughfare with the two little ones, Susan was lost to sight. I hurried down Plymouth Road and turned left into the park. It was crowded with people walking their dogs or sunbathing on the grass. Mothers and children were feeding ducks by the canal. But there was no sign of Susan. I'd lost her and I made my way back to the Butchers' Hall, cursing.

I stopped by Frank's stall on my way in, putting on a

smile. ‘Hello. Are you having a good day?’

‘Not at all bad, thank you,’ he replied with his usual bonhomie. ‘Have you been for a walk?’

‘I just thought I’d grab some fresh air.’ I picked one of his books. ‘May I?’

It was a biography of Baudelaire, and although I wasn’t particularly interested in French poetry at that moment, I pretended to look through it, admiring its tooled leather binding and, delicate onion-skin pages edged with gold. While Frank was dealing with another customer, I took a peek at the cardboard box that Susan had given him. He had placed it on a ledge behind his stall and I read the label. *A4 Envelopes*, was all it said. I’d already looked at a box of those when I’d broken into his workshop. I had a nasty feeling now that I should have paid them more attention.

I soon had another customer, and was busy wrapping a willow pattern plate in newspaper, when I saw Mr Dodgy Deal again, talking to Frank. As soon as my customer left, I glanced at my neighbours, Julie and Dennis. They were busy solving sudokus in their newspapers and nibbling flapjacks. By now it was around lunchtime and the crowd had thinned out, heading for the cafes outside. It was safe for me to leave my stall unattended. I crossed the hall and hung around as close to Frank as I dared, by a stall laden with costume jewellery. I pretended to look at earrings.

I caught only odd snatches of their conversation at first because the owner of the jewellery was a determined saleswoman and demanded my attention, but Gerry and Frank seemed to know each other very well. I picked up a pair of turquoise drops, just to keep the jewellery lady happy and pretended to give them serious consideration, holding them up to my ears in the mirror she whipped out for the purpose. Frank was saying something to Gerry about their *enterprise* and that it was important to keep it small. That's what made it successful, he was telling him, that there weren't too many people involved.

'We're not trying to compete with the big boys,' Gerry agreed. 'We mustn't get greedy.'

I put down the turquoise drops. 'Could I look at that amber ring?' I asked, pointing to the item furthest away on the display. Then Frank said, 'That's what I told young Scott.'

I listened more intently, my saleslady distracted for the moment by another potential customer.

'And look what happened to him,' Gerry said.

The ring wouldn't fit. The saleslady tried to find me a larger one.

'That was a very unfortunate incident,' Frank added as I tried on an ornate topaz.

Gerry grunted. 'Let's hope that sort of thing doesn't happen again, Frank. It's not in our interest.'

'Don't worry,' Frank assured him, as I took off the ring with a sorry shake of the head. 'I can promise it won't.'

I missed what was said next because of a couple passing behind me, chatting, but then I heard Gerry say, 'Tell her to keep her mouth shut if she knows what's good for her.'

'She will,' Frank responded

Were they talking about Susan? By now the lady on the jewellery stall was beginning to look at me as if I was wasting her time or she suspected I was malingering with intent to pinch something. I either had to buy something or move away. Frank and Gerry seemed to have finished their conversation, so I smiled in apology and did the latter. But I didn't return to my stall immediately. I genuinely needed a trip to the ladies now.

When I got home, I found a message on my answering-machine from Dean Collins, asking me to call. I did, thinking that there might be some news on Scott. 'Have you talked to Millie yet?' I asked.

Dean grunted. 'We can't find her.'

I felt a tug of disquiet. 'I hope nothing's happened to her.'

'I hope so too. But if the lass has gone to ground, either she killed Scott or she knows who did. We need to find her.'

'Perhaps she's just frightened. Have you asked Frank?'

'He says he hasn't seen her for days.' He sighed. 'Anyway, what I phoned you about was that motorbike.'

'You found it?'

He hesitated. 'We did but then we lost it again.'

'How?'

'Two constables were sent up to search the farm as soon as it was light. It seems our friend must have wheeled the bike into the barn. They found it hidden under some sacking. Then they got an urgent call out to a traffic accident and by the time they reported their find and we got someone else up there . . .'

'It had gone,' I finished for him.

'Yep. Local man driving by in his tractor reports seeing a grey Transporter van parked on the property, thought it was suspicious, so he gave us a call. It was about the right time so . . .'

'So, he's got his bike back. And he's still out there.'

'Seems like it. Never mind,' Dean added cheerfully, 'at least he hasn't got his gun.'

CHAPTER TWENTY-TWO

Sunday's rehearsal seemed more like a wake. We gathered on the lawn at Druid Lodge and held a minute's silence for Scott. During this brief interlude I saw several of the fairies cast furtive glances at Matthew, who stood as still as a rock, staring resolutely ahead, his inner tension given away by a pulse beating in his cheek. Then Gabriel addressed us all, lamenting the terrible tragedy that had occurred, the awful circumstances of Scott's death. In the middle of this speech, the police arrived, Cruella, Dean and a uniformed officer marching towards us across the lawn. *Please God, don't let them arrest Matthew,* I prayed devoutly. But they'd only come to take statements from various people they hadn't managed to track down since the last rehearsal. Morris gave them use of the music room for their interviews and they disappeared inside, Dean stopping for a brief word with Matthew on the way. Whatever he said to him, Matthew suddenly smiled.

'Just in case you're all wondering,' he announced with a touch of defiance, 'that was to tell me my alibi checked out.'

'I don't think any of us were in any doubt about it,' Gabriel told him, although it was quite obvious from the look on their faces that some people had been. There was a lot of shuffling of feet and supportive murmuring and Digby gave Matthew a matey pat on the shoulder.

Gabriel continued with his homily about Scott. He was convinced that Scott would have wanted us to carry on with the production. I don't know where his conviction sprang from, other than his own inclinations, but no one argued. If anyone felt uncomfortable with that, he went on, then now was the time to say. Nobody spoke. And if anyone felt like dropping out, he went on generously, we would all understand. No one moved.

But after a moment, Marian raised a hand. 'How are we going to carry on?' she ventured. 'With no Demetrius? And we still haven't got an Oberon.'

'These are problems we need to solve very quickly,' Gabriel admitted. 'I know I keep saying it, but if anyone knows someone who might be suitable, please persuade them to come along.'

Before we started rehearsal, I said hello to a young woman I noticed who was sitting apart from everyone else on the lawn, surveying what was going on with an air of detachment. She looked as if she might be Greek, with dark, almond-shaped eyes and a cloud of black curly hair. I guessed this was Gabriel's girlfriend, presumably the Darling that he talked to on the phone.

'I'm Naomi,' she offered in a low, husky voice. 'I'm so glad that the company has decided to carry on. I know it's what Gabriel wants.'

Well, he would, I thought cynically, he's getting paid.

'He was thrilled to be offered the opportunity to come down here and work with you all.'

That's certainly not the impression he gave but I didn't say so. 'Really?'

'Oh yes. He was grateful to get away. I think he was finding London too much.'

'And will you be staying down here too?' I asked.

She smiled. 'I'm only here for the weekend.'

'Well, I hope you enjoy the rehearsal. Nice to meet you.'

As rehearsals went, it wasn't one of the best. In fact, things went from bad to worse. Puck fell out of a tree and skinned her elbow, Bottom and Quince missed their entrances because they were being interviewed by the police, and then a feisty breeze got up, whipping away the actors' words.

'You'll have to get used to this,' Gabriel bellowed unsympathetically. 'We've got no control over the weather. It could be blowing a gale every night we perform.' He went on to make some point about voice projection when two of the lake's resident ducks chose to waddle across the lawn, quacking fussily as they led their ducklings down to the water. By now Gabriel had lost his sense of humour. He yelled at Emily when she wasn't loud enough and she fled into the house in tears. April Hardiman looked as if she wanted to follow her but had to remain, guarding the younger fairies, so it was Marian who hurried after her.

'Oh, for God's sake!' Gabriel muttered.

'Perhaps now is a good time to stop for tea?' Morris suggested.

'Oh, why not?' Gabriel hurled his script to the ground. 'We're not making any bloody progress out here.'

'Can't we get Emily a radio mic?' I asked Ricky as we trooped towards the house. 'Is it really out of the question?'

'The problem is, if we mic her up, her voice is going to sound unnatural compared with everyone else's. And it would complicate things technically, especially out here.' He grinned. 'The other problem is that people wearing radio mics have to remember to turn them off when they leave the stage, or the audience can hear everything they're saying in the dressing room.'

'I remember when Dartmoor Operatic did *The Gondoliers*,' Morris smiled impishly. 'Something went wrong during a duet and the audience could hear the two of them blaming each other when they got off stage.'

Ricky grinned. 'Going at it hammer and tongs, they were. Best laugh of the evening.'

As tea was served in the dining room, Emily reappeared, still looking tearful.

'You're back, are you?' Gabriel demanded heartlessly. 'Well, it's no good you crying, is it? That doesn't get us anywhere.'

'No, I'm sorry,' she responded in a trembling little voice. 'I will try to be louder.'

'This is not what that poor girl needs,' Elizabeth murmured as she came to stand beside me. 'She's on the verge of throwing in the towel as it is. He's going to lose her altogether if he can't handle her more sympathetically.'

Digby, standing close by as he tried to decide between various plates of sandwiches and slabs of cake, whispered, 'Such a pity, because her performance is coming along nicely. She just needs to support her diaphragm. Perhaps Mandy and I could help her out, suggest some exercises.'

Amanda, who clearly had no interest in sandwiches or cake, and had somehow gained possession of a brimming schooner of sherry rather than a teacup, added in her deep, mellow tones, 'That Gabriel Dark is an arrogant little prick.' I stifled a laugh. She might be a drunk and part-time shoplifter but I can't help liking Amanda.

I looked around for Naomi but there was no sign of her. I wondered if Gabriel would be looking after her, but the last I'd seen of him he was heading towards the patio lighting up a fag. Thinking that perhaps she didn't know refreshments were on offer, I went out into the garden to find her. I heard her voice, coming from a small courtyard at the side of the house where Ricky and Morris stow their bins, somewhere I guess she and Gabriel had gone to talk privately. She sounded furious. I know I should have crept away but I lingered for a listen.

'They were bloody bailiffs, Gabriel! They came to *my*

flat, trying to take *my* stuff to pay for *your* bloody debts!'

'I'm sorry,' he responded humbly.

'You've run off to hide down here and left me in London with all your shit. You promised me you'd stop all this.' Her voice was low and shaking. 'You promised you'd sort all this shit out!'

'And I will!' he stammered. 'I swear I will!'

'On your life, you promised me.'

'I know. I know. I've just had a run of bad luck, that's all.'

'You swore to me you'd stopped gambling. You said you'd get help.'

'I have.'

She gave a derisive laugh. 'Don't lie to me!'

'I have, I swear. It's just . . . well, I still owe money. Darling. I just need a little—'

'I am not loaning you any more money.'

'I just need to pay them back. If they catch up with me and I can't pay them . . .'

'If I give you money, you won't pay them back. You'll just gamble it away again.'

'For God's sake, Naomi!' Gabriel's voice ended on a sob. 'They're threatening to break my legs.'

Something like a groan broke from Naomi's lips. 'I may just break your neck.'

'Darling, please! This isn't a joke.'

'Oh, I know it's not a joke, Gabriel!' she sounded tearful, but they were tears of anger and frustration. 'I get phone calls. I get men turning up on my doorstep, banging on the door at all hours of the night, calling your name through the letter box, making threats. I've had enough, I really have! Now, either you get this sorted, or I am changing all the locks and your stuff's going out in the street.'

'Naomi, darling, please . . .'

Fascinating as all this was, I decided it was time I stopped eavesdropping. After all, it was their own private mess, no business of mine. I had enough mess of my own.

CHAPTER TWENTY-THREE

As if Mondays weren't busy enough, this one was made busier by a distress call from the Brownlows, who were expecting guests for dinner that night. Their house needed blitzing. The Brownlows are a pair of hospital doctors who, together with three teenage children, enjoy a breezily chaotic domestic life. No one in the family ever puts anything away. Any object, once put down, is likely to stay where it's put until it grows whiskers. The same carrier bag of Christmas decorations has been hanging on the kitchen doorknob since Twelfth Night and will probably continue to hang there until Christmas Eve. The only member of the household who possesses any tidying instinct is Goldie, their unimaginatively named retriever, who always brings me a present as soon as I let myself in through the front door. Today she appeared in the hall, plumy tail waving, a DVD, minus case, held gently in her soft mouth.

'Good girl,' I told her, stroking her noble head. 'Give. Thank you.'

There was a note left on the hall table.

Dear Juno. Please do what you can with the dining room, living room, kitchen and downstairs loo. Anyone who strays upstairs only has themselves to blame. Also, if he hasn't surfaced by the time you leave, could you go and wake Sleeping Beauty? He has a dental appointment this afternoon.

Thanks. Jo.

P.S. You do not have to kiss him.

I set to in the living room first, pushing back the sofa to see what might be lurking underneath. There's usually something. This time there were two dinner plates, complete with forks, crumbs and smears of ketchup, two one-pound coins, a crumpled tissue and a used plaster. I wonder if it's having to be scrupulously hygienic at work and constantly on the watch for germs that leads to such a cavalier disregard for them at home. Anyway, I gathered up the plates, and a few scummy-bottomed coffee mugs stuck to the window sill, and marched them into the kitchen to load them into the dishwasher. I had to unload it first, sorting the clean dishes waiting to come out after the last wash, from the dirty dishes someone had put in since.

I was scrubbing my way around the kitchen worktops, the dishwasher sloshing in happy accompaniment, when I heard the sound of the flush in the bathroom, shortly followed by the plod of heavy footsteps on the stairs and a truly hippo-sized yawn. Sleeping Beauty, it seemed, had arisen without any help from me.

'Hi, Juno,' he said, appearing in the kitchen doorway. 'Long time, no see.'

Chris is the Brownlow's eldest son and I haven't seen him since he left home to start college back in the autumn. He's tall and slim with light brown hair and a ready, charming grin. At that moment he was clad in the t-shirt and boxer shorts I imagine he had slept in. His legs looked very long and very pale. He opened the fridge door and took out a carton of orange juice. 'I don't suppose you fancy frying me breakfast?' he asked, smothering another yawn.

'You suppose correctly.'

He looked around for a glass as if he expected one to appear from the ether, then shrugged and drank straight from the carton. 'I'd pay you.'

'What with?' I asked cynically.

He considered for a moment. 'My body?'

'Save it for science.'

'You're nice!' he spluttered, almost choking on his orange juice.

I surveyed him, his slim body and boyish grin. 'What are you doing with yourself during the holidays? Got a job or anything?'

He shook his head. 'Nah! I'm just chilling.'

'Oh well, if you've got time on your hands,' I suggested, 'how do you fancy a spot of amateur dramatics?'

* * *

Henry Gillow doesn't look like a murderer, more like an ageing cherub, with innocent blue eyes, his soft, round face crowned by receding, crinkly hair. But what do murderers look like? During my visits to Dartmoor prison to see Henry, I couldn't pick them out. I couldn't separate the armed robbers and violent offenders from the petty fraudsters and drug addicts. Sometimes, looking around the visitors' hall I might encounter a face that was hostile, or an eye that looked back at me with too much interest, the kind of glance that made me want to look away, but mostly they looked no different from other men, some of them sad-looking, grey-faced under the harsh prison lighting.

'Hello, Henry,' I greeted him next afternoon. I was sitting about a table's width away from him, the table having been recently removed. It seems tabletops provide too much cover for visitors to pass smuggled items to inmates undetected. There were only a few other prisoners receiving visitors and they were seated far away from us, one in urgent conversation with an older woman who might have been his mother, another faced by a girl with a small child sitting on her knee; all of us watched over by the prison officer guarding the door. We visitors had all been through the same undignified process of being patted down, women having our handbags taken from us, put through a scanner and then into lockers.

Dartmoor Prison has been under threat of closure for years. Built on a wild, forbidding stretch of moor, it's too old to be modernised or humanised, to be brought up to modern standards of security, health or safety.

It's a grim fortress, high granite walls punctured by tiny windows, and it's only the ever-increasing size of the prison population that forces it to remain open. Voices and footsteps echo on the hard surfaces. Turning keys and steel gates clang. And there's a smell in the air, a mixture of disinfectant and school dinners. I wouldn't fancy being locked in there myself.

'I brought you some sweets,' I told Henry, 'but they wouldn't let me give them to you.' My bags of pineapple rock and liquorice comfits had been confiscated on arrival. Before being arrested, Henry had run an old-fashioned sweet shop and I thought they'd remind him of home.

'They'll be checking them to make sure they're not drugs,' he told me cheerily. 'I might get them later, once they've sampled a few.'

'What if I tried to send them by post?'

'Same thing,' he smiled sadly. 'All parcels must be addressed to the governor, and the contents are opened and checked.' I hadn't seen him for weeks and he looked as if he'd put on weight. Prison food was filling, he told me, too much carbohydrate.

I glanced at the prison warder who was keeping an eye on us. 'How are you, Henry? Are they treating you well?'

'Oh, I can't complain, you know.'

'Has your wife been to see you?'

He shook his head. 'No, no. I wouldn't encourage Marjorie to visit. She wouldn't like it here and it's a long way for her to come. She writes,' he added in a voice that suggested he wished she wouldn't, 'tells me how difficult

I've made things for her.'

'You mean running the shop on her own?'

'Well, that,' he admitted, 'although she has got her sister to help her.'

'Ah yes,' I remembered, 'Eunice.'

'It's more the sort of thing that some of the customers are saying. It's bound to upset her. I'm pleading temporary insanity, you know,' he added, looking rather pleased with himself. 'That's what she doesn't like, that people are saying I'm bonkers.'

'But if that plea helps you to get off . . .'

'I don't think there's much chance of that,' he said philosophically. 'They'll either lock me up for being a murderer or for being mad, it doesn't make much difference really, does it?' He gave another little smile. 'I don't mind. I get plenty of time to read. Although,' he added with a sigh, 'the prison library isn't exactly extensive.'

'Perhaps I could bring you some books.'

He shook his head. 'You're not allowed to bring books in. We can order new books on the Internet, from approved sellers, but we're not allowed anything hardback or second-hand.'

'In case it's been interfered with?'

'I suppose.'

There was a sudden disturbance at the end of the room. A prison officer had approached the man being visited by his wife and child and snatched a piece of paper from his grasp. It was a drawing the little girl had done for her daddy. Even from where I was sitting, I could see it was just a child's scribble, a few scrawled lines of crayon and a blob of paint. But the officer confiscated it. The wife protested loudly but he was adamant. 'You should have shown this to us on your way in,' he insisted, and folded it away in his pocket.

'What was all that about?' I asked.

Henry shook his head. 'There have been a lot of drugs smuggled into the prison lately and they're being very strict about visitors trying to bring anything in here.'

Confiscating a child's drawing seemed nothing short of vindictive to me. 'I could write to you,' I offered. 'I can't often visit but I could write, if you'd like that.'

'That would be something to look forward to, a letter from you, Juno, although,' he added sadly, 'it's not the same when you know your letter has already been read by someone else.'

'Do they open all prisoners' letters?'

'Some of them. Spot checks, you know. You can never be sure whether or not your letter might be opened. Well, except for official letters from your solicitor. They're protected by client privilege. They're not allowed to open those. Those are covered by Rule 39.'

'Rule 39?' I repeated, leaning forward. 'What's that?'

'Well, I don't exactly know what the rule says,' he admitted. 'All I know is that if you get a letter with your solicitor's address and *Rule 39 Letter* stamped on it, that means it contains confidential material and the prison staff can't open it.'

'I see.'

'Of course, they contact your solicitor to check they

have written to you. After all,' his face dimpled into a mischievous smile, 'anyone could get a rubber stamp made up with Rule 39 on it.'

'True,' I agreed, having stamped it on my own hand quite recently. 'That's very interesting, Henry.'

'Not really,' he sighed. Then he leant forward eagerly. 'That's enough about me. How is Ashburton's famous sleuth? Are you doing any detective work at the moment? Any interesting cases on the go?'

I told him about the drugs and gun at Daniel's farm, Josh Naylor's fall from Tavistock Viaduct, Scott's murder, and the suspicious Mr Frank Tinkler. Well, why not? It wasn't as if the poor bugger had much to keep him amused.

'I wish I wasn't stuck in here,' Henry lamented. 'If only I were free to assist you, to play Watson to your Holmes.' I think it was overhearing this last declaration that made the prison officer decide that my visit was at an end. 'Time's up,' he called abruptly. I said goodbye to Henry and promised solemnly that I would keep him up to date with my detecting activities. 'I think he's nuts,' I confided to the warder as he accompanied me from the visiting room. 'You're not likely to be letting him out any time soon, are you?'

He shook his head sternly, and I cast him a look of undying gratitude.

CHAPTER TWENTY-FOUR

Gabriel was all smiles at rehearsal next evening and not just because I'd dragged Chris Brownlow along who he immediately cast as Demetrius. He might not be as handsome as Scott, but he understood the text better and had a more natural delivery. It was also obvious from the first moment that Marian was going to find him a much easier person to get along with.

'And I think we may also have solved the problem of Oberon,' Gabriel beamed. 'I received a phone call from a young man who has heard about our problem and has played the part before. He wasn't able to come to rehearsal tonight, but I'm seeing him tomorrow, so we must keep our fingers crossed. There is, sadly, one other piece of news.' Gabriel paused for dramatic effect. 'I'm afraid Emily has resigned from the role of Titania.'

There was a shocked silence.

Elizabeth raised an eyebrow. 'It's more a case of constructive dismissal,' she murmured.

'She said she realised that she wasn't up to the role,' Gabriel added, 'and sadly, I was forced to agree with her. She tried her best, I'm sure, but between ourselves, since the auditions, I have been disappointed with her efforts.' He spread his hands in a helpless gesture. 'I can only blame myself for casting her.'

'Hypocritical bastard,' Ricky muttered. Then he glanced at me. 'You'd better start learning her lines.'

'No way,' I mouthed at him.

'I've been talking to my bosses at the Arts Council.' Gabriel carried on, seeming blithely oblivious to the change of atmosphere in the rehearsal room, 'and they agreed with me, that as time is growing short and we have no other potential Titania among the cast' – this caused the gang of fairies to flick indignant glances at each another – 'that the best thing would be to cast a professional actress in the role.'

Ricky and Morris looked at each other in surprise. It was obvious they hadn't been consulted. Elizabeth slid a glance in my direction. 'Can he do that?' she whispered. 'Isn't this supposed to be a community production?' I was too busy heaving a sigh of relief to care.

'And I'm very pleased to be able to announce,' Gabriel continued smoothly, 'that Naomi Walker, who I'm sure you all know from her work on television, as well as her visit here last Sunday, has agreed to come down to Ashburton to play the part.'

There was some excited chatter among the cast at

this and a few of them decided to applaud. Gabriel beamed. 'I can assure you that she will lend a great deal of distinction and professionalism to our production.'

How the hell has he managed that? I wondered. Naomi was on the point of chucking him out, not just from her flat but from her life, judging by what she'd said to him in the garden. It must have taken him more than his usual persuasive charm to talk her round. Perhaps, with all the trouble she'd had because of him, she decided to get out of London as well.

Gabriel clapped his hands together. 'Right, let's make a start, then, shall we?' He glanced over in our direction, 'If that little huddle in the corner of the room can bear to break things up. We've got a lot of ground to go over with Chris.'

'When will Miss Walker be joining us?' one of the fairies asked, made breathless by the excitement of the prospect.

'Not until the weekend, unfortunately. She has work commitments in London this week. Now, come along, everyone.'

Digby and Amanda walked into *Old Nick's* the next day, exactly as arranged. They'd come to provide a little diversion so that I could sneak into Frank's room. I didn't want to involve Pat or Sophie. Digby and Amanda were up for it as soon as I suggested it, and better still, didn't demand to know what it was all about. If I needed their assistance, Digby assured me, they were only too happy to render it, no questions asked. As it turned out, it wasn't a complete charade. They had some old and treasured volumes of Shakespeare that had fallen into a bad state of repair and needed rebinding. 'Frank,' I heard Sophie yell, 'you've got customers!'

I was already upstairs in the kitchen, pretending to give it a clean. I listened for Frank's footsteps as he went down and opened the kitchen door.

'Good lord!' I heard him say loudly as he laid eyes on the two waiting at the counter. 'Surely! It can't be . . . I recognise you two! You're from that television series . . . er, what was it called now?'

'*There's Only Room for Two*,' Amanda told him modestly, in a voice that said *oh, that old thing!* 'Amanda Waft.' I couldn't see her but I knew that she would be extending her long arm gracefully over the counter, presenting her hand for him to kiss.

'I'm honoured,' Frank responded gallantly.

'Digby Jerkin.' Digby would be wringing Frank's hand. 'Hello.'

I slipped into Frank's room as I heard him ask what he could do for them. They'd keep him chatting for ages, but I still wanted to be in and out as fast as I could. I headed straight for the shelves with the boxes of A4 envelopes and the one that Susan had given him in Tavistock. I took the lid off and felt a wave of disappointment; nothing more incriminating than the envelopes stated on the label. I slid one out carefully. It was a quality envelope, made in heavy, deckled paper and printed in curling script along the edge were the words *Padbury and Finch, Solicitors, Tavistock*. I slid the envelope back in, patting the top edge down gently until it lined up with the others. It was impossible to tell the box had been disturbed.

I checked the other box, the one I had only glanced into before. These envelopes were also printed, but with a different name and address: *Mr Leonard Newt, St Antony's Prison Trust, Merrivale Lane, Ashburton, Devon.* A registered charity number was printed in the top left corner.

'What are you doing in here?'

I nearly jumped out of my skin. 'Jesus, Pat! I didn't hear you come up the stairs.' I put the lid back on the box and stood up.

She scowled at me. 'I come up to make a coffee.'

'Ssh!' I ushered her out of the room and followed, leaving the door ajar as I had found it.

'What are you up to?' she asked, as I pulled her into the safety of the kitchen, 'poking about in Frank's room?'

'Nothing,' I said. 'I'm just being nosy.'

She eyed me suspiciously for a moment and then chuckled. 'Well, that's what you're good at.'

'D'you know a Merrivale Lane in Ashburton?'

'No such place. Leastways, I've never heard of it.'

'No,' I said, as I flipped on the kettle. 'Neither have I.'

When I got back downstairs Digby and Amanda still had Frank locked in conversation. I smiled to myself. Amanda was on form. Frank would probably never even miss the notebooks whose colourful covers I could spy lurking in the bottom of her shopping basket.

Later that day, when everyone, including Frank, had

gone home, I phoned the offices of Padbury and Finch, Solicitors in Tavistock. A woman answered the phone. I recognised her voice at once. 'Hello, Susan,' I said, and the call was disconnected.

Gabriel had not turned up by the time I arrived at rehearsal that evening, and everyone was standing around in groups, waiting for him. I was late because I'd been poring over a local map searching for Merrivale Lane. Pat was right, there was no such place in Ashburton. Nor was there any Mr Leonard Newt listed in the phonebook. Then I'd spent some time trawling the Internet trying to find St Antony's Prison Trust. It wasn't listed on any website and the registered charity number appeared to be fictitious. I was planning to return to my search as soon as rehearsal was over. 'Where is Gabriel?'

Ricky shrugged. 'He's late. He's not answering his phone. Let's hope he's on his way.'

'I wonder if we've got an Oberon yet,' Digby pondered. 'Wasn't he arranging to meet him sometime today?'

I thanked him and Amanda quietly for their good work that morning. 'You kept Frank out of the way for ages.'

'Any time,' Digby responded. 'Just say the word.'

'How's Emily?' I asked the group in general. 'Has anyone spoken to her since . . .?'

'I went round to see her.' It was Marian who spoke.

'Is she all right?'

'Still a bit tearful. Her father's furious about the way Emily's been treated.' She grinned. 'She had to beg him not to come here tonight and plant one on Gabriel.'

'She should have let him come,' Matthew put in. 'I feel like planting one on him myself.'

'But did she jump or was she pushed?' I asked.

'A bit of both, I think,' Marian responded. 'She's quite relieved, really. She hadn't been enjoying rehearsals with Gabriel picking on her all the time.'

April Hardiman was looking at her watch. 'He's very late. Do you think we ought to start without him? Some of these fairies will have to finish at nine and we're wasting time.'

Ricky agreed. 'C'mon, we'll run through Act Three. We can always start again when His Majesty arrives.'

But twenty minutes later he still hadn't. Everyone carried on rehearsing, apparently much happier without him. 'Why don't I slip around to his flat?' I asked Ricky. 'See if he's there? Perhaps he's fallen asleep or something.' To be honest I was a bit worried, remembering his conversation with Naomi. What if she'd changed her mind about playing Titania? What if the stress of his gambling got too much for him and he'd decided to end it all? What if the Devil had flown away with him?

Morris dug in his pocket and handed me a key. 'I had a spare cut, in case he lost it.'

'And it's above Mary's shop?' I hadn't been there myself.

'Yes, but you can't get to it from East Street. You need to go past it and turn first left and then left again into another little lane that runs behind.'

'I'll find it.'

'It's number 4a. It's got a blue door.'

'Thanks.'

'And if you find him dead drunk, I'm gonna sack the bugger,' Ricky warned. 'Arts Council or no Arts Council.'

It was a relief to get out of the stuffy rehearsal room into the open air. It was still early, the sky still light. I breathed in the spicy smell from the Indian takeaway just getting going across the street. The smell of curry always makes me ravenous, and the sandwich I'd munched while I was trawling the Internet seemed like a long time ago now. I headed up East Street, crossing over to Mary's gift shop and stopping for a brief look at the goodies in her window, then turned left and left again as instructed. It was a pretty lane, unlike the dark alley that runs down the side of *Old Nick's*, other properties fronting the cobbled walkway with pots of geraniums decorating the doorsteps and dangling flower-filled baskets hanging by the doors. There was obviously agreement among the residents about keeping the place looking pretty and well cared-for.

I found the blue door to 4a about halfway along and rang the doorbell. There was no response, so I used the key and let myself into a stone-flagged passage. I called Gabriel's name as I climbed the stairs into a bright, newly fitted kitchen. An open door led out onto a balcony overlooking the lane and a neighbour's garden. It was shaded from the evening sun by the walls, steeply sloping roofs and chimney pots that surrounded it, but would have been a pleasant place to sit earlier in the day, with a view of the green fields rising up behind the town. I noticed an empty wine glass sitting on a wrought iron table. 'Gabriel?' I called again.

It seemed he wasn't at home. He must have gone out and left the balcony door open. I made a mental note to lock it before I left. It wouldn't be difficult to climb the garden wall next door and break into the flat by clambering on to the balcony. I could do it easily. I went through into the living room and found myself gazing down St Lawrence Lane to the chapel tower. I lingered by the window for a few moments before I turned back into the room. It was a light and pleasant room, the walls washed in soft grey and lined with bookshelves. There was a faux wood-burner in the fireplace and a large sofa and coffee table. Gabriel's jacket was flung across the back of a chair, the silk lining turned uppermost, his specs folded up in his breast pocket. A dining table took up half of the room with a laptop on it, a scattering of papers, and a copy of *A Midsummer Night's Dream* placed face-down next to a half-drunk cup of coffee. It seemed he'd gone out without finishing it. And he hadn't taken his specs, which seemed strange. It was all a bit *Marie Celeste,* unless Gabriel was in the bedroom, deaf to my calls, either heavily asleep or dead drunk as Ricky had predicted. I went into the hall and stopped at the first door. I knocked.

'Gabriel?' I pushed the door open and put my head around it. The bed was empty and unmade, the duvet thrown back, trousers, underpants and socks scattered on top of it. Beyond the bedroom, a door led into what must be an en-suite. A woody, slightly citrus-tang hung in the air like aftershave or shower gel, something masculine and sophisticated. I knocked again. ‘Gabriel, are you in there? Are you all right?’ There was no response. ‘I’m coming in,’ I warned him and swung the door open into a large bathroom, revealing a floor chequered in black and white tiles shining with water. The room was dominated by a roll-top bath on scrolled feet, the window and the mirrors misted with steam. Two bare feet were sticking up from one end of the bath, on legs whose dark hairs were flattened with wetness. ‘Gabriel?’

He was lying in the bath, absolutely still, eyes staring up at me. He wasn’t dead drunk. Just dead. Someone had grabbed his legs, pulled him under and drowned him.

Instinctively I stepped back, slipping on the wet floor. I steadied myself, closing my eyes as I took in a juddering breath, then opened them again. The view hadn’t changed. Gabriel was still dead. His arms lay back beyond his head as if he’d been struggling to find a grip on the smooth and shining edge of the roll top. I stared. Somewhere in the room beyond, the Valkyries started to ride.

CHAPTER TWENTY-FIVE

Gabriel Dark never stood a chance. Because, basically, if you are in a deep bath and someone grabs hold of your legs and pulls you under the water, there is nothing you can do about it, no way you can fight back. And you wouldn't need great strength to do it either. A woman could do it, Cruella told me, staring accusingly from those frosty violet eyes as she took my statement.

Which left us with the question of who wanted him dead. I repeated the argument I'd overheard in the garden about Gabriel's gambling debts. 'Perhaps his creditors caught up with him.'

Cruella wasn't convinced. 'You don't kill someone who owes you money,' she objected. 'That way you'd never get your money back.'

'What if someone came here to threaten and intimidate him, to frighten him and it went wrong? He drowned during the struggle. He'd only need to inhale water once and—'

'Yes, thank you, Miss Browne.' Cruella obviously wasn't prepared to listen to any theories of mine. 'For now, we'll stick to the facts. We'll let you know if we need you again.'

I think she just wanted to get rid of me before her boss arrived.

I went up to Druid Lodge. I'd phoned Ricky earlier to tell him I wouldn't make it back to rehearsal, that I couldn't explain what was going on but I'd fill him and Morris in on what was happening when I arrived. Sophie, Elizabeth and Olly were there too, all curious. I gave them the grisly details. We sat around the breakfast room table, me cradling the glass of brandy Morris had insisted on giving me, while we pondered the question of who had murdered Gabriel Dark and why.

Ricky said he needed a fag. 'I often felt like killing him,' he admitted, lighting up and drawing thoughtfully on his cigarette, 'strangling him with my bare hands.'

Morris shuddered. 'You don't mean that.'

'I think we've all felt like strangling him at some point or other,' Elizabeth agreed calmly. 'He was never exactly endearing. But I think someone must have had a stronger motive than his poor people-handling skills for killing him.'

Ricky nodded. 'You can't help feeling sorry for the poor bugger.'

'But who would do a thing like that?' Sophie was almost tearful.

'You don't think Emily's dad did it?' Olly's blue eyes widened as he was struck by the notion. 'He threatened to sort Gabriel out.'

Ricky stood up and aimed his cigarette smoke out of the kitchen window. 'What about Emily herself?'

'Because Gabriel forced her to drop out?' I asked.

'I've known actresses who'd kill for less.'

Morris wasn't amused and tutted. 'Take no notice of him.'

'But she couldn't, surely?' I objected. 'I know Cruella thinks a woman could have drowned Gabriel, but *Emily*?'

'I know she ain't a great strapping wench like you,' Ricky responded, grinning, 'but don't let that fool you. She's a dancer and dancers are tough. You don't spend hours doing class all day without developing muscles like sprung steel.'

I laughed. 'You're not seriously considering Emily as a suspect?'

'What about Naomi?' Morris asked.

'You think she might have killed him?' From what I knew about her relationship with Gabriel, that was a lot more likely, but I didn't say so.

He sighed, agitated. 'No, I didn't mean that! Has anyone spoken to her? Has anyone told the poor girl?'

I sipped my brandy. 'The police will have contacted her by now.'

'Will she still be coming here,' Olly asked, 'to take part in the play?'

'I wouldn't have thought so.' Ricky took a final puff

on his fag and lobbed the butt out of the window. 'I bet she was only doing it as a favour to Gabriel. I'm sure she's got better career options open to her.'

'Besides,' Morris gave a mournful sigh, 'the poor girl wouldn't want to, not now.'

'She could have killed him, though,' Sophie frowned thoughtfully. 'Suppose she didn't go back to London on Sunday and they had an argument?'

I shook my head, remembering the steam rising from the bath, the misted-up mirrors. The water was still warm. When I found Gabriel, he could not have been dead very long. 'Wasn't Gabriel expecting a visitor this afternoon?' I asked. 'Wasn't he seeing someone about playing Oberon?'

'Yes, and that's a funny thing.' Ricky strolled back to the table. 'No one knows who he was. Gabriel said that a man had phoned him, someone who'd heard that we were short of an actor. He assumed that this person had heard about it through one of the cast . . .'

'That's right!' Olly held up a finger. 'He said he didn't know which of us to thank.'

'But we were talking about it when we were waiting for him to arrive,' Ricky went on, 'and no one knows who this person was.'

Sophie bit her lip. 'Perhaps Oberon was the killer.'

I said nothing. Whoever the killer was, he'd got into that flat undetected by Gabriel wallowing in his bath. Perhaps he had climbed up on to that balcony and got into the flat through the open kitchen door.

'We mustn't get too carried away,' Elizabeth smiled.

'The call from this potential Oberon was probably a coincidence. For all we know, Gabriel did meet him earlier in the day as planned. He might even have cast him.'

'He didn't turn up at rehearsal,' Sophie objected. She turned her dark eyes on Ricky.

'So, what's going to happen about the play now? We've got no Oberon, no Titania . . .'

'And no director,' Morris added.

'Yes, we have,' I said. 'We've got two people who should have been directing it in the first place.'

'But we're playing parts now,' Morris objected, 'and making the costumes.'

'That's never stopped you when you're doing a pantomime.'

'This is a bit different, love,' Ricky responded. 'We've never had two people murdered in a pantomime. Let's think about it for a bit, eh?'

'Perhaps we could get Emily back,' Sophie suggested. 'Now that Gabriel is . . . um . . .'

'This production is cursed!' Olly cried suddenly. 'First Scott, now Gabriel.' His blue eyes widened as he grabbed Sophie by the arm. 'Perhaps we're all gonna get picked off, one by one!'

'That's quite enough of that,' Elizabeth admonished him. 'Don't repeat that nonsense in rehearsal because some of those fairies are silly enough to believe it. Besides, this is no laughing matter. The poor man is dead. I think it's time to go home. You've got school in the morning.'

‘Last day of term,’ he objected cheerfully. ‘We won’t be doing much.’

‘Even so.’ Elizabeth offered Sophie a lift home and the party began to break up.

‘You all right, Princess?’ Ricky asked when the others had gone. ‘Can’t have been much fun finding him like that.’

‘Why don’t you stay the night,’ Morris offered, ‘instead of going home on your own?’

‘That’s very sweet of you,’ I responded, giving him a hug, ‘but I’m fine.’

Ricky was surveying me thoughtfully through narrowed eyes. ‘I don’t suppose it’s possible that he topped himself, is it?’

‘No,’ I answered, remembering Gabriel’s legs sticking up out of the bath, the water splashed about the floor during his struggle to survive. ‘I don’t think so for a minute.’

CHAPTER TWENTY-SIX

The Tavistock office of Padbury and Finch, Solicitors, was in Duke Street opposite a small cafe. This was handy for me as I could sit at a table near the window and watch the front door of the premises. Otherwise, I don't know what I would have done. It was impossible to park anywhere nearby, which ruled out the kerbside stake-out so often seen in detective series on TV, the kind of surveillance that involves someone taking photographs through the car window with a ridiculously long lens whilst the target remains oblivious of this process even though standing just a few feet away. But I hadn't come to take photographs. I'd come to watch for Susan coming out of the office. I would follow her and make her talk to me.

As it turned out I didn't need to follow her, she came to me. I'd been nursing a coffee for about an hour. It was around lunchtime and I was considering ordering a sandwich just to keep the waiting staff happy when Susan appeared at the door of the office and crossed the street. She didn't notice me as she came in, intent on heading to a table in the far corner. From the easy way she was greeted by staff, she must have been a regular customer. I waited until she'd seated herself comfortably and ordered from the menu before I got up and crossed the cafe to join her.

'Hello, Susan.' I took the chair opposite hers, effectively trapping her in her corner.

For a moment it seemed she couldn't speak, her eyes searching for escape like a trapped animal. When she found her voice, it was a desperate whisper. 'I can't . . . I can't talk to you. Please leave me alone.'

'You're in trouble. I want to help.'

'You can't. Please, just go away.'

'I heard what Frank said to you. I don't know what kind of hold he has over you, but—'

'You can't help me. No one can,' she whispered fiercely. 'You can only make things worse. If you want to help, then leave me alone . . .' Her voice broke suddenly and she put a hand to her mouth.

'Is everything all right?' the waitress asked as she passed.

'My friend isn't feeling too well,' I told her. 'Could she have a glass of water?'

'Of course.'

As she hurried away to fetch it, Susan fought to regain control. 'Please, I'm sure you mean well, but just go,' she begged.

Much as I felt for her distress, I ignored her plea and ploughed on. 'Let me tell you what I know so far. For reasons of his own, Frank Tinkler communicates with someone in prison and doesn't want his letters opened by prison staff. He sends envelopes stamped with Rule 39, which should guarantee client privilege and ensure they won't be opened, and to add authenticity, he gets you to supply him with stationery from Padbury and Finch. Now comes the tricky part, because of course, the prison authorities don't take these letters at face value. They ring your office to check that the letter has genuinely been sent by the solicitors in question. And this is where you come in . . .'

I paused, in case Susan wanted to speak, but she might have been carved in stone, her eyes downcast, her fingers gripping the edge of the table, only a tiny tremor at the corner of her mouth betraying the turmoil she was feeling inside. 'Because it's your job to answer the phone. You probably keep a record of Rule 39 letters as part of your duties. You're the person that confirms to the prison authorities that the letter is genuine . . . am I right?' I leant forward and whispered. 'If I were to speak to a policeman friend of mine, tell him to advise the prison authorities to start opening letters from Padbury and Finch . . .'

'God, no! Don't do that!' Her involuntary cry made other diners in the cafe turn their heads. She dropped her voice. 'If you do that, there will be an investigation. Frank will know . . . he'll blame me . . . he'll . . . you don't know what sort of man he is,' she ended bitterly.

'So, tell me,' I urged her. 'Tell me what hold he's got

over you. How is he making you do something that could lose you your job, end in prosecution?'

She took a sip of water from the glass that had been placed by her elbow and composed herself, taking a deep breath. 'My son, Jonathon, is in prison,' she began. 'He was in trouble with money and he . . .' she raised her shoulders in an ironic shrug, '*borrowed* some from his firm's funds. He thought that he could pay it back before it was discovered but he got caught and now he's serving a two-year sentence for embezzlement. After he'd been inside about a month, Frank contacted me and told me what he wanted me to do.'

'Did you know Frank? Before that, I mean?'

'I'd met him once or twice. My late husband had bought books from him in the past. He told me there was a way I could help Jonathon. When he told me what he wanted, I was horrified.' She shuddered at the memory. 'I refused, naturally. But then,' she took another deep breath, 'then Jonathon was beaten up – badly. The attack was filmed by an inmate on a mobile phone and Frank sent it to me. This would happen again, he told me, if I refused to co-operate.' She looked up and met my gaze for the first time, her eyes wretched. 'I had no choice.'

'I'm so sorry,' I said quietly.

Susan bit her lip, as if she might start to cry. I reached out a hand to her, but she waved it away. I let her compose herself again before I spoke. 'Do you know what this is about?' I asked. 'What's Frank up to?'

The waitress arrived with Susan's salad, but she pushed it to one side. 'I don't know,' she responded miserably. 'At first, it was just the occasional letter I was asked to verify. But now, there are several every month. I dare not refuse . . .'

'Who are these letters addressed to?'

'I don't know any names. Letters sent to prisoners are addressed to their prisoner numbers, not their names.'

'And you've no idea what these letters are about?'

She shrugged. 'I imagine it's something to do with smuggling things into prison – phones, weapons, drugs perhaps.' Her mouth twisted bitterly. 'Frank calls it his little sideline. He's very smug about it. He told me once that the way to keep everyone on his little *team* safe, was for each of us to know as little as possible.'

'He sends greetings cards to prisoners,' I told her. 'He runs a charity devoted to it. He calls it St Antony's. You don't know anything about that?'

She shook her head. 'All I know is that I'm not alone. He's blackmailing other women, other families. They have to do what he says, or their men inside will suffer.'

'Do you know a girl called Millie? She visits Frank from time to time and seems nervous of him. I wonder if you and she might be in the same boat?'

'I wouldn't know.'

'What about Gerry Deal? Has Frank ever mentioned him?'

'Gerry Deal?' Susan frowned. 'No. Doesn't he own second-hand shops?'

'He does. He and Frank seem to be good friends and Gerry has spent some time inside. He must fit into this somewhere.'

'The only other thing I know,' Susan began hesitantly, 'is that at one time Frank was smuggling things into prison hidden in books. But then the law changed.'

I nodded. 'You can't take books in to prisoners any more. They can only purchase books from approved sellers on the Internet.'

'He told me he'd had to find another way.'

I leant across the table. 'Frank has to be stopped,' I told her.

Susan raised her eyes to mine. 'All I care about is Jonathon.' She gripped my arm. 'I'm begging you. Don't tell the police. It could get him killed.'

'I won't,' I promised. 'Not yet, anyway. We'll have to find some way to get at Frank that bypasses Padbury and Finch.'

She gave me a pitying smile. 'Don't let him fool you. Underneath all the old-world charm, he's vicious. He'll take revenge if he's crossed. Be careful.'

'Did you try to kill him?'

The question shocked her, as I'd intended it should. She stared. 'What?'

'Last year someone tried to run him over, a woman driver with long blonde hair, possibly a wig. Was that you?'

'No, I swear . . .' She breathed out a sigh. 'God, I wish it had been me.'

I believed her. 'Do you know why Frank set himself up in my shop? He could have rented a space anywhere. Why pick on mine?'

'Because, like a lot of criminals, he's arrogant. It

amuses him to think he's carrying on what he's doing under the nose of someone like you. He thinks he can't be caught but he likes to dance along the edge of the abyss.'

'So, he's laughing at me?'

She smiled grimly. 'All the way to the bank.'

I drove from Tavistock back to Ashburton, the moor around me bathed in afternoon sunshine. But the far-reaching views, the mingling of golden gorse and purple of fresh-flowering heather set beneath a burning blue sky failed to snag my attention for more than a few moments. All I could think about was Frank running his dirty little enterprise from my shop. Presumably, this was what he'd been discussing with Gerry Deal, his jailbird chum. They'd talked about keeping away from the big boys, from organised criminals. They had their own nice little scam going and they wanted to keep it to themselves.

But for the life of me I couldn't see how Frank could be getting drugs, or anything else, into prison. It was easier to see how he might have smuggled things inside books. Pages could be hollowed out, small items secreted under covers or in spines. But all he sent now were little cards and envelopes. And letters, courtesy of Susan. Any packages, anything bulky, would surely be investigated by the prison staff. And as for his charity, the address didn't exist and neither did the official registration number. Hadn't anyone on the prison staff checked it out? Luke, the young gardener who had transformed the woodland at Druid Lodge, had spent time in prison. He told me that smuggling could only succeed if there was a bent screw somewhere. Frank must have help on the inside.

I pulled into a lay-by and stopped the car. I needed five minutes in the fresh air. A nearby tor, little more than a scattering of rocks shining yellow in the sunshine, beckoned from the top of a hill. I didn't bother putting on my walking boots, the ground was dry and my trainers coped with the stone-scattered trail that led to the summit.

From the top I could see fold after fold of furzy moorland fading into a misty blue heat haze, the road like a pale scar snaking across the landscape. I shaded my eyes against the sun but I could see not a single car and despite the shimmering blue day there was no sign of any other walkers. All around me was silent save for the distant bleating of sheep among the wind-ruffled grass. I sat on a rock and breathed in the air, feeling as if all of this wild beauty was mine. A movement caught my eye, a slow-worm sliding from a crevice to bask on the sun-warmed rock. It was a beautiful thing, slender, with smooth silvery skin and bright black eyes. I kept as still as I could, but it sensed my presence and slithered back into the shadows. I lingered for a little longer, tilting back my head to feel the sun on my face, the warmth on my closed eyelids, but I couldn't keep my thoughts away from Frank. Susan said it amused him to set up in my shop. *You carry on being amused, Frank*, I told him silently, *because I promise you, I am going to put a stop to you and your grubby little enterprise, whatever it is.*

Pat was on duty in *Old Nick's* when I got back, busily threading up beads from the glittering assortment on her tray. 'I'm making *bespoke* earrings now,' she told me with a coy smile. 'People come in and point to the beads and say "I want some made with those".'

I laughed. 'Are you selling more of them?'

'Oh, for definite.'

'Is Frank here?'

She nodded. 'I took him up a cup of tea just now. He's working on his posh orange cards. His granddaughter wants a guinea pig and I told him, we got dozens of 'em up at the farm, why don't he bring her over, she can choose...'

'Why do you call them posh?' I interrupted.

'Well, haven't you noticed?' Pat jerked her head at the display of his cards on the counter. 'He never makes any orange ones for sale down here. He makes 'em all colours but never orange.'

She was right, there were cards in every colour on display but none in orange. 'All them little cards he sends off for his charity,' she went on, 'they're all orange. I call 'em his posh ones.'

Those cards I'd seen lined up on Frank's table had been orange, Sunset Orange, a colour so expensive he kept it locked up in the safe, but only sent to men in prison.

CHAPTER TWENTY-SEVEN

If Oberon murdered Gabriel Dark, then it was a bit stupid of him to turn up at rehearsal that evening. Which he did. Although, at that stage, it wasn't really a rehearsal. Ricky and Morris had gathered the cast together to ask, for the second time in the life of this production, if they wanted to continue. Obviously, Gabriel's drowning took up a large part of the conversation.

'We've got only three weeks to go,' Ricky reminded everyone, 'and we still don't have a full cast.'

'Won't Miss Walker be playing Titania now?' one of the fairies asked him.

'I'm pretty sure she won't.'

'We'll be sending her condolences,' Morris added, 'and flowers, on behalf of all of us.'

'What about Emily, is she coming back?'

Then came a polite knock on the door. The young man

who walked in looked around the room uncertainly. 'Is Mr Dark here?' he asked. 'I'm Michael. I was supposed to meet him yesterday afternoon to audition for Oberon, but he didn't seem to be at home when I called.'

He was thin, rather beautiful and strangely elf-like, with large green eyes and high cheekbones, the tips of his ears just visible, protruding through thick, curling hair. He looked a dead ringer for the King of the Fairies and not like a murderer at all. Ricky explained to him that, owing to an unfortunate accident, Mr Dark would no longer be directing the production and asked him how he'd heard about it. From a friend of a friend of a friend, he said, someone at Exeter University where he was studying. He looked crestfallen. 'Does that mean the part has gone to someone else, then?'

'No, it hasn't. Did Gabriel say you've played the role before?'

'Yes, last year, with the National Youth Theatre.'

Ricky grinned. 'In that case, mate, consider the part yours.'

Emily walked in at that moment and a cheer went up around the room. 'Come in, my darling!' Morris bustled over to give her a hug and she looked as if she might cry.

'Oberon, meet Titania,' Ricky's smile included everyone in the room. 'Well, boys and girls, we're going to need a lot of extra rehearsal, but, if everyone's happy, let's get cracking.'

Shortly after I got home there was a phone call from Dean Collins.

'You might be right about how Gabriel Dark died. There

was water in his lungs but the only trauma to his body was around his ankle and knee, as if someone had grabbed hold of his leg and twisted hard. Possibly someone tried to put the frighteners on him and it went too far. He owed a lot of money all around, according to his girlfriend.'

'You've talked to her?'

'The local police up there have interviewed her. That's why he was so keen to get out of London, she says he leapt at the opportunity the Arts Council offered him. She also thinks that when she came down here at the weekend, she may have inadvertently led his killer to him.'

'How?'

'Someone had been following her about for days beforehand. She'd reported him to the police, thinking she'd picked up a stalker, some crazed fan type. She thought she spotted him at Paddington Station, but decided either she was being paranoid or she must have lost him in the crowd.'

'Could he have followed her all the way on the train?'

'I suppose it was just a case of keeping tabs on where she got off,' Dean responded. 'If Gabriel picked her up at the station, he could have followed them in a taxi all the way here.'

'God, poor Naomi, she must feel terrible.'

Dean was unsympathetic. 'These celebrity types make it too easy. Always on Facebook and Twitter. They give away too many clues, make themselves too easy to find.'

'So, you don't have any leads, then?'

'We've had a couple of detectives down from London

to look at the crime scene. Waste of time, really. Unless forensics turns up anything, they're more likely to find answers up there than down here. They've taken his laptop away.'

I changed the subject. 'Is there any progress on Scott's murder?'

'I'm afraid not. He'd never been in trouble, as far as we can tell. Which leads us back to Josh Naylor and our friend from Plymouth.'

The thought of Close-Shave made me feel queasy. 'No news on him, I suppose?'

'Not yet. But we'll find the bastard, don't worry.'

'What about the gun?'

'We're still waiting on test results. These things take time, you know.'

There was something else on my mind. I told Dean about my visit to Henry Gillow in prison.

He sounded horrified. 'What the hell are you visiting him for?'

'I'm sorry for him.'

He breathed a long sigh down the line. I knew he'd be shaking his head. I could just see him brushing a hand over the bristles at the back of his neck. 'He's a murderer, probably a psychopath. And in any case, you shouldn't be visiting him. Aren't you a witness?'

'No. Henry's admitted to his crime. His trial is just to determine whether he was mad or bad at the time he carried it out. I'm not a witness.'

He grunted. 'I'm still not sure . . .'

'Yes, well,' I said, determined not to be side-tracked,

‘tell me why a prison officer would confiscate a child’s drawing?’

He answered without hesitation. ‘Drugs.’

‘On a piece of paper?’ I said incredulously. ‘How? It was only a little kid’s scribble.’

‘You’d be amazed,’ he said. ‘It could have been painted on.’

‘Painted on?’

‘Sometimes—what’s that? Sorry?’ He was distracted by a voice in the background that I could clearly identify as Inspector Ford’s. ‘Oh, yes boss, right away! – I’ll have to go, Juno,’ he said to me. ‘I’ll talk to you later,’ and put the phone down.

‘Hell’s teeth!’ I declared to Bill as he sauntered in from my bedroom. ‘Just as I was about to find out something useful . . .’ Bill leapt on to my lap and stared at me meaningfully from his one emerald eye, but had to nudge me with his head before I realised my impatient fingertips were tapping up and down on the arm of my chair like the toes of a disgruntled tarantula. ‘Sorry, matey.’ I shoved him off my knee, where he was about to make himself comfortable, and reached for the laptop.

I spent a fascinating couple of hours reading about all sorts of drugs, and the ingenious ways in which they can be smuggled into prison. Eventually, I found the one I was looking for: Sublinutol. Also known as Sublinomide, Sublinutol is a prescription-only drug used to help wean drug addicts off heroin and other opioids. It has a variety of side effects, one of which is that it gets you high. Consequently, it’s a very desirable commodity in prisons. It comes in small, thin strips of film that are dissolved under the tongue. These can also be dissolved in water or mixed with ink or paint to create a liquid which can be painted on to paper, then rolled up and smoked as a joint. A common method of smuggling Sublinutol into prisons is to conceal squares of the film under postage stamps, or to paint it on children's drawings. One of the more interesting details mentioned about the sublingual film was its colour: orange.

I pictured Frank up in his room, burning the midnight oil with his bottle of Sunset Orange, painting Soblinutol on to his little greeting cards with their hearty, uplifting messages, or concealing tiny squares of film under the stamps of all those self-addressed envelopes. It didn't matter that the return address was fictitious. The envelopes were never meant to be sent back to anyone, were just a means of delivering the drug. And what about the Rule 39 letters? Did they contain Soblinutol too, an insurance, in case the charity envelopes didn't get through? There was only one person I could think of who might help me find out.

CHAPTER TWENTY-EIGHT

I had to make good use of Henry. While he was still on remand, he could receive up to three visits each week. Once he was convicted, and there wasn't much doubt that he would be, he'd only be entitled to two visits per month. I knew he'd be pleased to see me. Apart from his solicitor, no one else visits him.

'This is a delightful surprise, Juno,' he said, as I sat down. 'I wasn't expecting to see you again so soon.'

'I have an ulterior motive, Henry,' I admitted, lowering my voice. I glanced around at the guard by the door, but it was a Saturday, the visitors' hall was full of families and his attention was firmly fixed on a couple sitting at the far end. 'How do you fancy a spot of sleuthing?' I asked.

His eyes lit up like a kid at Christmas. 'Oh Juno! Please, tell me what you want me to do.'

‘I want to find out who’s receiving letters from a charity called St Antony’s Prison Trust. Have you ever heard of it?’

He shook his head. ‘No. No, I’m sorry, I haven’t. They try to keep us remand prisoners a bit separate, you know. I don’t mix with convicted prisoners much, except for Kenny of course,’ he added, brightening a little.

‘Who’s Kenny?’

‘I share his cell.’

‘What’s he in for?’

‘Burglary and aggravated assault but he’s very nice.’

‘I’ll take your word for it.’

‘He works in the library. He might know.’

‘Listen, Henry, I don’t want you to put yourself in any danger, so if this Kenny warns you to lay off . . .’

‘Why would it be dangerous to ask about a thing like that?’ he asked innocently.

‘Because I think the person running the charity is smuggling in drugs.’

He looked so excited I thought he was going to clap his flippers like a circus seal. ‘Of course, I’ll find out what I can. I’ll do my very best!’

‘Thanks. But if Kenny warns you not to go there, then don’t. Understand?’

‘You can rely on me,’ he vowed earnestly, which made me think that my warning to be careful had gone straight over his head. I repeated it.

‘I understand,’ he assured me, nodding enthusiastically.

‘Also, I want you to find out anything you can about a man called Gerry Deal.’

‘Gerry Deal,’ he repeated. ‘Right.’

‘He was in here some time ago for tax evasion. See if this Kenny remembers him. Anything you can find out about him . . .’

The guard by the door was giving me a hard stare so I changed the subject. I told Henry about Gabriel Dark’s murder.

‘And you found his body!’ He made it sound like a real treat. ‘Are you going to track down the murderer?’ He seemed genuinely disappointed when I said I was leaving that to the police. He slid a glance at the guard by the door. ‘You don’t think this murder may be linked to . . . um . . . to the other thing we were just talking about?’

‘No, I don’t think it is. Gabriel and Frank weren’t connected in any way and, apparently, Gabriel was in debt to some nasty characters in London. It seems they may have tracked him down by following his girlfriend.’

‘All this excitement,’ he breathed. ‘I do envy you so.’

‘Thanks, Henry. But I sometimes feel when it comes to excitement, I could do with a little less of it.’

I caught up with Elizabeth at the shop on Monday. Frank wasn’t in and neither was Pat. Sophie was occupied making sketches of Fergus, a charming cocker spaniel who’d been brought in to have his portrait painted, and so I was able to tell Elizabeth about my conversation with Susan without fear of being overheard.

‘You should tell all this to the police,’ she told me severely when I’d reported what she’d said, ‘so they can inform the prison authorities. Surely they can arrange protective custody for Susan's son?'

'We don't know who's involved in Frank's little scheme, remember. There will be men inside who'd hold a grudge if the Padbury and Finch letters were exposed and it all came to an end. There might even be prison staff involved.'

'What are you going to do?'

'Nothing until I know more.' I smiled. 'I have a native tracker on the trail as we speak.'

Elizabeth raised a sardonic eyebrow. 'I wonder who that might be. Let's just hope he's careful.'

'Indeed,' I agreed, 'I don't want him to land himself in it.'

'I was thinking more of him landing you in it,' she smiled grimly.

'I don't like these,' Maisie declared, her wrinkled face puckering in distaste as she sucked a throat lozenge. 'I only like them other ones.' She sucked throat sweets for a pastime, whether she had a sore throat or not.

'I'm sorry, Maisie,' I dumped her bags of shopping on the floor, 'but they were out of the blackcurrant flavour. I'll pop into the chemist in Sun Street and see if they've got any.'

'I don't like honey and lemon.'

'No, I'm sorry, I should have remembered.' I nudged Jacko's investigating snout from one of the carrier bags and lifted it up onto the safety of the kitchen table. Jacko continued to truffle about. One of the bags contained his chews and doggie biscuits and he knew I had a pig's ear in there somewhere.

'I don't mind them . . . um . . . what do they call 'em?' Maisie went on, still sucking remorselessly. 'They're all right.'

I opened the fridge to put away her tomatoes and ham. 'Well, what do they call 'em?'

'You know!' she cried testily. 'Them things in Australia.'

'Things in Australia,' I repeated vaguely.

By now she was getting impatient. 'You know! Fluffy toys!'

'Koalas?'

She nodded vigorously. 'Yes, them. Koalas. S'all they eat.'

'Eucalyptus?' I suggested as Jacko slyly filched his pig's ear from the depths of a carrier and carried the revolting thing triumphantly to his basket to demolish in peace.

'That's it! I don't mind the eucalyptus flavoured ones.'

Maisie and I usually reach an understanding in the end although increasingly these days we have to take the scenic route to get to it. I glanced at my watch. 'I've got time to nip to the chemist now. Do you have any prescriptions waiting?'

'I don't think so.'

'I'll check with the pharmacist. Jacko!' I called to him. 'You coming walkies?'

For once the magic word failed to have an effect. He glared at me from one beady eye and carried on gnawing piggy's ear. It took precedence over walkies, apparently. As I approached his basket he growled, just to make sure I'd got the point.

'Suit yourself.' It would be a much quicker and less hazardous trip to the chemist if I didn't have him on the end of the lead taking violent exception to every other canine we encountered. 'I won't be long,' I promised Maisie, who'd remembered she wanted some apples, anything but Golden Delicious because they were French, and went out.

I opted for patriotic Granny Smiths, nearly dropping them all in the doorway of the chemist's because who should be coming out, carrying a white bag that obviously contained prescriptions, but Frank. He was all smiles, standing back to hold the door open for me.

'Fancy meeting you here!' I stammered foolishly. 'I'm glad the age of chivalry isn't dead,' I added as he continued to hold the door open.

'My pleasure.' If he'd been wearing his hat, I'm sure he'd have tipped it. Then he sauntered off down the road, whistling. I couldn't help speculating about that white bag he carried. How did he get hold of Sublinutol, especially in the quantities he would need to keep his little scam going? He couldn't just walk into the local pharmacy and pick it up. It could only be obtained on prescription and Frank didn't strike me as a recovering drug addict. I realised the girl behind the counter was staring at me. Apparently, she'd already asked me twice what I wanted. I apologised and paid for Maisie's throat sweets.

Was there another Susan, I wondered, working in a pharmacy somewhere, blackmailed into helping Frank get hold of Sublinutol, perhaps a woman with long blonde hair who drove a green estate car and sometimes wore dark glasses?

CHAPTER TWENTY-NINE

It was my third visit to Henry in two weeks. He'd phoned me. He couldn't say too much because calls are routinely listened in on by prison staff. He just asked me to visit and he wouldn't have done that without good reason. He grinned when he saw me, despite the fact he was carrying his left arm in a sling.

I gazed at him in horror. 'Don't tell me you slipped in the shower.'

'No, on the stairs. I cracked an elbow.' He lowered his voice and added proudly, 'I was pushed.'

'Oh, Henry! You could have broken your neck.'

'Oh no, I don't think so. Kenny says that if anyone had wanted me seriously hurt, I would have been. This was just a warning for me to mind me own business.'

'This is my fault,' I muttered guiltily.

'Not at all. I was careless. Someone must have

overheard me asking questions.'

'Do you know who it was, I mean, who pushed you?'

He shook his head. 'There were lots of us on the stairs, going down for our lunch. I just felt this shove in my back. And even if I did know,' he added, lowering his voice to a whisper, 'I couldn't *grass*.' He smiled impishly, as if the whole thing was part of some *Boys' Own* adventure, and I wondered if what was protecting Henry, what allowed him to survive in such potentially dangerous surroundings, was the little bubble of unreality with which he surrounded himself. But in asking him to find out things for me, I had pierced that bubble, exposed him to real danger.

'You will be careful, won't you?'

'Don't worry about me.'

'Did you find out anything?' I hardly dared to ask.

He nodded enthusiastically. 'Everyone knows St Antony's Trust is just a way of getting Sublinutol into the prison, including,' he glanced over at the guard by the door and then back at me, 'one or two of the prison staff.'

'But they don't try to stop it?'

'Kenny says they get rewarded for turning a blind eye.'

'Well, that makes sense.'

'He knows several prisoners who receive mail from the trust and distribute cards and envelopes among the other cons.'

'With a nice little tab of Sublinutol under every stamp.' I thought for a moment. 'They must pay for them. Where does the money go? How does it get back out to the person sending the drugs in?'

Henry leant towards me, his round face serious, 'Kenny says there's one con who makes sure everyone pays up. His name is Drew.' He nodded at a yeti of a bloke slumped at a table not far away. 'That's him.' He was big and hairy and I was sure that when he stood up his knuckles would drag on the floor. But I was more fascinated by his visitor, the man sat talking to him.

'That's Gerry Deal,' I breathed.

'Is that him?' Henry had dropped his voice to a whisper. 'They used to share a cell. Don't stare at them, Juno, it's not a good idea.'

I looked back at Henry. 'They shared a cell?'

'Yes.' Henry smiled. 'Kenny said to stay away from Drew. He makes sure people pay up. But I don't think any money changes hands here *inside*. You see, each prisoner has an account that he can draw on to pay for things from the canteen, or things he has permission to buy online. And families can also pay money directly into this account from outside.'

'So, the families pay for the drugs and if they don't pay up their loved one doesn't get his fix?'

'I think there may also be threats of violence,' he added solemnly.

'Do you know if anyone receives their fix via Rule 39 letters?'

A prison officer walked past us at this point, so Henry didn't speak, simply nodded.

'Then if St Antony's Trust gets rumbled,' I whispered

when it was safe to speak again, ‘there’s still another way for the drugs to get in.’

He giggled. ‘It’s a sort of belt and braces approach.’

‘Thank you, Henry. That’s really useful.’

He rummaged furtively under his sling and drew out a folded scrap of paper. ‘That’s Kenny’s account number,’ he explained, passing it to me carefully, ‘I wonder if you wouldn’t mind, er . . . some small renumeration?’

‘Of course.’ I slipped the scrap of paper into my palm. ‘My pleasure. Ask him if he knows a prisoner called Jonathon, a young man doing two years for fraud.’

‘What do you want to know about him?’

‘He got beaten up quite badly some time ago. I want to know how he’s doing.’

‘Leave it to me,’ he said brightly.

‘Just be careful, Henry.’

He chuckled. ‘You know, it’s only since I’ve met you, Juno, that my life has become so very interesting.’

‘Yes, well, don’t let it become too interesting,’ I told him. ‘I don’t want you falling down any more stairs.’

‘Oh, don’t worry about me. You know I’d do anything for you, Juno.’ He was gazing at me with something perilously like adoration.

‘Um . . . well,’ I burbled inanely, ‘just stay out of trouble, Henry.’ He looked a bit crestfallen so I lowered my voice and added, ‘I’ll let you know if there’s anything else I need.’

The guard called time at that moment and I was able to make my escape, promising Henry that I’d visit him again soon.

There was a long queue of visitors waiting to retrieve

their bags from lockers on the way out. We shuffled forward slowly. Bored toddlers began to cry. I started feeling as if I'd been trapped inside for hours, found myself longing for daylight and fresh air. Then I spotted a familiar face further up the queue. I called out to her. 'Millie?'

She looked around, mouth opening a little as she saw me, then turned and hurried on. There was no barging through the queue of women and children ahead of me to catch her up, however much I cursed and fretted. I had to wait. Eventually I got to my locker, retrieved my bag and scrambled out through the prison door.

There was no sign of Millie in the car park. I cursed, looking around. I'd parked my van in the corner with its rear end facing a wall. As I made my way past the other parked cars, I saw a man standing by a blue Mercedes, also looking as if he'd lost somebody. It was Gerry Deal. He was frowning, muttering under his breath. He looked like a man in a seriously bad temper.

I crept around behind him and he didn't see me. As I slid between my van and the car parked next to it, a tiny sound made me turn my head. A pinched little face was staring up at me, Millie, crouching by my back bumper, hiding in the space between the van and the wall. She looked terrified. She put her finger to her lips in warning 'I don't want him to see me,' she hissed.

'Who? Gerry?' I asked softly.

'Don't look!' she pleaded. 'He mustn't see you looking.'

I squeezed down the side of the van. Fortunately, I'd

left enough room to open the rear door and I unlocked it, throwing my bag inside.

'If he sees me, he'll make me get in the car with him.' Millie's voice was shaking.

'Not while I'm around, he won't,' I promised her. 'Get in.'

She crawled into the back of the van and I closed the door after her and slipped into the driver's seat. I didn't need to tell her to lie down and cover herself with one of the dogs' old blankets. When I looked in the rear-view mirror, I could see she'd already done it. As I drove out of the car park, Gerry was still frowning around him, looking like thunder. 'Don't worry,' I told Millie, 'he hasn't seen us.'

Her voice was muffled under the blanket. 'He might follow us.'

'Where was he going?'

'Back home, I s'pose. He lives near Plymouth.'

'Then he'll take the Rundlestone road. He won't be following us. We're heading for Two Bridges.' I drove on for another few minutes, but there was no sign of the blue Mercedes in my rear-view mirror. Millie lay under the blanket, silent. It must be hot and stuffy under there, and smelly. 'I think it's safe for you to come out now,' I told her. 'I'll pull over as soon as I can. You'll be more comfortable riding in the front.' She said nothing but pulled the blanket off her tousled hair and peered cautiously out of the back window.

'Why were you hiding from Gerry?' I asked. 'Why are

you so afraid of him?'

'He gave me a lift to the prison,' was all she said.

'To visit your dad?'

She nodded. 'I never miss a visit. Not ever. Dad says it's only my visits keep him going. Scott used to take me only,' her voice trembled, 'only he can't no more. So I asked Gerry for a lift but I knew I'd have to go back with him afterwards. Then, when I saw you there, I thought—'

I glanced in the rear-view mirror. 'Hold on, Millie. Why would you have to go back with Gerry?'

She gave a tragic smile. 'It would be payment for the ride.' She hesitated, not looking at me.

'He'd stop in a lay-by somewhere. Afterwards, he'd give me the money to get a bus back home.'

'Jesus,' I breathed. 'How old are you?'

'Nineteen.'

Technically an adult, but even so. Gerry Deal was old enough to be her father, the thought of her with him made my flesh creep. I pulled in on the verge and turned around to look at her. 'This is coercion, Millie. Have you told anyone about this?'

She shook her head. 'I can't. I have to do what they tell me, otherwise something will happen to my dad . . .' Her voice rose in a child-like wail. 'If I talk to the police, I could get him killed.'

'They? You mean Gerry and Frank?'

She nodded miserably. 'But Frank doesn't—I mean, he's never touched me. I just run errands for him.'

'What kind of errands?'

She shook her head. 'I can't tell you.'

'Why don't you come up in the front with me?' I got out and opened up the back of the van, pulling her out by one arm and guiding her to the passenger seat. She was so much on edge I was afraid she might run off like a hare and I'd lose her in the wilds of Dartmoor.

As soon as she was safely strapped in the front seat, we got going again. 'Tell me about Gerry and Frank. They're in business together, aren't they?'

She looked down at the hands resting in her lap. Ragged patches of varnish shone on her fingernails but her cuticles were bitten and torn. 'I don't know anything, honest.' She was lying but I reckoned if I pushed too hard, she'd shut up like a clam.

I tried another tack. 'I'm so sorry about Scott.'

The poor kid moaned, her hands covering her face, her whole body suddenly convulsed by sobs. I pulled the van over, stopping in a rough circle of grit by the roadside, the only other vehicle a lonely ice-cream van. I tried to give her a hug but she pulled away from me, and all I could do was to sit, powerless to comfort her until her sobs subsided. I found a crumpled tissue in my pocket and handed it to her. 'Thanks,' she muttered, smearing the tears from her cheeks. She blew her nose and sat sniffing. I didn't know what to say next and came up with the only consolation that was available. 'Would you like an ice cream?'

She gazed at me from tear-drenched eyes for a moment, and then she nodded. I bought two large vanilla cones with chocolate flakes. She ate as if she hadn't eaten for days. ‘Do you drive?’ I asked her.

She looked up, surprised at the question. ‘No.’

‘It wasn’t you who tried to run Frank over, then?’

She stared. ‘Someone tried to run him over?’

‘A year ago. It was a woman driver, long blonde hair, dark glasses. She drove a dark green estate car. You don’t know her?’

Millie shook her head, a slow smile spreading across her face at the thought of Frank being run down. ‘No.’

‘You see, you’re not the only one who has to do what Frank says, who has someone they love in prison.’

Her smile disappeared. ‘I know that.’

As soon as we’d wiped our sticky fingers, I got back on the road. ‘You know the police are looking for you? They just want to know you’re OK,’ I added as she drew in a sharp breath, ‘and if you know anything about what happened to Scott.’

She started to cry again. ‘I don’t know anything! And I’m not talking to any police.’

‘All right, Millie. It’s OK, just calm down.’

We drove in silence for a minute or so, then she suddenly announced, ‘I feel sick.’

‘Really?’

She nodded. She’d downed that ice cream much too fast. There was a petrol station looming on our left and I pulled in to the forecourt. The van could do with filling up anyway. As I stopped by a pump, Millie leapt out, sprinting towards the loo with a hand to her mouth.

I filled up, went into the shop to pay, picked up a bottle of water for Millie and searched for some travel-sickness tablets, then had to wait while the bloke in front of me argued with the woman behind the counter about how much his fags and magazines had amounted to. He made her add it up a second time. I began to feel fretful. I hadn't seen Millie go back to the van and I was getting worried about her. I paid up as soon as Misery Guts ahead of me had got out of the way and went around the back of the shop to the loo to see how she was doing.

The ladies' toilet was green-tiled, surprisingly clean and pine-smelling and both cubicles were empty. There was no sign of Millie, just an open window high in the wall and the dusty footprint of a trainer on the babies' changing table beneath it. There was no sign of her outside. I raced around to the forecourt but there was no trace of her there either. Millie had done a bunk.

I found out from the girl in the shop that whilst I was around the back, she'd seen Millie get into the car. It was a white car, she said, with children inside and kids' bicycles strapped on the back. At least it wasn't a blue Mercedes.

I told the whole sorry tale to Dean when I got back to Ashburton and apologised for having lost her.

'At least she's alive,' he said. 'She might just have gone back to her dad's place. We'll check it out. Thanks Juno.'

He promised they'd find her. I wished I'd felt reassured. Finding her was one thing, getting her to tell what she knew was another.

CHAPTER THIRTY

'How easy is it to steal prescriptions?' I tried the question with a smile.

Elizabeth gave me one of her steely glances. As she works in a doctors' surgery, I thought she'd be the best person to ask. 'Why do you want to know?'

We were in the kitchen in the house she shares with Olly. I'd invited myself in and sat nursing a coffee. 'My interest is purely academic.'

'Juno, no interest of yours is ever purely academic.' She folded her arms resolutely. 'What is this about?'

I hadn't updated her on my discoveries about Sublinutol or all I had learnt from Henry but I could see I was going to have to give information if I wanted to get any in return.

'What I want to know,' I added when I'd told her all, 'is how Frank is getting hold of the drug in the first place. It's prescription only.'

'I see. Well, the answer to your question,' Elizabeth responded crisply, 'is that it's not easy at all. Blank prescription forms are effectively blank cheques and are kept under lock and key. Each prescription has a serial number . . .'

'I know.' I must have taken scores of prescriptions to the chemist for various clients over the years, but I'd never really scrutinised them in detail until earlier that morning when I'd had a thorough peruse of Maisie's.

'. . . Those serial numbers are logged before the prescription pads are loaded into the computer,' she went on. 'Most prescriptions are printed out on the computer these days, and many of them are emailed straight to the pharmacy.'

'Then there's no chance for them to be forged or interfered with en route?'

'None.'

My nicely cooked-up theory was crumbling into dust 'Doesn't anyone write them by hand anymore?' I asked glumly.

Elizabeth thought for a moment, idly fiddling with a gold earring. 'Doctors on call doing home visits would have a prescription pad in the car. They would have to write it by hand. But like any drugs they carry, that pad would be kept locked up.'

'And a doctor on call usually has a driver,' I added glumly, 'so the car is never left unattended.'

'Exactly.'

We were silent for a moment, listening to the

melancholy strains of Olly's bassoon drifting from the living room. He was practising for his next exam.

'You know, during the summer, while the holidaymakers are here,' Elizabeth went on, 'we get visitors registering at the surgery as temporary residents, so they can access their medicines while they're away from home. But there are others who try it on, drug addicts who register at several surgeries under false names and addresses so they can obtain multiple prescriptions. Often to sell them on.' She gave a wry smile. 'They do tend to get caught fairly quickly. Pharmacists are trained to look out for irregularities and they'd be suspicious of anyone turning up with too many prescriptions, or coming from too far away.'

'But if they visited different pharmacies, spread the load?'

'They would be wise to stay local. Genuine patients get their prescriptions from the pharmacies closest to home.'

Whilst I pondered this, the music across the hall stopped and Olly burst into the kitchen, carrying a flute. 'Oh hello, Juno,' he said brightly, 'I didn't know you were here.'

'Hail Thisbe!' I cried.

'Nay, faith, let me not play a woman, I have a beard coming,' he quoted at me, adopting a female voice that was even more high-pitched than his own. It was the line that had convulsed the audience at the audition and won him the part he wanted. He began hunting through a pile of papers that had been left on the kitchen table. 'They done my costume yet?'

'They're working on it.'

Elizabeth smiled. 'What are you looking for?'

'My music for the play.'

'I'm glad we're having live music.' Olly's music teacher at school had written it. 'I didn't realise you played the flute.'

'I don't, not properly. Ah!' He grabbed what he was looking for. 'It's all odd notes and toots and bells but I suppose it'll sound all right.' It seemed that when he wasn't onstage as Flute the bellows-mender, he'd be lurking behind the bushes with the other musicians.

'It'll be atmospheric,' I told him. 'Olly,' I added hastily before he dived back into the other room. 'Do you know Scott's girlfriend? She might have gone to your school, probably in Scott's year. Her name's Millie. She comes into the shop to see Frank.'

He was nodding. 'Yeh. Millie Stevens. She dropped out of the sixth form.'

'D'you know why?'

He shrugged. 'Drugs, probably. She was a bit of a sad case.'

You have no idea, I told him silently, as he disappeared with his flute and his music.

'Going back to what we were talking about earlier,' Elizabeth went on as soon as Olly was out of earshot, 'you think there must be another Susan, working at a doctor's surgery or pharmacy, who's being blackmailed into obtaining prescriptions for Frank?'

'Well, that's my theory. But I can't prove that the

orange cards turning up in prison come from Frank, the sender's address is fictitious. The police would need to catch him with the stuff in his possession. For all I know, that little safe of his is stuffed full of drugs and prescription pads. But they can't carry out a search of his room based on my suspicions. They need just cause.'

'What you really need,' she said, her grey eyes twinkling, 'is to get hold of one of these little orange cards.'

'I'm pretty certain Frank would know if a card went missing. He may not put serial numbers on them, but I bet he knows exactly how many he's got at any one time. He's not stupid. He'd know I was on to him and the last thing I want to do is give him a chance to destroy the evidence and put himself in the clear.'

Elizabeth sighed. 'It's a problem.'

I didn't say anything, but I think I'd already worked out how getting hold of one of his cards could be managed. It was just, a bit like understanding what Maisie is on about at times, I would have to take the long way round to get it.

I decided it was time I replaced my old brown sofa and invested in a new one. I pulled Van Blanc into the forecourt of Gerry Deal's shop in Preston late the next afternoon.

There were two sofas standing on the forecourt, one beige and boring, the other an alarming shade of purple. I didn't fancy that one, it would clash with my hair.

The beige one was a bit dull. Although, I had to

concede, as I bounced around on its cushions, more comfortable than the one I had at present. But I reckoned it was too big. I'd never get it through the flat door. I decided to look inside.

The shop was cluttered with an assortment of second-hand three-piece suites, cane conservatory chairs, coffee tables and wall units, as well as washing machines, fridges, beds, an army of bedside cabinets, standard lamps and several widescreen televisions. None of these items were new, but the sad thing was that none of them looked very old either, as if they had fallen out of fashion too soon, or the owners had been forced to part with them before the dreams of owning them had faded. A sign on the wall advertised house clearances; another pointed through to a back room, proclaiming Antiques and Vintage. As I toured the aisles I was observed, without much interest, by a couple behind the counter who would presumably sell me things if I wanted. If I didn't, I sensed they weren't bothered. They certainly didn't offer to help.

'Quiet this afternoon,' I observed.

The female half of the couple, a plump teenager with pink hair, smiled and muttered, 'Yeh.'

'Gerry not about?' I asked.

The male half, a youth not much older, obviously thought he'd better show an interest if I was on first name terms with his boss. 'No, we don't see Mr Deal much. He's mostly down at our Plymouth branches.' He grinned weakly. 'It's busier there.'

'We see Mrs Deal more,' the pink-haired half volunteered.

'Sometimes.' She turned to him for confirmation. 'Don't we, Andy?'

'They're both involved in the business, then?'

'Oh yes,' she assured me. 'Although Mrs Deal is more the antiques side of things.'

'Is there anything in particular you're looking for?' Andy asked.

'Just browsing,' I smiled. 'Is it OK if I look out the back?'

I wandered through to the back room, where I couldn't see anything that I would describe as either antique or vintage. The furniture was reproduction, much of it stained dark oak, but I doubt if there was anything more than thirty years old. A Clarice Cliff design tea set was spread out over one table but that was reproduction too. I picked up a set of brass fire irons, machine-made, probably about ten years old, selected a particularly revolting figurine from a sideboard full of ornaments and wrinkled my face at the price tag. Only one item caught my eye, a picture on the wall. To be precise, a frame containing six cigarette cards of golfers, handsomely mounted. Gerry's wife obviously didn't like it as much as he'd thought. It was bearing a price tag considerably in excess of the one I'd been asking before Gerry Deal beat me down and bought it for less. 'Cheeky bastard,' I breathed softly.

I heard a slight kerfuffle in the main showroom. 'Bloody hell, Kelly!' Andy's voice sounded loud in alarm. They're here! Both of them, Mr and Mrs!'

Kelly let out a strangled moan. I stuck my head around

the corner for a look as she grabbed a cloth and a can of spray polish and started squirting like a hyperactive skunk. Andy began rearranging standard lamps as if he'd been engaged in this vital and time-consuming work all afternoon.

Mrs Deal preceded her husband into the shop. Despite the summer heat she wore a cream wool suit with tights and high heels. And she was well-weighted with bling: gold buttons on the jacket, gold earrings, chunky necklace, bristling gold charm-bracelet, and gold chains on her handbag. She was expertly made-up and as she marched into the shop not a hair on her head moved, lacquered to within an inch of its life.

There comes a time in every woman's existence, I think, when she needs to make a compromise with nature, to realise that, unless she is fortunate enough to be born with Mediterranean skin tones, it's probably not a good idea to keep on dyeing the hair jet-black. It's counterproductive, just emphasises the wrinkles. But Mrs Deal was obviously not a woman to compromise in the fight against nature. She was going down fighting.

'Oh, do stop it, you two!' she yelled at her unfortunate staff. 'You're not fooling anyone.'

Andy cleared his throat and jerked his head in our direction. Mrs Deal, realising that there was a customer in the shop, was suddenly all smiles. 'Oh, good afternoon,' she cooed, arching thickly pencilled black brows and adopting a voice of friendly concern. 'Are you being looked after all right?'

'Perfectly,' I assured her.

Gerry came in at this moment, carrying a large print, a pastel mess of flowers in a shiny pink frame. 'Andy can put this on the wall,' he said to no one in particular. Behind his Mercedes, a van had drawn up and a chunky youth was unloading dining chairs from the back, bringing them into the shop two at a time. 'All right, Kelly, love?' Gerry asked, grinning. I felt sick. I hoped he hadn't been getting her into his Mercedes, stopping in any lay-bys. And if he had, did Mrs Deal know anything about it? Maybe that was the reason for her coal-black hair – desperation. He caught sight of me and a flicker of suspicion crossed his features. Then he smiled. 'Well, look who it is!' He opened his arms wide and for a horrible moment I thought he was going to try to hug me. 'It's Miss Hard Bargain from Tavistock.'

'Not hard enough,' I responded, nodding at the cigarette cards on the wall.

He obviously thought better of the hug. 'Ah well, business!' He laughed, spreading his hands in a helpless gesture. 'Cheryl,' he said to his wife, 'meet Juno Browne.'

I was sure I hadn't introduced myself to Gerry at the fair in Tavistock. He must have got my name from Frank. 'Actually, I'm from Ashburton. I've got a shop there.'

Cheryl tried to sound as if she gave a damn. 'Oh, yes?'

'Frank rents space there. You know Frank Tinkler?' Now I had her interest. She flicked a heavily mascaraed glance at her husband. I turned to Gerry. 'You and he are friends, I believe.'

'We've known each other a long time,' he laughed. 'In the trade, you know.'

'Trade?' Antiques or drugs, I wondered.

'Antiques, old books,' he explained, 'always running into one another, me and Frank.'

'I thought you two were in business together,' I said innocently. 'Some kind of *enterprise* . . .' I let the last word hang.

Gerry chuckled but his eyes bore into mine. 'Not really.'

'Oh? I must've heard that wrong, then.'

'Heard?' Cheryl's voice was sharp. 'Heard where?'

'I don't remember.' I shrugged and laughed, 'from someone in the trade, I expect.'

Gerry was still smiling, that glint of gold showing at the back of his mouth, but his eyes never left mine. 'You got a twin sister?' he asked.

'No.' I frowned. 'Why d'you ask?'

'The other day I saw a girl looked just like you – and there can't be many of those, can there?'

I shrugged. 'I don't know what you mean.'

'In Princetown it was, outside the prison. I'd been visiting a friend and I was just driving away. But that couldn't have been you, could it?'

'Couldn't it?'

He didn't answer, just continued to stare. I could easily deny it, but there was no point. 'I don't think that's any of your business,' I told him.

'Fair enough.' He nodded slowly to himself. 'So, what was it you wanted in here, exactly?'

CHAPTER THIRTY-ONE

Elizabeth collared me in rehearsal that evening as soon as we stopped for a break and drew me away from the others. 'I had a word with a colleague at the surgery,' she told me, 'about prescriptions.' She smiled. 'She didn't ask why I wanted to know, just assumed my interest was academic.'

'And?'

'She felt that an opioid substitute like Sublinutol would initially be prescribed by a specialist drugs unit – whose prescriptions are blue, by the way – but once a patient had stabilised, he or she would probably be passed on to an ordinary GP for prescriptions.'

'Then Frank could be getting hold of Soblinutol directly from a drugs unit?'

'Or from an addict. My colleague pointed out that prescriptions are also issued in hospitals – these would be the familiar green ones – but these are kept under lock and key like the drugs, usually the responsibility of a ward sister.'

'So, our other Susan could be a nurse in a hospital, or someone working in a drugs unit, an addict, or a GP?' I frowned. It was quite a wide choice.

'Or all of the above,' Elizabeth pointed out.

'I don't suppose Frank could be making his own prescriptions? Forging them?'

'Apparently the coloured paper is difficult to forge. I can't see him faking it with marbling ink, to be honest.'

This was frustrating. I cogitated for a moment. 'Perhaps he's stealing it at source, direct from the company that makes it.'

Elizabeth raised her brows. 'If it's that easy to obtain, why isn't he selling it on the street? Why in prisons where it's so difficult to smuggle it in?'

'We don't know he *isn't* selling it on the street,' I pointed out, 'but in prison he can get more for it. Prisoners don't have a choice of supplier. If they're desperate, they'll pay anything. Or their poor families will.'

I'd forgotten about the sofa situation until I came home from rehearsal and found the purple one staring at me in the hall. Gerry stung me a hundred quid for it. Adam helped me lug it as far as the hall but then we decided we'd better make room for it first by removing my old brown one. That had got as far as the landing before I'd run out of time. I'd promised him we'd sort it out later.

I knocked on his door. Kate had already gone to bed

but he helped me drag it up the stairs. It took a bit of huffing and puffing but his superior strength counted and we got it on to the landing in no time. It took twice as long to manoeuvre it through the doorway and into the living room. We both stood staring at it. 'Not sure about the colour,' he frowned. 'Purple.'

'I might get a throw to go over it.'

He glanced at my hair. 'I think you should. What's happening to the one on the landing?'

'Don't know. Tip, probably.'

Adam scratched his beard. 'Leave it on the landing for now. It's not in anybody's way.'

I thanked him and wished him goodnight. Then I collapsed on my new sofa. Bill leapt up, sniffing his way along the back. He decided to mark it as his territory by starting to shred the fabric with his claws until I yelled at him and pushed him off. I bounced on the cushions experimentally. Not bad. But I wouldn't have bought it if Gerry Deal hadn't turned up at his shop. It was a high price to pay for the slightly smug feeling that I might have rattled his cage.

I got a call before bedtime. 'Sorry, I know it's late,' Dean apologised, 'but I thought you'd want to hear this. That gun you found, ballistics matched it to bullets left at the scene of an armed robbery in Newquay two years ago, and . . .' he added, pausing for dramatic effect, 'guess whose fingerprints we've found on the grip?'

'My friend with the motorbike?'

'Spot on.'

'That's fantastic,' I said, not entirely without sarcasm.

'Any nearer catching him?'

'Not at present,' he admitted.

'Well, keep up the good work,' I encouraged him, 'and let's hope he doesn't hold a grudge.'

I gave Henry explicit instructions. I was back in the visitors' hall, same watchful prison officers, same smell of school dinners. He gazed at me solemnly, his cherubic little face deadly serious, repeating after me everything I said.

'You do not do this yourself,' I told him firmly. 'You get Kenny to do it. Tell him I've already put the payment in his account, with a bit extra for himself.'

Henry nodded.

'Then what do you do next?' I asked.

'I phone my solicitor,' he said obediently. 'I tell him I want to see him.'

'And what do you ask him to do?'

Henry repeated exactly what I'd told him, his face wreathed in smiles. 'This is so exciting!'

'We don't want exciting, Henry.'

'No,' he said dutifully, losing the smiles, 'no, of course not.'

'Did you find out anything about Jonathon?'

'Jonathon Blake. Kenny says he keeps his nose clean. He'll be coming up for parole shortly.'

'That's brilliant, Henry. Thanks.' I glanced at the prison officer standing by the door. 'Now, you're clear on exactly what you have to do?'

He repeated it all again.

'Splendid. That's perfect,' I said, as I got up to take my leave. 'Don't forget, Henry. I'm relying on you.'

I got back to the shop in the late afternoon. Sophie was busy on the portrait of Fergus the spaniel. We'd had quite a profitable day, apparently. I was richer by a 1920s clothes brush holder and a WW2 field telephone. I asked if Frank was upstairs. 'Yes. He asked if you would be coming in.' Sophie frowned. 'He's a bit snappy today,' she confided, lowering her voice.

'Not his usual charming self?'

'No.'

I hid a smile. 'I'd better go up and see what he wants.'

I didn't need to knock on his door, it was open. He wasn't working on his little orange cards, but marbling a large piece of paper, peeling it back from its tray of mysterious liquid to reveal a design of feathery swirls in shades of yellow and brown. He laid it down on the table and turned to look at me, picking up a cloth and slowly wiping his hands.

He knew that I knew. I could tell. He couldn't know how much I knew, but he knew I was on to him. I could read it in his fixed smile, his speculative stare. I'd been visiting the prison and I'd been to Gerry Deal's and he knew. No point in worrying about alerting him now, he was already on his guard. 'How's the new sofa?' he asked.

'Oh, settling in.' I smiled too. 'How did you know about that?'

'My friend Gerry just happened to phone,' he answered

lightly. 'He mentioned you'd been in his shop.'

'Ah! Did he?' I imagined he'd been on the phone to Frank as soon as I was out of his door.

'He also said you'd been visiting someone in prison.'

'Well, he saw me in Princetown,' I corrected. 'But as I said to him, it was none of his business.'

'Nor mine,' Frank acknowledged with a self-deprecating smile.

'Quite . . . as a matter of fact,' I continued after a moment, 'I do visit someone there. A friend. I see him quite often.'

'A friend?' He gave a sad little shake of his head. 'Such a worry, having someone you care about in prison.' He added slowly, 'It can be such a violent place.'

Don't you dare threaten me, I told him silently. 'So I understand.'

'Some prisoners' families, or friends, will do almost anything, pay almost anything, to keep their loved ones safe.'

Bastard. 'Really?'

'You see, it's never ourselves we worry about, is it? It's the people we love that we don't want to get hurt.' His tone was silky. He was enjoying this conversation and despite my determination to appear imperturbable, a spider crawled down my spine.

'I have observed,' I said, trying to sound matter-of-fact, 'how very accident-prone some prisoners are.' *Go on, tell me you can keep my friend safe*, I urged him silently, *try to fucking blackmail me*. I think he might have been on the point of trying it, but I saw a flicker of uncertainty in his eyes, and he drew back from the edge of the precipice. He gave a little laugh. ‘My, my, Juno! What a very strange conversation we seem to have wandered into.’

‘We do, don’t we?’ I agreed, smiling. ‘It’s such a hard life for men in prison,’ I added, as I headed for the door. ‘No wonder they find your little orange cards so uplifting.’

CHAPTER THIRTY-TWO

There is only one cash machine in Ashburton, in St Lawrence Lane outside of the post office. Like a watering hole on the Serengeti, all wildlife turns up there eventually. Gerry's purple sofa had cleaned me out and I needed cash. Rehearsal had gone on late, it was already dark, the clear sky brightened by a full moon. I keyed in the amount I wanted and as I stood waiting for the machine to disgorge, I heard someone coming around the corner from East Street, someone with light hurried footsteps, a female tapping of heels, someone almost running. It was Millie. As she rounded the corner she trailed to a stop, turning to look behind her, her little face pinched and worried. I called her name. Startled, she stared for a moment. I pocketed my card as the machine spat it out. I thought perhaps she couldn't see me in the shadows. 'It's me, Juno.' She took off like a hare, straight down St Lawrence Lane.

'Millie, wait!' I could hear the machine counting my cash, frustratingly slow to deliver. I swore at the bloody thing to hurry up. As it finally gave me my money, Millie sprinting off into the distance, I realised that it wasn't me she was running from. A man came charging around the corner, roaring her name. He thundered past me like a train, powerful legs moving like pistons, big feet pounding the pavement. Millie disappeared down a side turning and I heard him swear. He was a chunky-looking lad. I didn't get a look at his face.

'Hey!' I yelled, grabbing my cash and thrusting it into my pocket. I didn't stop to count it, just took off after him, my shoulder bag a weighty annoyance hanging, bouncing with every step. He was far ahead of me, chasing Millie down the narrow path that threaded its way between the churchyard and the recreation ground. Not a place where she could outrun him, but it offered places to hide.

The churchyard opened up on my right, the pointed spears of its enclosing railings silver-tipped by the moon. Ahead of me, the t-shirt of the man ahead glowed pale in the moonlight, showing me his broad back. I slowed to a walk. He was standing by the little iron gate that led into the churchyard, drawing breath, peering into the shadows around him. Had Millie jumped the wall into the park, or run into the churchyard to hide? I recognised him as he turned. He'd been at Gerry Deal's shop, unloading chairs. He'd helped me load that purple sofa into the back of my van.

'Millie!' he yelled. 'Don't be such a stupid cow. You know I'm going to find you.'

I could see her, crouched behind a tombstone, her back flat against the upright slab, her head bowed, elbows in, arms pulled tight around her knees, trying to make herself as small as possible. He made a decision and clumped a few steps up the churchyard path. 'Millie?' He was only yards from where she crouched, her whole body clenched as tight as a fist. *Stay still*, I willed her silently, *don't move*.

'The longer I've got to mess about like this,' he threatened, 'the worse it's going to be.'

Amongst the shadowy gravestones a vixen screamed, a raw, savage sound that made him wheel around, swearing. It startled Millie. She stumbled into a run, springing away from the shelter of the tombstone, dodging around the graves, I could hear the ragged sobbing of her breath. I ran too, heading for the churchyard gate as her pursuer caught her up. He grabbed her by one arm, dragging her into the shadows, and shoved her up against the church wall. Millie whimpered.

'Hey you!' I yelled, yanking the torch from my bag. 'What do you think you're doing?'

He squinted in the bright light I shone in his face, held up a hand. 'What's it to you?' he demanded. 'Mind your own business.'

'She doesn't want to talk to you.' I nodded at Millie cowering in the corner. 'I suggest you sod off.'

He took a step towards me then, puffing out his chest, holding his arms away from his body like a gunslinger ready to draw. He didn't frighten me. He was all swagger. For real menace he should take lessons from Close-Shave. I flipped out my phone and it lit up obligingly, tinkling its little song despite the fact that the battery was low and it probably wouldn't work. 'I'm calling the police.'

'And telling them what?'

'You chased her, you grabbed her, you pushed her – that's assault. I also heard you threaten her. Oh yes, and you're an associate of known felon Gerry Deal, that should help.' I began to press buttons.

He scowled, considering his options. A couple appeared, rounding the corner of the church, an elderly pair with two little terriers on the lead enjoying their last trot around before bedtime. The presence of witnesses was enough to make Chunky think twice. He rounded on Millie, pointing. 'Don't think this is over,' he warned her and shouldered his way past me out on to the street.

'Is everything all right?' the couple asked in one voice, the mild, inoffensive voice of someone who hopes it is all right and doesn't really want to get involved if it isn't.

'Fine, thanks.' I assured them. 'Goodnight.' I slipped an arm through Millie's before she could run off. 'That was a fine trick you pulled on me at the garage,' I muttered.

She shrugged, sullen as a child.

'Has our friend gone, d'you think?' I steered us both away, around the church and into the glow cast by the lamps of West Street. I looked up and down the road but couldn't see him lurking anywhere. 'What's his name, anyway?'

‘Brendan,’ she breathed. When I gave her an enquiring glance, she shrugged. ‘Just Brendan.’

‘Right. Well, if Just Brendan has buggered off, it’s time you and I had another talk.’

She hung back, resisting the pull of my arm. ‘I told you, I don’t know anything.’

She tried to bolt then but I hung on tight. Her arm felt thin as a twig, I was afraid I might snap it. ‘Relax, Millie. Nothing bad is going to happen, I promise. Let’s go somewhere where we can sit and have a drink. We could go back to my place . . .’

She shook her head. ‘I don’t want to.’

I really wanted her indoors, somewhere where she couldn’t run off, but she was shivering, from fright not cold, and I took pity on her, walked back into the churchyard and found a bench overlooking the tombstones. ‘We’ll just sit here, then.’ I pulled her down gently, my arm still linked in hers. ‘Tell me about Frank.’

‘I can’t say anything,’ she cried out in fright. ‘He’ll kill me.’

‘Frank? I promise you he won’t.’

She began to cry, a hand to her mouth, and I fished in my pocket, found a crumpled tissue and pushed it into her hand. ‘Listen, Frank has to be stopped and you can help me stop him.’

She shook her head.

‘You’ve got no choice, Millie, if you don’t, you’ll never be free of him.’

She sobbed softly and for a few moments I let her get on with it, then tried a comforting hand on her arm.

She stiffened but didn't shake me off. 'Tell me about Sublinutol – you help him to get it, don't you?'

'I pick up the prescriptions,' she sniffed, staring at the ground, 'take them to the chemists, then I deliver the stuff to him.'

'Where do you get these prescriptions filled, not all in the same place?'

'No. I go all over, on the bus. I'm at it all day sometimes, Plymouth, Ivybridge, Tavistock . . . wherever I can get away with it.' She gave the ghost of a laugh. 'Frank thinks it's funny, making me run about. The more I have to run about for him, the better he likes it.'

'That's because he's a control freak. Don't pharmacists ever get suspicious? Don't you ever get challenged?'

She shrugged her thin shoulders. 'Now and again. But then I don't go back to those places.'

'And who writes these prescriptions?'

'Different people. I can't say.'

'I'm not asking you to name names.'

She hesitated. 'There's a woman works in the drug rehab place, she used to look after my dad. That's where I get them mostly. And there's a doctor, she . . . and . . . I don't know how many people. They all have to do what Frank says . . .'

'Because they have men in prison.'

'We have to do anything he wants.' She was slowly shredding the tissue between her fingers, tiny scraps falling between her feet. 'And I'm not the only one Frank's got running about either.' She gave a pathetic little laugh. 'He's like a horrible great spider, it's like we're all flies trapped in his web.'

'And where does Gerry Deal fit into all this?'

'He set it all up with Frank. When he was in prison, he made the contacts. They're in it together.'

'Have you heard them mention a man called Drew?'

She nodded, more tiny shreds of tissue falling to the ground. 'Gerry met him in prison.'

'Do you know what a Rule 39 letter is?'

She shook her head miserably.

'It's a letter the prison authorities can't open. I think that's how Frank and Gerry communicate with Drew.' She didn't offer any comment. I just let her sit. Something moved between the graves, slunk in the shadows, a cat perhaps, or the vixen that had screamed.

'Brendan works for Gerry. Why was he chasing you?'

She smeared a tear across her cheek. 'Gerry sent him to fetch me. I didn't want to go.'

I took her hand. It was cold as stone. She might have been a little carved angel, keeping watch over the gravestones, her sharp features outlined by the moon, her eyes black hollows.

'They'll both get what's coming to them, Gerry and Frank,' I promised her, 'for what they've done to you, and to all the others. Look, why don't you let me take you to talk to someone—'

She writhed to drag herself free from my restraining arm, a living, terrified girl again. 'Not the police. I won't talk to the police. My dad—'

I stood up, struggling to keep hold of her. 'Trust me, Millie. Frank will never know. You'll get protection.'

She laughed scornfully, shrill laughter turning to sobs as she tried to shake me off. 'He'll kill me, just like he killed Scott . . .' She sank down on the bench again, as if all the fight was gone from her, washed away in a flood of weeping.

'Frank killed Scott?' I shook her gently but she moaned, shaking her head. 'How do you know that? Millie, tell me!'

She couldn't speak. I thought her racking sobs would fracture her fragile body, break my heart. 'What happened?' I tried again. After a minute I lifted the curtain of hair that hid her face and tucked it behind her ear. 'What happened to Scott?' I repeated softly. I gave her another tissue. She blew her nose, then took a couple of deep breaths. 'Take your time,' I told her. 'Did you see Scott that night?'

'For a bit. He was really scared. He'd been with Josh when they'd lost the drugs, up at that old place.'

'Moorview Farm?'

She slid a knowing glance at me. 'You know all about that, don't you? But Scott didn't realise it was you who'd frightened them off, not till later. Then, when they killed Josh . . .'

'Who killed him? Not Frank and Gerry?'

She shook her head. 'It was nothing to do with them. I don't know who killed Josh. Some drugs people. Frank told Scott not to have anything to do with Josh, said he was stupid, that he'd lead him into trouble . . .' She gulped back a sob. 'Josh thought he was going to make big money. He'd got into some gang in Plymouth. He was dealing heroin and cocaine on the streets. Anyway, these people, they knew he and Scott were mates. They told Scott he had to find their stuff or they'd kill him too . . .'

'Did Scott ever talk about a gun?'

She nodded. 'He tore the place apart but he couldn't find it. He was terrified they'd come after him . . .'

'But he never mentioned a name?'

She shrugged. 'There was some bloke rode a motorbike that Scott was scared of, but I never heard a name. Anyway, he came back from that stupid rehearsal and he told me everything was going to be all right. He was so relieved. He was nearly crying. Frank had told him he knew where the gun was.' She sniffed and turned to look at me, smearing tears from her cheeks. 'He said that *you'd* found it . . .'

'Me? Well, I did.' I frowned. 'But that wasn't until after Scott was killed. And I took it to the police. How would Frank know about it?'

Millie shook her head. 'He didn't know. He was lying. He told Scott he'd overheard you in the shop, telling someone you'd found the gun in the farmhouse and you'd taken it away, hidden it in the woods where you go walking with the dogs. Frank convinced him he knew the place, and if he went there with him that night, they could find it, easy. He said they had to do it fast, because they never knew when you might come back and move it.' Her shoulders shook as she suppressed another bout of tears. Her thin chest heaved and she gulped, a deep breath. 'Scott was so happy. He told me all his troubles were over. He went off to meet Frank and . . . he never came back.' Her voice shook pitifully. She began rocking back and forth on the bench. 'I know it was Frank killed him,' she cried passionately. 'I know it!'

I stared at moonlit tombstones. 'But why would Frank want to kill Scott?' I asked.

'He'd told him to stay away from those drug dealers. He reckoned that if they found out about his own business, his and Gerry's, that they'd want a piece of it. He was afraid they'd try to take over, be too powerful to fight, that they'd lose control . . .'

'You mean he killed Scott because he thought he was a liability?'

'I suppose.' Her voice was flat, all cried out. She turned to stare at me from eyes empty of all emotion. 'And if he finds out I told you, he'll kill me too.'

'He won't.' I sat thinking things through. 'Does Brendan know where you live?'

She hung her head helplessly. 'Yes, he knows.'

'Is there somewhere else you can go? Somewhere safe, that he and Frank and Gerry don't know about?'

'I got an auntie in Plymouth, but I haven't seen her for a long time.'

'Ring her. Let her know you're coming. I'll drive you there now.'

'But it's late.'

'She won't mind. We'll go to your place, pick up what you need, then I'll take you straight there.'

'I don't want to go back to my place. There's nothing I need.'

'I want you to stay with your aunt until you hear from me, OK?'

'OK.' She frowned at me. 'What are you going to do?'

'I don't know,' I admitted, 'I'm making this up as I go along.'

It was nearly two in the morning by the time I got back from Plymouth. Millie knew her aunt's address in Cowley, but hadn't visited her for so long she'd only retained a hazy idea of how to get there, and neither of us had satnav on our phones. It was dark, quiet and there weren't many people around to stop and ask. After twenty minutes of driving in circles we were forced to pull over and phone auntie for directions. Eventually we found the house, the only one in the street with any lights on. I stopped long enough to see Millie enveloped in a welcoming hug by a plump lady in a dressing gown, then I pulled in and made a phone call to Ashburton police station. But neither Inspector Ford, Cruella or Dean were available. It seemed they were all out on a job. I left a message on Dean's phone, telling him to call me back immediately. It was urgent, I told him. I knew who had killed Scott Pritchard.

It seemed like a long drive back from Plymouth in the dark. I hoped Millie would have the sense to stay put, stay safe. Whilst I'd been focusing on her, I'd felt fine. But on the journey back, I felt strangely nervous. I couldn't stop thinking about Close-Shave, wondering where he was and what he was up to. A motorbike roared past me and my stomach flipped as if I'd driven over a humpback bridge. 'For God's sake, woman,' I told myself severely, 'get a grip!'

A sick anger was growing inside me, thinking of what Millie had told me, what Frank and Gerry had put her through, and Susan, and other women like them. And Frank had killed Scott, a boy he'd known since he was a small child, because he feared he might involve him in a hostile takeover. He was a cold-hearted bastard. It was strange, really. Close-Shave wore menace like a second skin. One look at him was enough to make warning signs flash before your eyes: this animal is dangerous. But Frank, with his Panama hat and courteous, old-world charm, no one would think him capable of blackmail, extortion, murder, of causing so much misery. I wondered if Jean Tinkler, that pleasant, rather faded woman, knew what he did, knew what her husband's hobby really was.

I should have gone home, driven back to my purple sofa and Bill, waited for the police to call me back. But I felt compelled to drive down Shadow Lane. I stopped outside *Old Nick's*. There was a light shining in the upstairs window.

I parked the van down the lane, out of sight. It was so quiet I could hear the faint electric buzz from the solitary streetlight. The air was still warm. I slid down the alley at the side of the shop to the Sun Street end where I knew my phone would pick up a signal. I tried Dean again. Left another message. As I pocketed the phone, I noticed a car parked half on the pavement, a Mercedes, a faint glow of light from a street lamp showing its colour. Gerry's car.

I sneaked soft-footed up the alley, back towards the

shop. I'd almost reached the side door when it swung open, flooding the cobbles and stone wall opposite with an oblong of yellow light. I ducked behind a big recycling bin. Peering warily over the lid I saw the chunky and unmistakeable outline of Just Brendan as he stood in the alleyway, carrying a large canvas bag, clutching it to his chest. I flattened myself against the wall, but he thumped past me, puffing beneath his burden, looking neither right nor left.

A moment later, Gerry appeared, clutching his car keys, his forehead shiny and sweaty in the light. He looked agitated. 'Two minutes, Frank, that's all!' he hissed and bustled on past me. It seemed some kind of exodus was going on. Brendan must have told them I was with Millie. They knew the game was up. This was their getaway. Only Frank was left inside now. He'd stabbed Scott. What I wondered, as I slid inside the door and closed it softly behind me, was whether he still had the knife.

CHAPTER THIRTY-THREE

I stood at the foot of the stairs, looking up. Frank's room was in darkness, the door flung wide. Where was he? Had he heard me come in? Was he waiting for me up there in the dark, knife at the ready? I glanced down the corridor that led into the shop. No movement, no shadow, only Mavis the mannequin, silently pointing the way to the storeroom and she wasn't giving anything away.

My heart started to hammer as I climbed the stairs. I stopped on the landing by the bathroom door and creaked it open. The moonlight through the frosted window glinted on the mirror and the basin taps; no Frank lurking behind the door. I breathed out a sigh. I turned up the second flight, towards his room, treading as if I was walking on glass, slowly, placing each foot with care. I reached the doorway and stood looking in.

The dim glow through the window lit a pale rectangle of polished floor.

The kitchen door creaked behind me. I had no time to turn before a violent shove between the shoulder blades pitched me forward, sent me stumbling into the room, colliding with the table, its legs scraping as I shunted it a foot across the floor. The door slammed behind me. I was in darkness. Was Frank there in the dark with me? I turned. The light on the landing framed the door with a thin ribbon of gold. Then I heard the click of the padlock, the spinning of the numerals as Frank lined them up. He was outside on the landing. I flung myself at the door, rattling the handle.

'Calm down, my dear,' he answered with infuriating composure. 'We both know I could have killed you a moment ago. But I chose not to. Don't make me regret my decision.'

'Just as you killed Scott?'

There was a moment of silence before he spoke. 'A cruel necessity, I admit, but I really don't think the boy had any long-term prospects.'

I banged on the door. 'Let me out!'

'You're perfectly safe,' he responded. 'You'll just have to wait until morning for someone to release you.'

'Frank!'

'Goodbye, Juno. Knowing you has been most . . .' he paused as if searching for an appropriate word, '. . . entertaining.'

His footsteps retreated down the stairs, the side door slammed. I flung my shoulder uselessly against the door, kicked at the wood in fury and then slumped to my knees. After a few moments of useless and pathetic cursing, I dragged myself to my feet and fumbled for the light switch. At least I could see what Frank had been up to.

The safe was open. He had cleared it out. I was staring into an empty metal void. I guess anything of value – the money and drugs – had been taken out in that canvas bag Brendan carried. Everything else, the books, papers, cards, the boxes of envelopes, inks, even the bottle of Sunset Orange, had been left behind. It was as if he and Gerry didn't care about the evidence. And what had triggered their departure? It couldn't just be the fear of Millie's revelations. Had Frank received some warning from the prison? Had Henry moved faster carrying out my instructions than I'd anticipated? One thing was for sure, by morning Frank wasn't going to be found Chez Tinkler.

And I wasn't waiting until morning to be let out. I crossed to the window, ready to throw up the sash, only to discover that at some point Frank had fitted a lock on it. There was no key. I tried pushing against the transom, but it didn't yield. I didn't want to break my own window, but it seemed I had no choice. I looked around for something to break it with. The only viable object was one of the shallow metal trays that Frank used for marbling. I picked one up, angled it slantwise, took a step back and rammed the corner of it against the glass. The pane cracked. I tried again and this time it fractured. I pushed the tray through again and again, squinting in case of flying glass, knocking out jagged splinters which crashed on to the pavement below.

You would think a noise like that would at least wake the neighbours. But it seemed the citizens of Ashburton slumbered, undisturbed, save for a dog whose echoing bark I could hear from streets away. I cautiously stuck my head out of the frame. My only option was to climb down to street level if I could do it without breaking my neck. Terrific. I was considering whether the nearest drainpipe would hold my weight without my ripping it from the wall when flashing blue lights announced the arrival of my rescuers.

It took two uniformed officers nearly half an hour to get me out, from the time I threw my keys down to let them in the side door, to finding my toolbox and drilling off the lock plate. It seemed that after Dean had picked up my message, they'd been sent around to my house and already knocked up a sleeping Adam in a desperate attempt to find me.

Dean couldn't come himself because, along with Cruella and the inspector, he was on an operation in Plymouth. In fact, at the moment that I had been dropping Millie off with auntie, they'd been pinning an uncooperative Close-Shave to the pavement prior to his arrest. They were still there apparently, taking stock of all the illegal goodies in a lock-up garage they'd discovered the keys to on his person.

I made good use of my time while I was waiting to be released, carefully arranged the cards and envelopes printed with the charity's bogus address on the table and placed the bottle of Sunset Orange in plain view. I didn't want the police to miss anything. I hid the *Rule 39 Letter* stamp in my pocket and the box of *Padbury and Finch* envelopes out of sight behind a stack of paper. I didn't want them to find those.

Henry had followed my instructions to the letter. His solicitor had arrived at Ashburton police station earlier with one of Frank's orange cards and its stamped, addressed envelope – both purchased in prison by Kenny from Drew on Henry's behalf. He told the police he had information that the card and the envelope contained Sublinutol in different forms, that the address on the envelope was fictitious and that it had in fact been sent by a Mr Frank Tinkler from *Old Nick's* in Shadow Lane.

At the station I gave the inspector and Cruella a slightly elasticated version of the truth – a kind of one-size-fits-all. I told them that I'd learnt about the smuggled Soblinutol from Henry in prison and had put two and two together when I saw that Frank was sending out mail to prisoners from a fictitious address. I also mentioned his association with Gerry Deal. Cruella eyed me with the upmost suspicion through all this, her arched black eyebrows disappearing into her fringe. It was clear the inspector could also smell a rat. He knew I wasn't telling them everything. I didn't mention Susan, the Rule 39 letters or Padbury and Finch. But I gave them Millie's address in Plymouth, so that they could learn from her about how Frank and Gerry ran their business and the murder of Scott Pritchard. They sent a female officer to interview her – not Cruella, thank God, but an officer trained in dealing with victims of abuse.

A full investigation would be launched at the prison into what had been going on with St Antony's Trust, but as long as there was no mention of Rule 39 letters or Padbury and Finch, I reckoned Susan and Jonathon Blake were in the clear. Frank and Gerry's little enterprise was stuffed. Except that my efforts to terminate it had been a complete waste of time because the two of them had disappeared anyway. At least I'd given Henry some excitement.

At dawn, when police called at Frank's house he was already long gone, a tearful Jean protesting that she hadn't seen him since he'd slipped out to the pub the night before. 'We'll get him,' Dean promised me robustly. 'He can't have got far.'

In fact, this wasn't true. Frank and Gerry had planned their escape in advance. Gerry's wife Cheryl was quick to realise she wasn't intended to be a part of their new lives, and sullenly revealed the existence of her husband's Cessna plane, which he kept at a private flying club near Exeter. By the time the police got there it had already disappeared, without filing a flight plan, and was later found abandoned at a disused airfield not far from Heathrow. The whereabouts of Frank and Gerry were unknown. If they'd boarded an international flight, they had done so under assumed identities. Airport CCTV surveillance might spot them, but searching through it would take considerable time. Frank, it seemed, had got away with murder.

CHAPTER THIRTY-FOUR

The devil is in the detail, this particular detail being Just Brendan. He seemed to have disappeared from the face of the earth. Possibly he'd gone to ground. The other possibility was that being of no further use to his masters, they had disposed of him. Police were still looking.

It was a week since Frank and Gerry had flown off into the blue. During that time the St Anthony's Trust Sublinutol smuggling enterprise had been exposed, without revealing Susan's involvement, or the use of the Rule 39 letters. And if Drew had any sense, he'd keep his mouth shut. Police discovered Frank had been running an identical operation at prisons in Exeter, Channings Wood, and at Horfield in Bristol.

The only slightly dodgy moment came when the police discovered the box of Padbury and Finch envelopes. I hadn't had a chance to remove from Frank's room before they began their search. I made up a story about hearing Frank complain that the printer had delivered a box of wrong envelopes instead of the ones he'd ordered. Later I phoned Susan on the quiet and warned her not to overreact if the police contacted her office. They don't know anything about the Rule 39 letters, I assured her, just tell them you noticed your last order of envelopes from the printers was a box short. She cried with relief when she learnt that Frank had disappeared. Jonathon was shortly to be paroled. I checked in on Henry and he was still in one piece, so it seemed that all was well.

I was waiting to shut up shop. It was the evening of the first technical rehearsal for *A Midsummer Night's Dream* and Sophie had wanted to get off early, to try on her costume. She hadn't seen it yet. I knew she'd love it. I'd helped to make it, a classical Grecian dress in soft pink, with a secret pocket sewn in for her inhaler. As Ricky had put it, we didn't want her coming over all wheezy on us.

There were only a few minutes to go before closing time, I'd already started counting the float. I was feeling quite smug. At auction, a set of rare cricketers' cigarette cards fetched four times their estimated value and a single American Beauty, ten times. In fact, they have paid for the repair of my window, my rent at home, and all the bills at the shop for the next quarter. I was sitting at the counter, contemplating my good fortune and considering the purchase of a quilt or throw to cover up that purple sofa, when the bell on the shop door jangled. Standing in the doorway was a man who looked like he'd been sofa-surfing for the last seven days, surviving on lager and fags. 'Brendan!' I breathed, shocked at how grimy and hungover he looked. 'What are you doing here?'

He said nothing, just turned the shop sign so that from the outside it read 'closed'.

Not good, I decided and stood up slowly. 'The police are looking for you,' I warned him. He sniggered, I could sense he was edgy, his gaze roving restlessly around the shop, checking I was alone. The pupils of his eyes were like pinpoints. He was high on something. 'What do you want?'

'I've got a message for you.' His voice was hoarse. 'From Frank.'

'Where is Frank?'

He gave a derisive snort. He was nervous, working up to something, a smear of sweat on his top lip, the fingers of his left hand twitching. He had something concealed in his right, something he was holding behind his back. I decided to come out from behind the counter. While it offered me some protection, it was a confined space and I didn't want to get trapped behind it if Brendan was about to turn violent. I concentrated on keeping my breathing steady.

'What's the message?' I asked.

'This.' He charged towards me, a kitchen knife in his hand. I dodged backwards as he swept the blade from side to side in a flailing arc, releasing a breathy grunt with each swipe of his arm. I grabbed Sophie's chair and raised it up before me like a lion-tamer, jabbing its legs towards his face. He stumbled, crashing into Pat's table.

With an inward moan I saw the printer's tray tip up and a myriad tiny glass beads pour down onto the floor in a glittering rainbow, scattering colours across its shiny surface. Brendan tried to right himself, but skated on the beads, his feet slipping under him, the knife flying from his grip. It fell under Sophie's table. I dropped the chair, scrabbling across the floor, reaching out, my fingers at full stretch. Brendan grabbed me by the leg, and dragged me towards him. I aimed a kick with my free foot and caught him a glancing blow on the shoulder but he didn't stop. He was trying to climb over my body to reach the knife. My fingertips touched it, and the whole knife spun on the floor like the needle of a compass. I couldn't reach the handle. Brendan grabbed my hair, jerking my head back. It bloody hurt, I felt as if he was going to tear off my scalp. I heard the shop bell jangling wildly. I scraped the back of his hand with my nails. He winced but he didn't let go. His grip just tightened, his weight pinning me to the ground. I could scarcely breathe. I clutched at his wrist but couldn't tear his hands from my head. I struggled to get a grip on his little finger, to curl mine around it, to bend it back, snap it. Then something like the hand of God smote Brendan on the back of the head and he pitched forward on top of me, his hands gone slack.

I felt as if I was lying under a dead whale. Then his inert body was hauled off me. I rolled over, gasping, and found myself staring up at a frowning Dean Collins. 'You all right, Juno?'

I struggled to sit up, feeling my head to check if I still

had any hair. 'Think so.' I let him pull me to my feet, where I clutched on to his solid arm for a few moments, getting my breath and waiting for the giddy walls of the shop to settle. Dean grabbed the chair with a free arm and pushed me down on to it. I gazed at the unconscious Brendan. 'What did you hit him with?'

'This thing.'

I surveyed the two broken halves of Pat's tray. 'Oh, shit! . . . Thanks,' I added, a little belatedly. Brendan lay like a heap of blubber, not moving, and I prodded his bulk with my toe. 'You haven't killed him, have you? Are you allowed to hit people like that?'

Dean sniffed, unconcerned. 'He was trying to kill you. Anyway, you heard me call out "police" and warn him to desist, didn't you?'

I hadn't, as a matter of fact. All I could remember was the jangling of the bell. ''Course I did,' I said.

By now Dean was busy muttering into his police radio and after a short interval the relevant people arrived to lug a groaning Brendan off to hospital, treat his concussion, then arrest him.

'So, did you just happen to be passing?' I asked as the ambulance drove away.

'No, I came around to tell you the good news about Karl Richardson.'

'Who's Karl Richardson?'

'The guy with the motorbike?'

He meant Close-Shave. 'Right. So?'

'We've arrested him for the murder of Josh Naylor.'

'You've got evidence?'

'Witness statement. One of the guys we picked up when we raided Karl's lock-up was on the viaduct that night. He was prepared to do a deal, to testify.' He hooked out the knife from under Sophie's desk and dropped it into an evidence bag. 'And this could be the knife that killed Scott Pritchard.' He grinned. 'Quite a satisfactory day, all in all.'

'I'm glad you think so, Officer,' I said, surveying the mess on the floor. It was all right for him. I had to go and find the dustpan and brush, and work out exactly how I was going to explain this mess to Pat.

The rehearsal that night was the first where the cast were all in costume and I was there in case any last-minute adjustments were needed. I sat on the grass with my trusty notepad. We would aim for a full run-through of the play, Ricky told the assembled company, but we might have to stop in places as this was our first attempt with lights and sound fully rigged.

'Just be aware that there are lights on the ground and up in the trees. Do not touch any of 'em. Those lamps get very hot. There are also cables snaking everywhere, so try not to trip over, especially you fairies when you're darting about. We'll probably have to do a bit of tweaking as we go along, so don't be surprised if you hear me yelling at you to move your arse. It'll only be because you're not standing in the light. And don't take any notice of odd bods wandering about you haven't seen before – they're technicians. Just ignore 'em and try not to get in their way.' He consulted a pad of notes. 'The only other note is for you, Emily, my love. When you come off between scenes, don't forget to turn that bloody microphone off, or we'll hear everything that's going on backstage.' Ricky and Morris had decided that the radio mic was the lesser of the two evils.

'It's a bit difficult to get at actually,' Emily responded, 'under this dress.' The flesh-coloured microphone bud was hidden in her hair, wired to a control box that she wore at the back of her waist where it wouldn't be seen.

'Perhaps someone can give you a hand with it? Oh, thanks April!' He gave a thumbs-up as she raised her arm. 'Right, everybody happy? Any questions?' He looked around but there was no response. Everyone was keen to get on with it. 'Right, let's give it a go.'

It was a fine evening, still warm, the acting area on the lawn bathed in sunshine. There was no need for lights as the play started. But as the sun gradually sank lower and the woods filled with shadows, they began to come up slowly, gradually building, casting shafts of blue and green between the trees, creating glowing caves of purple amongst the foliage and reflecting golden gleams on the still dark surface of the lake. Further off in the woods, tiny white lights winked like fireflies. It was magical, except when some odd bod wearing a t-shirt and headphones popped up amongst the fairies, or when Ricky, resplendent in his robes as Duke of Athens, yelled out that we'd have to stop and do that bit again.

It was going really well. So far, no had one tripped over any cables or crashed into any lights. I only made two notes about costumes: the hem of Marian's dress was coming down and Marcus was wearing trainers. We were in the middle of the scene with the four lovers when a young female voice floated from amongst the trees. 'Do you think I've got time to go to the toilet before I'm on again?' It was one of the fairies. Emily had forgotten to turn off her microphone.

'Well, I should think so, dear, if you hurry.' That was April's voice. The four lovers carried on valiantly despite the interruptions.

I signalled to Morris, who was out front watching, that I'd slip down and tell Emily to turn the mic off and he gave me a thumbs up. But before I reached the lakeside path there came an almighty crash from somewhere in the trees, followed by a loud wailing.

'Mandy! Mandy!' I heard Digby's voice raised in alarm. 'Darling, are you all right?'

'Oh, Christ on a bike!' That was Ricky. 'What's happened?'

The four lovers gave up and wandered off into the trees to find out what was going on. I heard Sophie's voice. 'What's the matter?'

'It's Amanda,' said a fairy, 'she tripped over a footlight.'

By the time Morris and I arrived, it seemed the entire cast was gathered around Amanda who was lying on the ground, moaning. Digby was kneeling next to her, holding her hand, whilst April, a first-aider, was gingerly feeling her ankle.

'I think it's broken,' she pronounced.

Amanda lay back in Digby's arms, sobbing. 'I'm so sorry!' she moaned. 'I've let everyone down.'

'Nonsense, darling,' Digby reassured her. 'It's not your fault.'

'No, of course it's not,' Ricky added, not quite as convinced.

Various people volunteered to drive Amanda to hospital but Digby was concerned about causing further injury to her ankle when fitting her into a car. In the end, we called an ambulance.

'Was she pissed?' I muttered slyly to Ricky as we waited for it to arrive.

'I did catch her taking a little nip from her hip flask before we started,' he confided in a whisper, 'just to steady her nerves, she said.'

The paramedics arrived and confirmed that Amanda's ankle was indeed broken. Once she and Digby had been seen safely into the ambulance and it had begun trundling across the lawn, I asked the question that was on everyone's lips. 'What do we do now?'

Ricky was silent a moment, while he gave me what I can only describe as a significant look.

'That's up to you, my love.'

The whole company had gone quiet, everyone had turned to look at me. Morris was blinking like a nervous owl. 'It's only a very small part,' he ventured softly.

'Oh, fuck!' I murmured.

‘My sentiments exactly,’ Ricky nodded. ‘I don’t know how we’re going to fit those tits of yours into Amanda’s costume.’

CHAPTER THIRTY-FIVE

Amanda, it turned out, had not been drunk. Digby assured everyone of that, though no one in the cast had actually voiced the idea out loud. Amanda, he insisted, was a professional to her fingertips and would never drink before a rehearsal. It seemed that her stilted way of walking was not compatible with the woodland floor. In other words, she'd tripped over a cable and crashed into a footlight and now I had three days to learn her bloody lines.

'Four days will quickly steep themselves in night; Four nights will quickly dream away the time. . .'

I was repeating them like a mantra as I walked the dogs, all the time I worked. At the Brownlows' house I had Chris following me around with the script, feeding me cues while I cleaned his parents' bathroom. In the shop, Sophie tested me over and over. Meanwhile, Ricky and Morris were running me up a new costume.

'At least we don't have to worry about covering up the scrawny bits like we did with Amanda,' Ricky told me genially. 'We're going for something more youthful, a bit more daring. We thought leopard skin.'

He was only saying this to wind me up.

'Hippolyta was the Queen of the Amazons,' Morris teased with a coy smile. 'We couldn't really do it with Mandy, but she should wear something warlike.'

In the end they came up with a draped Grecian dress in burnt orange crêpe, with a bronze-coloured corset over the top which looked like armour, leather wrist-guards and a belt slung around my hips from which hung a dagger. Also, a heavy gold necklace, a small crown and dangly earrings.

'You look amazing!' Sophie told me when I ventured out into the garden for the first time. I'd actually been standing in front of the mirror for several minutes before I felt confident enough to let Ricky drag me out in front of the others and I knew she was right. I looked amazing. The rest of the cast applauded. All I had to do now was remember the fucking words.

'Daniel will go wild with desire,' Ricky whispered.

This was an interesting point. Daniel was supposed to be coming down to see the play, but I hadn't heard from him in ages. I'd been texting him, and leaving messages, asking him when he was coming, offering to pick him up from Exeter airport, or the station if he was flying to Bristol and was coming down by train. *Just let me know,* I'd texted. But he didn't. And his silence was odd.

I hoped he was all right. I hadn't told him I was playing Hippolyta. I was torn between wanting it to be a surprise and the dread I was going to mess up and ruin the entire play, in which case I'd rather he didn't see it at all. In the end, I decided I'd better let the cat out of the bag, so at least he was prepared. I messaged him and got back, *I'll be there Saturday*. Saturday was the final night of the play. I had two rehearsals and four performances before then to get it right.

We dedicated our performances to Gabriel, whose killer had still not been found, and to Scott, cast and crew gathering to hold hands every night before the play began.

The play was surprisingly brilliant. The audience laughed in all the right places and were warm and generous in their applause. Every night we had fine weather. No one tripped over any cables, Emily never forgot to turn off her microphone again and Bloody Eric only needed prompting twice. I was steered around the set each night, my elderly bridegroom's hand firmly on my arm, to make sure I didn't wander off into the wrong place. I've never had any trouble making myself heard, so that was not a problem. Amanda graciously turned up at dress rehearsal, her leg in a cast, and sat out front. She was absurdly lavish in her praise of my performance but hoped I didn't mind if she gave me one or two notes. I didn't. I needed all the help I could get. I had four and a half lines at the beginning of Act I and then, thank God, I was not seen or heard again until Act IV Scene

1, when I had half a dozen more. After that it was just a few one-liners in the last act and I was done.

On opening night, I felt sick with fright. I was so nervous I was still shaking at the curtain call. By the middle of the week, I was starting to enjoy myself a bit. Most of all I enjoyed the wave of relief that swept through me as we took our bows and it meant that another night was over. I was looking forward to Daniel's coming on Saturday. He didn't. He turned up on Friday.

I didn't spot him sitting amongst the mass of picnickers, and as it grew dark and the stage lights came up, it became impossible to see the audience anyway. They were lost among the shadows of the lawn. I didn't know Daniel was there until the show was over. The audience had drifted away and the cast were heading towards the house to change out of their costumes. Sophie and I were chatting and it was Soph who noticed him first, hovering at the edge of the paved terrace that bordered the lawn.

'Look who's here!' she giggled, nudging me.

'Daniel!' I laughed. 'I didn't think you were coming until tomorrow.' I could tell something was wrong. He didn't smile. I thought he looked on edge, but Sophie grabbed my arm and began pulling me in his direction.

'What do you think of Juno?' she asked playfully. 'Doesn't she look magnificent?'

'Truly magnificent,' he repeated, but there was a flatness in his voice and his expression was hard to read. He made no move towards me. I stared into those grey eyes and could see the storm brewing. 'Sophie, would you excuse us?' he asked, without taking his eyes from mine. 'Juno and I need to talk.'

'Oh . . . yes,' she faltered, looking from him to me and back again, sensing the atmosphere. 'I'll see you later,' she added, squeezing my hand, and dashed off into the house.

Daniel surveyed me in silence. 'Was I that bad?' I asked after I'd endured this for a few moments.

At last, he smiled. 'No of course not. You were fine. Everyone was fine. It was a great show, you should all be proud. And you,' he sighed deeply, 'you look beautiful.'

'Thank you,' I smiled as I took a step towards him. He didn't budge. 'What's the matter?'

Olly came trudging up the lawn, Thisbe's white dress pulled on over Flute's homespun clothes, the long plaits of his red woollen wig swinging as he walked. He stopped to give me a high five. 'It went great tonight, didn't it, Juno? Hello, Daniel. D'you enjoy it?'

'Yes, Olly, well done,' he answered stiffly. 'It was wonderful.'

Olly didn't linger but called to Marcus who came puffing after him, still encased in his Wall costume, and the two of them jogged into the house together.

'What's the matter?' I repeated when they were out of earshot. 'What's wrong?' I closed up to him and put my hands on his arms. 'You haven't been answering my calls. Has something bad happened?'

'I've been talking to the police.'

I tried to mask my feeling of disquiet. 'What about?'

'About everything.' He sighed wearily. 'About Frank Tinkler, Karl Richardson . . .'

‘Oh.’ I let my hands drop. Now I knew why he was angry.

He turned away from me and began pacing the terrace like a panther. ‘You promised me you would try to stay out of trouble, that you wouldn’t put yourself at risk.’

‘I didn’t.’

‘Don’t lie, Juno, please. You went into the shop alone, knowing Tinkler was there, knowing that he’d murdered Scott Pritchard. What is it with you?’ he demanded angrily. ‘Do you get some kind of weird kick out of putting yourself in danger?’

‘No, of course not!’

‘Just tell me, why did you go into the shop? What the hell was in your mind at that moment?’

‘I just thought I might be able to stop him . . . somehow,’ I added weakly. ‘I don’t know. I was angry.’ I was getting angry again.

‘And I begged you not to go up to the farmhouse.’ He shook his head. ‘A gun, for God’s sake!’

Dean and the inspector had promised not to reveal my part in finding that weapon. I frowned. ‘Have you been talking to Cruella?’

‘I wanted to get the facts.’

‘And you wouldn’t get them from me?’

He gave a bitter laugh. ‘No, I don’t think I would.’

I bit my lip. I hadn’t told him that Brendan had tried to kill me. I could feel myself blushing. He gave a despairing sigh, running a hand through his hair. ‘I can’t trust you, Juno.’

‘That’s not fair. I don’t go looking for these things.’

‘Maybe not. But you seem to attract them, draw trouble to you like a magnet. I learnt yesterday—’

‘Yesterday?’ I cut in.

He paused for a moment, flicked me an almost sheepish glance. ‘I got here yesterday morning. I stayed last night at the farmhouse.’

‘You’ve been here since yesterday morning?’ I couldn’t believe it. ‘You don’t answer my calls, you sneak down here on the quiet and then, instead of coming to me, asking me about all this, you go behind my back and get it from Cruella.’

‘Don’t you understand? I hate it when you put yourself in danger.’

I understood. He’d lost Claire. He didn’t want to lose me too. ‘Look, Daniel, I’m sorry. I’m so sorry. The last thing I want to do is cause you any pain . . .’

‘And what’s this about you nearly getting stabbed the other day? If Dean Collins hadn’t happened to walk in . . .’

Cruella again. I could just imagine the smirk on her horrible little mouth as she told him everything. My anger flared. ‘You have no right to sneak around behind my back talking to her!’

‘It seems like it’s the only way I’m going to find out the truth.’

‘You can’t control what I do.’

He’d been pacing, his back to me, but he turned at this, staring. ‘I’m not trying to control you.’ His voice was quiet with anger. ‘I know you will always do exactly what you want to do.’

He was right, and the fact that he was right just made it worse. 'You told me once that if I didn't do the things I do, I wouldn't be me.'

He gave a hollow laugh. 'No, you wouldn't, and that is exactly the point.'

'Meaning what?'

'Meaning, I can't live with it. I can't bear it, Juno, worrying about you all the time, worrying what the hell you're up to.' He stopped suddenly, his shoulders slumping. He looked defeated, drained. 'Christ, isn't it enough I had to drag you out of a river?'

My voice shook. 'I thought we agreed never to speak about that.'

He gave a bitter laugh. 'Well, it seems you've been able to put it out of your mind.'

I felt as if he'd struck me. Tears pricked my eyes. 'Daniel, I'm sorry.' I reached out a hand to his cheek. 'You're right. I don't stop to think, to consider the consequences.'

He drew back from me. 'You're never going to change, Juno.'

'I'll try.'

He shook his head. 'I went through hell and back when Claire died, and I am not going through it again with you.' His chest heaved in a deep sigh. 'This isn't going to work.'

His words were scaring me. 'What isn't?'

'You and me,' he said simply. 'You and me.'

I felt as if I was in free fall down a lift shaft, I wanted to clutch at something for support.

‘I can’t bear it. Juno. . .’ He hesitated for a moment and reached out to touch my hair. His eyes were sad. ‘I’m sorry, Miss Browne with an “e”.’ Then he turned away.

‘Daniel!’ I called after him. He kept on walking. ‘Daniel!’

A crowd of fairies, still in their costumes, ran out to dance on the lawn, surrounding him. He had to force his way through them. They grabbed me by the arms, wanting me to join their dance, to whirl around with them. I pulled away, my eyes still fixed on Daniel’s departing back, on his tall figure walking away from me. I wanted to run after him, to plead with him, tell him that we could make it work, beg him to give me another chance. But I felt as if I’d been turned to stone. I couldn’t move. And besides, I knew he wouldn’t listen.

CHAPTER THIRTY-SIX

The week after the play was over, I received a very strange letter. It arrived at the shop, sent by airmail and carrying an exotic stamp. The postmark was too heavily smudged to make out.

But on the back of the envelope the sender had written St Antony's Prison Trust, so I knew it who it was from. I unstuck the flap carefully, in case something horrible jumped out, and drew out the single page letter. The handwriting was in blue ink, meticulous and neat.

Dear Juno,

It is always wise to have an escape plan. Gerry and I put ours in place some time ago, around the same time as we moved our funds offshore. Ours was an efficiently run and profitable little enterprise and over the years we built up quite a nest egg.

But we were always prepared for the possibility that it might come to a sudden end and, as I have said, we had made plans accordingly. As they have doubtless realised by now, these plans did not include either Mrs Tinkler or Mrs Deal, both of whom have been left adequately provided for.

You may wonder why I am writing. I am aware that Brendan bungled my little message to you, but I am sure you got the point. I just want you to know that while your meddling and interference may have put a temporary stop to our activities, you haven't won. After all, it is I who am enjoying this tropical paradise and you who are stuck in Ashburton. This is a place which holds many exciting business opportunities for two enterprising gentlemen such as Gerry and myself, and has no extradition treaty with the United Kingdom.

With the Very Best Wishes

Frank

I gave the letter to the police. Frank and Gerry, it turned out, were living in the Dominican Republic.

'Don't think we've given up on Tinkler,' Inspector Ford told me fiercely. 'He might think he's shaken us off, but he's wanted for murder, and extradition treaty or not, we're not going to stop trying.' He grunted. 'I can't get over his bloody nerve. He kills Scott Pritchard in cold blood and then walks into this station, cool as you please, to give us a statement a few hours later.' He allowed himself a rare smile. 'The only comfort is, if he and Deal try to start up in business again in a place like that, they may find they've bitten off more than they can chew. The drugs gangs over there don't take any prisoners.'

Indeed, after all the misery that they had inflicted, the thought that Frank and Gerry might end up getting horribly slaughtered in some kind of drugs war, was a comfort.

It was about the only comfort to be had. I felt as if my heart had been hollowed out with a spoon. I realised now that however much I loved being with him, I'd hardly thought about Daniel when he wasn't around. But now he was all I could think about. I fell asleep thinking about him and he was my first thought on waking. On the final night of the play, I'd scanned the audience as we were taking our bows, peering out into the darkness, hoping that he would be there. Or that he might relent and come knocking on my door. I said nothing to anyone, but I must have worn a widow's face and I fooled none of the people who knew me too well.

'He's just pissed off about all that malarky you're always getting up to,' Ricky told me chirpily. 'He'll come around, you'll see.'

I don't think so. Scorpio – passionate, committed, obstinate, inclined to be unforgiving – are not the coming-around sort. I drove up to Halshanger Common because I couldn't stop myself. There was no sign of the space-bug. In its place stood a smart new caravan about twice its size. Men in hard hats were erecting scaffolding around the farmhouse. A digger was cutting a trench for new drains, maybe putting in a damp course. Work was finally under way. There was no sign of Daniel, though, or his car.

I returned that evening, just as the light was failing. His car was in the drive, and there were lights on in the caravan, music playing on the radio. After all this time, he'd actually made it to Moorview Farm, to living there. I had thought I would be there too, spending nights in that caravan snug in each other's arms, that I'd become a part of turning that cold, empty shell of a building into a home. And now, would Daniel even speak to me?

A bark came from inside. Lottie sensed I was there. She barked again, loud and insistent, demanding to be let out. The door opened and she hurtled towards me, racing down the path, barking joyously. I crouched down as she flung herself towards me and my arms were filled with wagging, wriggling whippet. Lottie and I adore each other. In a way she'd brought Daniel and me together. I hugged her warm body hard. 'Oh Lottie, I have missed you,' I whispered.

'Lottie.' Her master's voice. Daniel was framed in the doorway of the caravan. He didn't move. 'Lottie come here.'

I stood up. With the light behind him I couldn't see his face, just an impression of a statue, immovable, carved in stone. I took a step towards him, my lips forming his name. 'Daniel, can't we talk? Please?'

It was as if I hadn't spoken. 'Lottie,' he repeated, clicking his fingers. 'Lottie! Come here now.'

I smoothed her warm head. 'Go on,' I told her softly. 'You'd better go. Good girl.'

She trotted up the path, then stopped to look back at me from dark, soulful eyes, tilting her head as if to question why I wasn't coming too.

'Go on,' I repeated and she slunk inside.

For a moment Daniel stared. Then he turned his back on me and closed the door.

I stood feeling numb, humiliated in some idiotic way, although I'd have gladly swallowed my pride if he'd been prepared to talk. After what seemed like an age, staring at the closed caravan door, I walked back to the van. I sat, my forehead resting on the steering wheel, letting hot tears fall silently. Daniel would be living here. We were certain to come across each other in the town. How could we meet and behave like strangers? I wiped my eyes, catching my reflection in the rear-view mirror as I turned the key in the ignition. 'This is going to be great,' I told myself.

It was Elizabeth, and only Elizabeth, who knew the whole story. She was the only one who knew about Millie, about Susan. I showed her Frank's letter before I took it to the police.

'It's the vanity of the man that is so astonishing,' she said, raising her eyebrows as she read, 'writing to you just to crow like this. He's obviously a narcissist on top of everything else.'

'I just wish for Millie's sake, and for Scott's family, I'd been able to stop him.'

'You scuppered his little enterprise, that's the point. If it hadn't been for you, Frank would still be carrying on, and Susan, Millie and other women . . . women whose names we will never know . . . who will never know *you* . . .' she smiled, 'women in dark glasses and blonde wigs, driven to desperate acts, would still be compelled to do his bidding. Don't beat yourself up because he got away.'

I supposed she was right. Millie was now living with her aunt, and talking about going back to college, so at least some good had come of it all.

Yesterday, I bought myself a beautiful quilt, in shades of green, and threw it over my sofa. It looks great, hides most of the purple. My only remaining relative, my cousin Brian, is coming home on leave soon before he takes up his next diplomatic appointment abroad. He'll be in London for two months and has invited me to visit him there. It means I'll have to put up with his hag-wife Marcia, but I think I just might accept his invitation. Apart from the fact that it will be wonderful to see Brian again, right now the thought of museums, galleries, shops, theatres and restaurants seems unusually attractive.

In the end it was Chris Brownlow who took up the offer of a job helping Adam with breakfasts at *Sunflowers*. He's only earning pocket money, but he's still got most of the day to laze around, which seems to compensate. I haven't seen Daniel. Kate and Adam say he's not going into *Sunflowers* to pinch their Wi-Fi, so he must be going somewhere else to work. I still feel raw, but as each day goes by, I find I'm more angry than anything else. I can't forget the shutting of that door, the swift brutality with which he ended our relationship. After all, I'm still the same woman he fell in love with.

I try to occupy my mind with other things. Kate and Adam's baby will be due soon and I'm finally getting around to putting the wild tangle of their back garden in order, something I promised to do when I first moved in. It's on my 'to do' list, along with valuing the rest of the cigarette cards and finding Pat another printer's tray. It took Sophie and me days to help her sort out all those beads, sieving the different sizes into plastic bags for now.

I feel I've been neglecting Pat, thinking too much about my own problems. So, I've devised a plan for raising money for her animal sanctuary, for Honeysuckle Farm. It involves Ricky and Morris holding a huge garden party, inviting lots of rich people and plying them with expensive food and drink. Local celebrities Digby and Amanda could come and mingle and Pat would bring along some animals for everyone to meet. I'm thinking about an adoption scheme, where people can sponsor a particular animal and pay regularly towards its upkeep. I haven't told Ricky and Morris they are going to do this yet. The thought of donkeys on their lawn and geese in the flower beds might not appeal too much at first. They might need a bit of persuasion. They came into the shop today and insisted I joined them for lunch. An excellent opportunity to broach the subject. We walked along the street together and I linked my arms through theirs.

'Are you all right, Princess?' Ricky asked me.

The clock of St Andrew's church began striking twelve. I waited for it to finish striking before I answered, 'Yes, I'm fine.'

We stopped at the junction where North Street meets East and West Street, pondering which particular lunch establishment to favour with our custom, which way to turn. 'I've got a proposition for you two,' I began.

Ricky raised his eyes to heaven. 'Oh Gawd.'

'Take no notice of him, Juno,' Morris tutted. 'What is it, my love?'

I took a deep breath. 'Well, it's about Pat's animal sanctuary . . .'

ACKNOWLEDGEMENTS

I would like to thank Jolyon Tuck for his help with all things legal and Dr Kate Austin for her help with all things pharmaceutical. My usual thanks go to Susie, Fliss, Claire and the terrific team at Allison and Busby and my wonderful agent Teresa Chris, who keeps me on the straight and narrow. Thanks go to Martin, as always, for his love and support and to Di Davies for her unfailing encouragement and enthusiasm for my work. I'd also like to thank, once again, the people of Ashburton, who are so tolerant in letting me elasticate their streets to fit in Juno's world.

STEPHANIE AUSTIN graduated from Bristol University with a degree in English and Education and has enjoyed a varied career as an artist, astrologer and trader in antiques and crafts. More respectable professions include teaching and working for Devon Schools Library Service. When not writing, she is involved in local amateur theatre as an actor and director. She lives on the English Riviera in Devon where she attempts to be a competent gardener and cook.